BAD APPLE

ANTHONY
BRUNO

BAD
APPLE

A NOVEL

Delacorte ▬ Press

Published by
Delacorte Press
Bantam Doubleday Dell Publishing Group, Inc.
1540 Broadway
New York, New York 10036

The trademark Delacorte Press® is registered in the U.S. Patent and
Trademark Office.

Library of Congress Cataloging in Publication Data

Bruno, Anthony.
    Bad apple / Anthony Bruno.
      p.   cm.
    ISBN 0-385-30508-7
    1. Gibbons, Cuthbert (Fictitious character)—Fiction. 2. Tozzi, Mike
(Fictitious character)—Fiction.   3. Government investigators—United
States—Fiction.   I. Title.
PS3552.R82B336   1994
813'.54—dc20   93-42616
                                                                    CIP

Manufactured in the United States of America
Published simultaneously in Canada

November 1994

10 9 8 7 6 5 4 3 2 1
BVG

For Shuji Maruyama Sensei
and all the aikidoka of
Aikido Kokikai International

ONE

Gary Petersen ran his fingers along the grip bumps in the steering wheel as he stared down at the backpack on the floor on the passenger side. It was a kid's backpack, blue and yellow, made out of some kind of cheap material that probably wouldn't last a whole school year, not with his kids. On the outside there was a goofy-looking picture of Cookie Monster. Inside there was $130,000 in cash. Petersen's thumb made a soft tomtom sound on the steering wheel. He kept doing it because it filled the quiet. His wife was right, he thought. He ought to have his head examined.

He checked his watch again even though he knew it couldn't be more than a few minutes later than the last time he'd looked at it. It was just something to do while he waited. The parking lot was dark outside. The Vince Lombardi Service Area off the New Jersey Turnpike didn't get much car traffic in the wee hours of the morning, especially on this side of the lot where the trailer trucks parked. Two rows of eighteen-wheelers were angle-parked, shoulder to shoulder, the truckers inside bunked for the night. A lot of them kept their running lights on—must be some kind of insurance regulation, Petersen figured—so they wouldn't get broadsided in the dark. That wasn't very likely here, though. They kept the lot pretty well lit. Except here, where he was parked, way over by the edge of the lot where the seven-foot cattails grew.

Petersen glanced up at the headlights sailing across the sky on the elevated section of the Turnpike. They looked like UFOs up there. In the rearview mirror he could see the Manhattan skyline across the Hudson. The top of the Empire State Building was lit in orange and yellow for Thanksgiving. He glanced at his watch again. Technically it was already Wednesday. Thanksgiving was a day away. They were having it up at his in-laws' in Connecticut this year. He hoped to hell he could make it. Whenever you're on an undercover like this, anything's liable to happen. Some mob guy calls you on Thanksgiving morning and says he has to see you right away, there's nothing you can do. Can't make excuses. You have to go.

Now that he thought about it, he should've made it part of his cover that he had a sick mother or something, something life-or-death that could buy him some personal time when he needed it. It would've come in handy with Tony Bells. Bells was fucking crazy. Calls up in the middle of the night, meet me here in twenty minutes, meet me there in a half-hour. And never during the day. The guy was like a fucking vampire. It would be just like him to call on Thanksgiving and say they had to meet that night. Shit. Petersen couldn't do that to his wife. Bad enough she'd have to drive all the way up to her parents' alone with the kids, but then she'd have to hear her father's shit about how she was gonna end up a widow one of these days because of what her husband did for a living. He could hear the old man now: "The FBI's got desk jobs, haven't they? Why doesn't he get a desk job?" What a pain. Next time he'd remember to have a sick mother.

He stared out at the deserted parking lot again. So where the fuck was Bells? Did he want the money or not?

It was getting cold out there. Petersen turned the engine back on, and as he reached over to turn up the heat, he caught his own reflection in the rearview mirror, just his eyes. They were dark, evil-looking eyes with thick eyebrows to match. Amazing. He was Irish on his mother's side, Swedish and German on his father's side, and he comes out looking like Popeye's archenemy, Bluto. All he needed was the beard. Every one of his cousins was either blond or redhead, and all of them had light eyes. A couple of dirty blondes, but that's as dark as they got. How the hell he turned out the way he did, no one could figure. His mother said she thought someone had married a black Irishman a couple of generations back and that's why he'd turned out the way he did. Who the hell knew? All he knew was that he never looked like a Petersen or a Flynn or a Schmidt. Whenever he went under-cover, he was either an Italian or a Greek. This time he was Greek. Teddy Katapoulos.

He kept looking at his eyes in the rearview mirror, turning his face one way, then the other, examining himself. Something wasn't right. He wondered if he looked scared or tired or what. He sat back and frowned, wondering why the hell he was won-dering this. He wasn't tired and he certainly wasn't scared. He'd done lots of undercovers before. This was by no means his first. And there was nothing to be nervous about, not tonight. He'd been alone with Tony Bells before—that wasn't it. Sure, the guy was creepy, but so what? That's just the way he is. Sort of like that actor, Christopher Walken. Creepy, but smooth about it. Bells would be perfect as Dracula, somebody like that. It wasn't like he or Walken sucked blood in real life—they just made you believe that they could. In reality, Bells was just another scum-bag mob loan shark. That's all. A creepy-looking, scumbag Ma-fia loan shark. But very smooth.

Petersen glanced down at the Cookie Monster backpack on

3

the floor. It used to be his daughter's favorite when she was in kindergarten—she used to sleep with the damn thing. It was baby stuff now, though. She was nine going on twenty-one and heavily into Ren and Stimpy. Whoever the hell they were.

He focused on Cookie Monster's googly eyes and remembered when he used to tiptoe into his daughter's bedroom to take the backpack out of her bed. There really was nothing to be nervous about tonight. He was gonna be giving Bells what he wanted. $130,000 at half a point a week. Bells would turn around and loan it to someone else for a point, point and a half a week. In a year, Bells could clear sixty-five grand off that money. He wanted this cash. Loan sharks are always on the lookout for "investors" like "Teddy Katapoulos," guys who want to get a good return on their money but who don't want the hassles of loan-sharking it themselves. It works out nice for both parties.

Except in this case.

Tony Bells didn't know that the money he would be getting was courtesy of the FBI, and that "Teddy Katapoulos" was one of a dozen undercover agents taking part in Operation Shark Bite, a special task force targeting loan-sharking in the New York area, coordinated by the Manhattan field office's Organized Crime Unit. Undercover agents had infiltrated the loan-sharking activities of two crime families so far, the Luccarellis and the Giovinazzos. Some agents were working for loan sharks, some were borrowing from loan sharks, and some, like Petersen, were working with loan sharks, lending them money to "build their books."

For a change, Petersen was on the safe end of this operation, relatively speaking. The undercover guys who were taking out loans with the intention of not paying them back in order to elicit threats and violence from their shylocks, *they* were the ones holding the shitty end of the stick. They were the guys who had to watch themselves. Still, Petersen didn't feel completely at ease waiting here in a parking lot in the middle of the night. He could never be at ease with Bells. No one could.

Supposedly, Tony "Bells" Bellavita wasn't even a made man. The FBI and NYPD both had him classified as only a "Luccarelli associate." But unlike most mob associates, Bells didn't work under a soldier. He was connected directly to a capo, Armand "Buddha" Stanzione, and from the few wiretaps they had of conversations between these two, they seemed pretty tight. Bells didn't seem to bow and scrape to Stanzione the way most underlings did with their captains, which was very unusual. But of course that was why Bells had been targeted by Operation Shark Bite. He had a direct line to a capo. No middlemen. If they got the goods on Bells, there was a good chance they could take down Buddha Stanzione with him.

Petersen remembered one of the tapes they had of Bells talking to Buddha at a "social club" in the Down Neck section of Newark. There were a lot of long silences on that tape, the kind of gaps that give you *accida* thinking that the equipment malfunctioned and you've lost everything. But that wasn't it on this one. Stanzione was definitely a man of few words—that's why they called him "Buddha"—and Bells could be just as bad. He would do this thing where he'd just look at you. Wouldn't say a thing, just look at you. Creepy as hell. When Petersen first listened to that tape, he could just see Bells giving Stanzione that look, and after he went over it a few times, Petersen noticed that every time Bells didn't talk on the tape, it was Buddha who'd started up the conversation again. It seemed strange that a mere associate would be able to pull this kind of shit with a capo, especially a cutthroat mother like Buddha. But Bells seemed to get away with this kind of disrespect. *Very* strange.

Petersen turned down the heat and checked the time again. It was almost quarter after two. He wondered if he should just call it a night and take off because it didn't look like Bells was coming. Just as well, he thought. He'd rather meet him in daylight to tell the truth. Friggin' Bells, though, he likes to do things at night and always on the road somewhere. Says he's gotta have privacy, total privacy when he does business. Well, next time Petersen was gonna insist on meeting during the day. After all, he was the one providing the cash. No more coddling after this.

He switched on his headlights and reached for the shift when he noticed a pair of moving headlights in his rearview mirror. The approaching car had just turned off the access road and pulled into the lot. Petersen felt a ghost hand clutch his stomach. Was it Bells? He half-hoped it wasn't.

The headlights swept the lot, moving slowly, heading toward him. The car pulled up right behind his, and because the high beams were on, Petersen had to turn away from the glare in his rearview mirror. He glanced into his side mirror, which wasn't quite as bad. He heard the car's engine shut off, but the headlights stayed on. Petersen kept his engine running.

The driver's-side door opened and the driver got out, but in the glare of the high beams, Petersen could only see the approaching silhouette in a long overcoat, his breath visible on the cold night air. Count Dracula makes his entrance, Petersen thought wryly. Frigging scumbag.

Petersen looked down at the armrest in his door and hit the automatic door locks, unlocking the passenger side for his guest. He turned to his right, expecting to see Bells coming around the back of his car to the passenger side, but he was startled when he saw the dark overcoat right next to him on the other side of the driver's window. Petersen hit the button and lowered his window. He squinted and bent his head down so he could see the man's face above the roof line.

"I was just about to take off. What happened?"

No answer.

Then he saw the hand coming out of the overcoat pocket, and that other hand in his stomach squeezed hard because in that split second he sensed what was coming. The first shot sounded like a balloon popping. Petersen didn't even hear the next two, they came so fast. He didn't even see the gun.

Slumped across the seats, he knew he'd been shot, but he didn't know where. He was aware of the car door opening then, and he did feel a hand leaning on his hip, but he couldn't move. He was all clenched up, his whole body.

Shit, he thought, grinding his teeth. His father-in-law was really gonna bust his wife's balls now. Shit!

He blinked with watery eyes as the royal-blue blur of the Cookie Monster backpack was dragged over the transmission hump. He thought about going for the gun in his belt just before he blacked out.

TWO

"Bert, are you all right?"

FBI Special Agent Cuthbert Gibbons took the icebag off his cheek and glared at his boss, Brant Ivers, over the roof of Gary Petersen's white Mercury. "I'm fine," he growled.

"Are you sure?"

"Yes."

The assistant director in charge of the FBI's Manhattan field office just looked at him. "You look like you're in a lot of pain, Bert. Go home if you're not feeling well."

"I said I'm fine."

Ivers furrowed his brows as he pulled up the zipper on his tan suede jacket. He let out a sigh, and his breath materialized over his head like a dialogue balloon in the funny papers. "We have enough problems here tonight, Bert. Let's not make it any worse, shall we? Why not just go home and see a dentist first thing in the morning? I don't want to have to order you to go."

Then don't, Gibbons thought.

He put the icebag back on his face and held his tongue. Not because Ivers was his boss. He never had any problem telling off this aging preppy shitass. He was keeping his yap closed because his tooth was killing him, one of the back molars on the bottom. Without warning it would start hurting like a bastard. There was

8

a dull, throbbing pain that was pretty constant, and that he could put up with, but when it started to scream—like right now—all he could do was clench up his face and bear it until it passed.

Gibbons's wife had told him to go to the dentist when it started to give him trouble, but he'd been too busy to take the time off. Now he wished he had listened to Lorraine. Of course, he'd never admit to her that she might have been right about something. When it came to being right, Gibbons believed that women should never be encouraged. It could just lead to other things.

"Go home, Bert. We can handle things here." Ivers was giving him the fatherly routine now. That was almost funny since Gibbons had at least five years on him, maybe more.

When Gibbons didn't answer him, Ivers switched to a motherly tone. "Now, Bert, don't be so stubborn."

Gibbons tried to ignore him. He hated it when people called him "Bert" because he hated his first name, which was actually Cuthbert, and he had always hated it. He was Gibbons, just Gibbons, and he must've told that to Ivers at least a hundred times over the years, but he wasn't gonna say it anymore. His tooth hurt too much, and this self-absorbed, self-promoting asshole was just too dense to get it. Besides, compared to what had gone down here tonight, Ivers's deliberate stupidity about Gibbons's name wasn't worth mentioning. An agent had been shot tonight, an agent on a sensitive undercover. That was what mattered to Gibbons right now. Not his name or his tooth or his stupid boob of a boss. An agent had been shot.

Gibbons peered through the Mercury's passenger side window at the bloodstained seats. He stepped back to see if there was anything in the backseat, and the glass mirrored his own face. Gibbons inspected his reflection. His face was pretty swollen on one side. Didn't make him any uglier, though. He was pretty ugly to begin with. Mostly bald, with small mean eyes. Nose like a big chili pepper hanging over thin bloodless lips. The beginnings of a baby turkey wattle starting to grow under his chin. He pulled his open shirt collar together, then let it go. He'd forgotten to grab a tie when he ran out of the house, and he always felt naked without a tie. Unlike shitass Ivers, Gibbons had come up through the ranks when J. Edgar was in charge, back in the days when FBI agents did not go anywhere without a tie, a suitcoat, shined shoes, and a hat. Wearing a tie was a habit Gibbons had never gotten out of. It was a habit that a lot of the younger agents, particularly the undercover jockeys, had a hard time getting into. Gibbons glanced over the roof at the assistant director in charge in his crewneck sweater and wondered what his excuse was.

Ivers was standing with the two New Jersey state troopers who had been the first ones on the scene. He looked real cute taking down notes on a clipboard in his tan suede jacket, bottle-green Shetland sweater, pressed jeans, and oxblood tassel loafers. If he didn't have that big square head of his and that phony-looking dye job with the artfully graying temples, he'd look like a Ralph Lauren ad. What an asshole.

Ivers was just wasting those troopers' time with that stupid clipboard because Gibbons had already gotten all the particulars when he first got there. A trucker from South Carolina named Nelson had been asleep in his rig when he heard somebody leaning on his horn. He ran out with an aluminum baseball bat intent on bashing some Yankee head in when he found Gary Petersen slumped against his steering wheel, bleeding all over the place. The trucker ran back to his rig and called for an ambulance on his CB. Petersen was semiconscious when the trucker got back to the car. He said he opened the door and hunkered down next to the wounded man, held his hand, and kept him talking until the rescue squad got there. The trucker also said he didn't see a soul in the parking lot when he first came out with the bat.

Gibbons had gotten all this directly from the trucker, and he'd already told Ivers, but Ivers was the big cheese here, and he had to *look* like he was in charge. The clipboard was a good prop for a big cheese.

Gibbons winced as another wave of screaming pain carved its way through his jaw. It was the kind of pain that made him think of power tools—lathes and routers and crap like that. He tilted his head back and looked straight up at the sky, holding the icebag to his face and blinking at the glare from the pole lights until it finally subsided. The damn tooth hurt like a bastard, but he had no right to complain. Not when Gary Petersen was in an emergency room, fighting for his life.

Gibbons's face was clenched again, but not because of his tooth. He was steamed. Petersen shouldn't have been shot. This should *not* have happened. Petersen wasn't supposed to have been in any danger at this stage in his undercover. Ivers had already speculated that this could've been a simple armed robbery, a plain case of bad luck, Petersen being in the wrong place at the wrong time. Well, the asshole could theorize and postulate all he wanted with that goddamn clipboard of his, but as far as Gibbons was concerned, there was only one plausible reason for Petersen being shot. His cover had been blown. Period.

But even if Petersen's cover had been blown, this still shouldn't have happened. Gibbons had worked organized crime for over twenty-five years, and he knew better than anyone that there were unwritten rules between the Mafia and the law, and Rule Number One was that wiseguys do not kill cops, not even undercover cops. They could beat a cop silly if they ever caught one trying to infiltrate their ranks, but that was the extent of it.

No mob boss anywhere would ever sanction a hit on a cop or a fed. It just wasn't done. None of them want the kind of heat something like this creates. But shooting Petersen was a severe breach in that unwritten contract, and whoever was responsible was gonna suffer.

Gibbons had seen things like this before. Every few years some cowboy comes along who thinks he's invincible, that he can get away with killing a cop. But it always ends up ugly. Whoever shot Petersen may not realize it, but he'd be better off if he turned himself in. At least he'd get a trial. If the mob finds him first, they'll go straight to sentencing, and wiseguys are firm believers in capital punishment.

Of course, the way Gibbons was feeling right now, he wouldn't mind having the bastard alone in a room for fifteen minutes before the legal process officially kicked in. Back in the old days, they used to stop the clock for special cases like this. But then the Supreme Court stepped in and said suspects had rights. Gibbons didn't exactly disagree with that. He just felt that cops should have rights, too. Like the right to temporarily break the rules when bad guys break them first. It was only fair.

Ivers walked around the front of the Mercury to where Gibbons was standing. The heels of his loafers made a nice click on the asphalt. Very tony. "Bert, has McDaniels arrived yet?"

Gibbons shook his head. "He's on his way." McDaniels was Petersen's partner.

Ivers sighed and looked down at his clipboard. "What do you know about Petersen's assignment here tonight?"

Gibbons frowned and shrugged. "I know what you know. He was meeting Tony Bellavita to give him some cash. I don't know how much."

"Were those bills marked?"

Gibbons shrugged. "I don't know the particulars. McDaniels will know."

Ivers pressed his lips together and stared down at his clipboard. He muttered something to himself.

Gibbons rattled the icebag. The ice had mostly melted, but it was still pretty cold. The only problem was, it didn't seem to be doing much good for his throbbing tooth. Shit.

Out of the corner of his eye, Gibbons noticed a dark blue van pulling into the lot. One of the troopers flagged it down and went over to the driver's side. It was about forty feet away, headlights on, motor running.

Ivers was pressing his knuckle into his lower lip, intent on his clipboard. He looked up suddenly and stared at Gibbons from under his brow. "We've got a big problem here, Bert."

No kidding. Gibbons put the icebag back on his face.

"We've got eleven undercover agents out on this operation. If Petersen was shot because his cover was blown—and at this point, I suppose we have to assume that that's the most logical reason—then every other agent out there is in jeopardy. If they uncovered Petersen, they may have uncovered others."

Gibbons rolled his eyes and nodded. Outstanding deduction, Sherlock.

"Now the question is, do we pull in those other agents and shut down Shark Bite, or do we leave them in place until we know more? It would be a damn shame to scrap Shark Bite after all the work and preparation that went into it. Some of those men spent years working their way in. I'd hate to lose all that time and effort. It would take us a good long time to get men in as deep as we have them now. But on the other hand, we can't leave them out in the cold if there's some trigger-happy wiseguy on the loose who knows who they are."

"Ummm." Gibbons was only half-listening. He was paying

more attention to that blue van. The second trooper had gone over to join the conversation. The first one was pointing at the white Mercury. Gibbons kneaded the icebag as he kept an eye on the van, wondering what the story was over there.

Ivers was tapping the clipboard with the end of a gold Cross pen. "What's Tozzi's current status, Bert?"

Same as usual, he's an asshole.

Gibbons squeezed his eyes shut then as another screamer suddenly drilled through his tooth. This time he was convinced the mere mention of Tozzi's name had brought it on. Tozzi was the longest-running of all the partners Gibbons had ever had, almost ten years now, and sometimes Gibbons couldn't believe he and Tozzi had been together that long and hadn't killed each other yet. Until Tozzi came along, Gibbons had never been able to keep a partner for more than three days in a row. True, Tozzi was an asshole, a hardhead, and a hotdog who wouldn't know how to follow an order if his life depended on it—and it frequently did. Still, Tozzi was better than every other agent Gibbons had ever worked with. Even though he did have his head up his ass most of the time, at least Tozzi's heart was in the right place. Too bad he was Gibbons's wife's first cousin. Partnering with the guy was one thing. Being related to him was sort of like having a rash that wouldn't go away.

"Bert?"

"Huh?"

"Tozzi's current status—what is it?"

"He's teamed up with an informant, a mutt named DeFresco who's connected to the Luccarellis. DeFresco's introducing Tozzi as his partner in a porno video venture. They're trying to borrow money from Buddha Stanzione with the intention of falling behind in their vig payments. Tozzi wants to get Stanzione's number-one shy to threaten him, maybe even rough him up a little, and get it all on tape."

"And who is this shylock?"

"Take a guess. Tony Bells."

"Bellavita? The person Petersen was meeting here tonight?"

"None other than."

"Where's Tozzi now?"

"Right this minute?"

"Yes, right this minute."

"Home in bed if he's got any brains." Which is doubtful.

"Well, call him and let him know what happened to Petersen. Find out if he's been introduced to Bellavita yet. If he has, tell him to pull back until we find out what happened here tonight. We certainly don't want him to be Bellavita's next victim. In fact, let's get word to all the undercover men working on Shark Bite. Pull back until we know more. In the meantime I'm ordering a manhunt for Bellavita. I want him in custody for questioning ASAP."

Gibbons's eyelids drooped. Ivers sounded so tough and determined whenever he used words like *manhunt*. Like Tyrone Power in all those old war movies. Of course, the manhunt *had* to be done—that went without question. If they didn't find Tony Bells, the mob guys sure would, and that would be the end of him. And from Gibbons's point of view, life without parole was preferable to the death penalty. Better to make the son of a bitch suffer every single day for the rest of his life than to put him out of his misery in a muzzle flash. The only thing Gibbons had a problem with was calling Tozzi. He knew how Tozzi's warped mind worked. You tell the guy to put it in reverse, he'll put it in drive and floor it. If he finds out about what happened to Petersen, he won't pull back and lay low. Not Tozzi. Putting Tony Bells's head on a plate will become his personal crusade.

But that was all right, Gibbons figured. He'd been looking for an excuse to shoot the dumb bastard in the foot to keep him from doing something stupid.

"Now, Bert, I have a list of all the undercover men on Shark Bite. Tell me where . . ."

Gibbons was listening, but all of a sudden Ivers's voice started to fade out as another screamer started building up steam. It rumbled through his head like a B-52 coming out of the clouds with a full load. The bomb-bay doors were open, and the fat boys tumbled out, speeding through the sky, zeroing in on Gibbons's tooth. The initial explosion made sweat bead on his freckled forehead despite the November cold; the ones that followed came so fast, they rolled together into one big annihilating wave of excruciating killer pain.

"Bert? Bert? Are you all right?"

Gibbons held on to his jaw and kept his eyes squeezed shut until the pain finally went back to being a manageable dull ache. The first thing he focused on when he opened his eyes was that blue van. It was parked now, as close to Petersen's car as it could get. The back end was open, and two guys were loading themselves down with some kind of equipment. At first, Gibbons thought they might be forensic people from the state, but on second glance, they didn't look right. Leather jackets, jeans, running shoes. One of them had funny-looking gold-rim glasses, too trendy for any bone-picker he'd ever met. Then he saw one of them hoist a video camera onto his shoulder, and he realized who these guys were. A freelance film team, ambulance-chasers who prowl the streets all night looking for juicy disaster footage that they can peddle to the local TV news shows. Fucking bloodsuckers.

Gibbons charged around the white Mercury and started

shouting, "Hey! Hey! Pack up your gear and get the hell out of here."

The sound man, the one with the trendy glasses, gave him a dirty look and raised his boom mike on a stick as if he were going to defend himself with it. The cameraman, a tall, lanky guy in his early thirties with floppy blond hair, flashed a too-friendly smile and sauntered over toward the yellow tape that the state police had used to cordon off the crime scene.

"What's the problem, man?" the cameraman said. "We're just here to cover the story."

Gibbons watched the guy's eyes darting to the interior of the car. He was looking for something gory. The worst part about it was that the sneaky bastard was making like the camera wasn't rolling. Who the hell did he think he was kidding?

Gibbons moved in and cut him off, blocking his view of the car. He couldn't take pictures now, for chrissake. The forensics guys hadn't even gotten here yet. "Take a hike, the two of you. Now get going."

"C'mon, man. We're just doing our job."

"Do it somewhere else."

The cameraman ignored Gibbons and pointed the camera around him, going for the interior of Petersen's car.

"Hey, I'm warning you two little shitasses—"

"Bert!" Ivers called from the other side of the car.

Gibbons stepped in front of the video cam and put his hand over the lens. The camera guy reared back, moved to the side, and kept shooting. "Hey, I don't know who the fuck you think you are, man, but we've got a right to be here. Freedom of the press—you ever hear of it?" The guy kept shooting.

Suddenly the B-52 made another run on Gibbons's tooth. It came fast and without warning this time. The pain was beyond belief. Gibbons clenched his fist, his face twisted, and hammered the car door with a King Kong backswing.

"Get out of the way, will you, man? This is news."

"He's ruining my reading," the soundman complained.

Ivers called over the roof of the car. "Let the state police deal with them, Bert."

The cameraman craned his body over the yellow police tape, shooting into the open window on the driver's side. Gibbons saw red. He went for Excalibur, his prized .38 Colt Cobra, the gun he'd used his entire career as an FBI agent in violation of the standard-issue weaponry rules, and he stuck the muzzle into the lens of the video cam. Gibbons growled, low and mean. "Move on. Now. Or I'll blow your fucking eyes out."

"Jesus Christ!" The soundman clutched his headset and hightailed it back to the van.

The cameraman dropped the unit to his waist and glared at Gibbons. "What the fuck is your problem, man? We're only trying to get a story."

"Move on."

The cameraman started to backstep toward the van. "You're gonna hear from our lawyer, man. This is a clear violation of our freedom of the press rights. A *clear* violation."

"You can write to Ann Landers for all I care. Just get the hell outta here." Gibbons kept Excalibur leveled on the two bloodsuckers until they packed up and drove off.

Ivers came up behind him. "Put your weapon away, Bert. That was uncalled for."

"No, it wasn't." Gibbons holstered his gun and turned on him. "Gary Petersen deserves better than twenty seconds' worth of footage of his bloody car seat in a stupid TV report that doesn't say anything about anything sandwiched in between some garbage about what Madonna had for lunch and a commercial for Ex-Lax. The guy's got a wife and kids. He's a decent guy and a damn good agent, but nobody's gonna say shit about that because nobody gives a shit about the guy who takes the bullet. It's always the other guy, the one who pulls the trigger, who gets all the press. The victim is always just a prop for the bad guy in these things."

Ivers took off his half-glasses. "I agree with you entirely, Bert. But that cameraman was right, too. The First Amendment guarantees his right to cover this event as a journalist."

Gibbons was looking around on the ground, grumbling. "Yeah, well, maybe the Supreme Court will get around to fixing that, too."

"What?"

Gibbons found his icebag on the pavement by the front of the car. "Never mind." He brushed off the bag and put it back on his cheek.

That was the goddamn problem with this country, he thought. Everybody knows his rights, even when it's wrong.

THREE

Tozzi's arm lay on the table in front of him like a dead fish. The squeezed lime wedge in the glass of dark rum in front of him looked like a dead fish, too, a little green one. He stared down at his watch. It took a few seconds for the time to register in his brain. Twenty minutes to four. In the morning. He closed his weary eyes. This was nuts.

The place was called Joey's Starlight Lounge, but the only light in there came from behind the bar, and it gave everybody who got near it a sinister Phantom of the Opera kind of look. Joey's Starlight Lounge was a peek-a-boo bar where topless dancers in g-strings shook their booties with their hands over their nipples. When a patron at the bar gave a girl a buck, he'd get a peek. For five, he could have a gander. For ten, he could get up close. For twenty, he could touch. But right now there was hardly anyone there, and Annette, the only girl on duty, was sitting in a folding chair behind the bar, wearing a Seton Hall warm-up jacket to cover her assets, reading a paperback copy of *King Lear*. She had jet-black hair chopped at the collar, and she said she was studying acting at Juilliard. She worked here, she said, because she refused to waitress, and the tips were a lot better.

Tozzi finished off what was left of his drink, which was pretty

20

watery now that all the ice had melted. That was okay. He was just thirsty.

He looked into the bottom of his empty glass and saw his reflection under the little dead lime. The dark hair was getting thinner every day, but it still covered what it was supposed to. The dark deep-set eyes were tired, so they were even more deep-set and that much more suspicious. Heavy brows, Roman nose, slightly thick lips—a thug if there ever was one. But not a bad-looking thug. He wasn't DeNiro, of course, but he wasn't a toad either. Not on a good day.

Tozzi leaned out of the booth where he was sitting and squinted into the gloom in the back room. It was even darker back there, but in the dim light of a wall sconce he could make out the two figures huddled over a table, clasping their glasses in front of them. He couldn't see the muscle, but he knew they were back there, too, four of them, all bruisers. The thin guy was Tony Bells, the loan shark. The little guy was his boss, Buddha Stanzione. Tozzi knew what they were talking about. Him.

Tozzi scanned the bar, looking for his "partner," but the only person at the bar was Stanley Sukowski, Tony Bells's driver. Stanley wasn't a made guy and never would be because he was half-Polish. He was what they called a "mob associate." Stanley was the loan shark's right-hand man, and he was friendly enough, considering that his primary function was collection agent, which meant legbreaker. Tozzi had first met him last summer at a picnic Bells had thrown for a few of his associates, and Stanley had been wearing a T-shirt he said his daughter had given him for his birthday. It had a big picture of the Tazmanian Devil on the front, that hairy evil-looking cartoon charcter with the teeth and the big slathering jaws who was always trying to eat Bugs Bunny. Stanley, with his pronounced underbite, nonexistent neck, and squat build, actually looked quite a bit like the

Tazmanian Devil, Tozzi had thought at the time, and now he always thought of that T-shirt whenever he saw Stanley.

Tozzi nodded at Stanley, who nodded back, and wondered where the hell his "partner," Mr. Fuckhead DeFresco, had gone. Bobby "Freshy" DeFresco and he were supposedly in the porno distribution business. Freshy knew Bells from their old neighborhood in Bayonne, and he was the one who was going to get them their "business loan" from Tony Bells. It was all "in the bag," Freshy kept saying. "In . . . the . . . bag."

In the bag, my ass, Tozzi thought. Nothing was in the bag. Bells didn't know shit about "Mike Santoro," Tozzi's undercover name, and the loan shark must've had some doubts about him, otherwise he wouldn't be having this meeting with Buddha. They were asking to borrow $150,000 at a point and a half a week, which was not the preferred bad-guy rate. What Tozzi couldn't figure out was why Bells needed Buddha Stanzione's okay on this. As far as Tozzi knew, Bells had a free hand to loan money as he saw fit. Why all of a sudden was this case different?

Either Bells was nervous about lending to a partnership where he really didn't know one of the partners, or he felt that Freshy, the other partner, was such a fuck-up, he couldn't be trusted with that much money. But that was why Tozzi was sitting here, drinking a drink he didn't need, waiting for the dawn's early light. He was waiting to hear what Buddha Stanzione's decision would be. If they said yes, Operation Shark Bite would be one notch closer to hauling in a big one, a capo in the Luccarelli family. If they said no, Tozzi will have wasted a lot of time for nothing.

Staring into the gloom, cradling his face in his palm, Tozzi let out a tired sigh. This was really fucking nuts when you thought about it. Going undercover was nuts. Who in his right mind would ever depend on a screwball like Freshy DeFresco for anything? Who in his right mind would play around with someone as violent and short-tempered as Buddha Stanzione? Who in his right mind would come within fifty feet of that nut Bells? Who in his right mind would go undercover inside the Mafia, intending to borrow money from them and not pay it back, *hoping* that they would threaten to shoot out his kneecaps? He had to be nuts. That's all there was to it. He was nuts.

His eyes drooped, and he almost started to doze. This *was* crazy. He needed to get some sleep. Maybe "Mike Santoro" the pornmeister could stay up all night waiting for a couple of wiseguys to make up their goddamn minds, but Mike Tozzi had another life, a real life, and he needed to get some sleep. That night, just about sixteen hours from now, he was finally going to be testing for his black belt in aikido, and he'd be damned if he was going to miss it this time. The last time Sensei came over from Japan to preside over testing, Tozzi had been limping around on a cane after having been shot in the leg in the line of duty. That was eight months ago. After five and a half years of martial arts training, working his way up through the ranks, *kyu* by *kyu*, Tozzi had had to wait eight more months before Sensei came back and he could test for his black belt. Eight more months. It wasn't the worst thing that had ever happened to him, and when he was philosophical about it, he felt that maybe it was a good thing that he'd had to wait. That it built character, gave him a little humility, gave him a chance to sand off some of the rough edges in his techniques. But deep down, he knew that was bullshit. He wanted to test, badly. And to be absolutely honest about it, for the last eight months, he'd felt like a kid who'd been kept back and had to repeat a grade. It wasn't fair. In fact, it sucked.

As he started to doze off, he imagined how his test would go that night. The gym would be crowded, at least a hundred and fifty people in white *gi* uniforms sitting along the edges of the mats. After all the lower belts were finished testing, the black-belt tests would begin. Tozzi's name would be called, and he'd run out to the middle of the mat. After Sensei tested his posture, Tozzi would then run through all the formal techniques with a partner, dealing with all kinds of attacks, including *tanto-tori*, knife attacks. After that he would perform *bokken kata*, a formal movement exercise done with a wooden sword. Then at last the big part of the test would come, the part that everyone both dreaded and looked forward to at the same time: *randori*, free-style against multiple attackers.

To earn the rank of *shodan*, the first level in the black-belt ranks, you had to take on five opponents simultaneously. But unlike other schools of aikido, where the guy being tested had to make eye contact with his attackers before they could attack, thereby assuring that they came at you one at a time, in Tozzi's school, Aikido Kokikai, they attacked at will, using any of the various attacks that were used in technique practice.

Tozzi pictured his attackers lined up on the mat, most of them seasoned black belts, all sitting *seiza* on their knees in a row. Tozzi would also be sitting *seiza*, facing them, about twenty-five feet away. They would all be staring at him, mean-faced, trying to psyche him out, but he wouldn't let himself be intimidated by such blatant tactics. He was centered. His attitude was positive. His mind was free and open. He had no strategy, no special techniques, no tricks he intended to use. His only goal was to get out of the way and take each one as he came, throwing him efficiently and automatically, keeping a rhythm and not linger-ing over any particular attacker. He'd keep moving and make them come to him, make them commit their attacks and com-promise their own balance. He wouldn't fall into the typical trap of getting caught flat-footed and allowing them to gang up on him, each attacker grabbing two fistfuls of his *gi* jacket and dragging him down. No, he'd stay light and mobile. He wouldn't let them catch him. He would just throw and move on to the next attacker, throw and move on. That was his only strategy.

Sitting *seiza* before his attackers, he would pause to take a deep breath, filling his diaphragm and letting it out slowly through his mouth until finally he was ready. He'd be psyched, but he'd also be relaxed. He was ready to become a black belt. The five attackers would be ready, too, waiting for his bow, the signal for the *randori* to begin. Tozzi would take another deep breath and let it out slowly, settling deeper into his center. All he'd have to do now was bow.

He'd scan his attackers one last time, making eye contact with each grim face. He was ready. Calmly he'd bow, and they'd all jump to their feet, rushing at him full-tilt. He'd stand up and wait, wait for them to come to him. He was calm, ready. The first black belt would run up to him, his fist balled. Tozzi would force himself to wait. The punch would come full force, aimed right at his—

"Hey, Mike!"

Tozzi's eyes shot open. He looked all around him. It wasn't the bright lights of the gym or the wide blue expanse of the mats. It was the murky gloom of Joey's Starlight Lounge in Hoboken. Shit.

"Hey, Mike. What the hell you doing, sleepin'?"

Tozzi opened his eyes again and gazed blankly at the goofball moon face on the other side of the booth. He closed his eyes again and sighed. Friggin' Freshy.

"Wake up, man. Jesus Christ! You can't fall asleep now. What if Buddha wants to talk to you?"

"Buddha doesn't talk to anyone who isn't made." Tozzi cleared his throat. "You know that."

"Yeah, that's true, that's true. But he might make an exception. You never know, Mike. You never know."

Freshy DeFresco rattled the ice in his favorite drink, a Rusty Nail, scotch and Galliano. He was a skinny kid with a concave chest that even a sweater and sport coat couldn't hide. He had a round face with watery basset hound eyes and a perpetual three days' growth of beard. A small-time hood, Freshy was barely thirty, if that, and he was already half-bald to the crown of his head, but he kept the mousy brown hair long in back and tied it in a shitty little two-inch ponytail. Even with the diamond stud in his ear, he was still the uncoolest asshole Tozzi had ever met. He was jittery and fidgety, always playing with something in his hand or bouncing his knee or doing something to drive you crazy, and he wasted so much time figuring out all the "angles," he didn't know if he was coming or going anymore. Freshy made Barney Fife look suave.

Freshy took a quick sip of his Rusty Nail, then went back to rattling the ice. "Something wrong, Mike? What're you looking at me like that for? Huh?"

Tozzi stared at him through half-closed lids. He didn't trust Freshy as far as he could spit. Despite all Freshy's testimonials that he was a changed man and that he was ready to work for the good guys from now on, Tozzi didn't believe a word of it. He'd heard this rap a hundred times before from other guys who'd been flipped by the law. They get themselves in a jam, go to trial, and end up facing serious time for the first time in their lives, and all of a sudden they get religion. They call every cop and fed they can think of, begging to make a deal, promising to do anything—rat on their old associates, testify in court against a bigger fish, make introductions for an undercover cop—anything to get a reduced sentence. Guys like Freshy think they can go to heaven on brownie points. Of course, when you're facing three to seven for fencing stolen property, the thought of getting credit for time served plus parole and a promise of witness relocation when it's all over probably does sound like heaven.

Still, Tozzi had been burned before by mutts like Freshy. Crooks don't get religion; they just get scared. And when they get scared, they'll do anything and say anything to save their sorry little asses. Put a guy like this back on the street so that he can help you, and nine times out of ten the guy will play both ends to the middle, telling the cops what they want to hear, then turning around and telling the bad guys what they want to hear. It was a matter of survival and paranoia. Bad guys who flip never really believe in their heart of hearts that the good guys can protect them, and Freshy was probably no different. Tozzi was willing to bet that in that fucked-up head of his, Freshy thought he was just looking out for his own best interests. Just in case the Bureau decided to cut him loose, he wanted to make sure he had something to fall back on. And that was to be expected, up to a point. Just as long as he didn't try to make *big* brownie points with Buddha Stanzione and Tony Bells by telling them who Mike Santoro really was.

"Mikey, whatta'ya keep looking at me like that for? I didn't do nothin'."

"Where you been?"

Freshy jerked his thumb at the front door. "I just had to go get something. Something for Bells."

"What?"

"Whatta'ya mean, what?"

"What did you go get for Bells?"

"A turkey."

"A what?"

"A turkey, a turkey. It's gonna be Thanksgiving. People eat turkey. What'sa matta, you don't eat turkey? I got a good deal on some fresh turkeys. I figured I'd give Bells one. You know, goodwill toward men and all that jazz. Grease the wheels, you know."

"You're full of shit."

"I swear on my mother's eyes, Mike. I just went home to get him a turkey. I'll show you. I got a whole bunch of 'em in my trunk."

"You're full of shit. You don't have any friggin' turkeys. They'd go bad in the trunk."

Freshy rattled his ice. "Nah! Whatta'ya, kidding? It's friggin' cold out there. They stay nice and cold in my trunk. C'mon. I'll go show you." Freshy didn't make a move to get out of the booth.

"Frig you, you lying bastard."

Freshy threw up his hands and rolled his eyes. "Why the hell don't you ever believe me, Mike? Why?"

"Because you're a goddamn liar."

"I am not."

"Yes, you are."

"When did I ever lie to you? When?"

"If you got a turkey for Bells, why don't you give one to Buddha? Grease his wheels, too."

Freshy shook his head. "Can't do that."

" 'Cause you don't have any turkeys. That's why."

"Man, you don't understand shit." Freshy looked down and rubbed his brow, suddenly distraught. He took another quick sip. "Listen to me, Mike. Buddha Stanzione, you don't even talk to. I mean, what if I gave him a turkey and it turned out to be bad? You know, smelly, rotten? I'd be fucking dead. He'd eat *me* for Thanksgiving."

"You just told me they stay nice and cold in your trunk."

"Yeah, but you never know about these things, Mike. You

drive around, the car heats up, the trunk gets hot, there go the turkeys. It could happen, man. You never know. I don't wanna get whacked just 'cause I gave the guy salmon Manila or something like that. Not me, man."

Tozzi leaned on the tabletop and put his face in Freshy's. "Keep on lying, Fresh. Go 'head, keep it up."

"I ain't lying, man. You wanna fuckin' turkey, I'll give you one. C'mon."

"Cut the shit and listen to me." Tozzi lowered his voice. "If I find out you're fucking around with me, Freshy, I'll cut you loose, and I'll make sure Buddha and Bells know you were cooperating with us. You hear me?"

Freshy blinked in confusion. "I'm shocked to be hearing this, Mike. This isn't you talking. Haven't I played straight with you so far? Did I get you the introduction to Bells or what? Did I convince him that we were doing porno together or what? Is he or is he not at this very moment sitting in that back room back there trying to get some money out of Buddha for us? That's what you wanted, right? So what the hell else do you want from me? If you want me to do more, then you gotta tell me what. I'm not Mr. Mysterioso, the mind-reader."

Tozzi rubbed his tired eyes. "You're right, Fresh. You did do all that. But what I wanna know is, what else you been doing? What're you telling Bells behind my back?"

"Nothing!"

"Then keep it that way. You hear me?"

"I can't believe you're saying this to me."

"Don't try to play both sides to the middle, Fresh. It won't work. I'll cut you loose and feed you to the sharks. I swear to God, I will."

Freshy rattled his ice and thought about it for a second. Then a big grin opened up under his long sharp woodpecker nose.

There were gaps between all his front teeth. "You won't cut me loose, Mike. You think you will, but I know you, Mike. You won't."

"Oh, no? Why won't I?"

"Because."

"Because why?"

"Because you got a hard-on for my sister, that's why."

Tozzi sat back and scowled. "Get the fuck outta here."

"C'mon, c'mon, c'mon. Don't try to bullshit me, Mike. I seen how you look at her, man. It's obvious."

"Get outta here."

"C'mon, Mike. Be honest. You already put the moves on her, didn't you? I know she took you up to her apartment once. C'mon, deny it. I dare you."

Tozzi gave him the finger, then picked up his glass and tilted in back into his mouth. Ice slivers slid onto his tongue. He wanted to put out a few of Freshy's crooked yellow teeth to shut him up, but not with Buddha and Tony Bells sitting back there. He and Freshy were supposed to be partners, buddies. The little fuck.

He chomped on the ice and stared down at the squeezed lime in his glass. Freshy was an asshole, but in this case he was right. He did have a hard-on for Gina DeFresco. He'd been catching himself daydreaming about her a lot lately. Too bad she didn't give a shit about him, though.

"Hey, Mike?"

Tozzi glared up at Freshy. "Shut up." Thank God his sister didn't look like him.

"No, man, I wasn't gonna say nothing about Gina. Forget about that. I'm sorry I even brought it up."

"Shut up anyway."

"Yeah, but I just wanna know one thing."

30

Tozzi sighed, struggling to keep his eyes open. "What?"

"Seriously. You wanna turkey or not?"

"No."

"Free, I mean."

"No!"

"Okay, okay, I was just asking. You don't have to get nasty about it."

Freshy shrugged and fidgeted, rattling his ice chips and looking hurt.

Tozzi ignored him and leaned out the side of the booth to see what was going on in the back room. Buddha Stanzione and Tony Bells were still huddled at that table, still talking. He wondered what the hell was taking them so long to make up their minds. He looked at the Budweiser clock over the bar. It was after four. Christ, if he didn't get some sleep, he could forget about his black-belt test. He squinted into the gloom to see their faces, but he couldn't make out their expressions. What the hell were they doing back there?

FOUR

Tozzi picked up his empty glass with the dead-fish lime in it and got out of the booth.

Freshy looked up at him, surprised. "Where you going?"

"I gotta go to the bathroom." He went over to Stanley the Tazmanian Devil sitting at the bar.

Stanley growled, "Whatta'ya want?" Real friendly.

Tozzi nodded toward the back room where Buddha and Bells were having their meeting. The men's room was back there. "I gotta go to the bathroom."

Stanley's glance slid down to Tozzi's crotch. Stanley was the guard dog here, and his orders were to keep everyone out of the back room. He nodded toward the front door. "Go outside."

Tozzi made a face and put some distress in his voice. "I gotta take a shit."

The Tazmanian Devil rubbed his jaw, thinking it over. He shook his head. "Go outside."

"C'mon, Stanley. I really gotta go."

Stanley stared at his crotch again as if he were looking for proof.

"C'mon, Stanley. I'm dying here."

Stanley frowned and thought about it some more, then got off

32

his stool. "Wait here." He went toward the back room and stood in the archway, waiting to be noticed.

Buddha noticed him, but said nothing.

Bells followed Buddha's gaze to the legbreaker standing in the archway. "What?" He was annoyed with the intrusion.

"Sorry to interrupt, Bells, but Santoro says he needs the john." Stanley shrugged. It was beyond his control.

"Tell him to go outside."

"He says he's gotta do . . . you know, the other thing."

Bells frowned and looked to Buddha. The capo shrugged, unconcerned. "Let him go."

Stanley moved out of the archway between the rooms and let Tozzi pass. He muttered under his breath, "Be quick."

Tozzi walked into the room sideways, facing Bells and Buddha as he moved toward the men's room. "Thank you, Mr. Stanzione. I appreciate it."

Bells and Buddha just stared at him, waiting for him to go into the bathroom so they could continue their discussion. From the far end of the room, Buddha's four gorillas stared at him, too.

Tozzi went into the tiny men's room and closed the door behind him, locking it with a paint-encrusted eyehook. The bathroom was even more decrepit than the rest of Joey's Starlight Lounge. It was freezing in there, and the floor was sticky. The urinal was covered with spiderweb cracks and full of ice chips, the door on the toilet stall was long gone, and a plastic bucket under the sink was overflowing with used brown-paper towels. Despite the cold, the room smelled to high heaven of piss and disinfectant.

Tozzi dumped the old lime in his glass into the toilet and shook out the last drops of ice water. He stepped up on the toilet and looked out the small grimy window. Outside, in a side lot hidden from the street by overgrown hedges, two identical cars were parked, a black Lincoln Continental Town Car and a gray one. Buddha's motorcade.

Tozzi got down and went to the warped wooden door. Through the slit where the door didn't quite meet the frame, Tozzi was able to see Buddha and Bells sitting at their table. He put the rim of his empty glass against the door, careful not to make any noise, then put his ear to the base of the glass. Low-tech surveillance, but the best he could do on the spur of the moment.

He listened for a full minute, but all he could hear was the jukebox playing softly out in the bar. He took his ear off the glass and looked through the slit. Buddha and Bells were just sitting there, not saying anything. They seemed to be waiting each other out.

Bells was looking down at something on the floor between him and Buddha. Tozzi got up on his toes to see what was so interesting. He furrowed his brows when he finally spotted the blue and yellow kid's backpack. There was some goofy-looking character on the front of the backpack, a fuzzy blue thing with googly eyes and a cookie in its paw. The crazy eyes reminded him of Freshy DeFresco's when he wanted something.

Buddha was moving a pair of salt and pepper shakers around the tabletop as if they were chess pieces. He seemed to be lost in thought, intent on the salt and pepper. Only his fingers moved. For a little guy, Buddha had a big face, but the face seldom moved, except for the eyes. Even his dyed-black hair, which he combed in a slight pompadour, seldom moved. From his build, you'd expect Buddha to be a wiry kind of a guy, but Buddha didn't say much and he didn't move much—that was why they called him Buddha. He was like one of those statues. Of course, the name was deceptive. Snakes don't move much either, not until they strike.

It looked like Bells was waiting for Buddha to make the first move. He just sat there with his arms folded on the table, a trace of a grin on his face as he watched the capo move the salt and pepper shakers around the table. They were waiting each other out.

Tozzi went back and forth between squinting through the crack in the door and putting his ear to the glass, waiting for one of them to say something.

After a while, Buddha's glance slid down to the backpack on the floor, lingered there for a moment, then floated back up. He looked Bells in the eye. "Your wife come back yet?" His voice croaked from underuse.

Bells shook his head.

"What's it been? Month, month and a half?"

Bells raised his eyebrows and shrugged. "She ain't coming back. She left everything—wedding ring, engagement ring—everything."

"That's too bad. What was it, another guy?"

"Margie? I dunno, maybe. Who knows? She was a wack and a half. I only hope she's happy wherever she is."

Buddha picked up the salt shaker and stared at it. "Pretty girl. She always seemed like a nice kid."

Bells didn't respond, and they fell back into silence.

No wonder this meeting was taking so goddamn long, Tozzi thought.

Buddha looked down at that backpack again, then clicked the glass salt shaker against the pepper shaker for a little while. Finally he pointed at the backpack with his chin. "I don't think so. Not this time."

Bells stared at him as if he were crazy. "Why not?"

35

Buddha frowned and shook his head. No was no.

"You're being stupid," Bells said.

Buddha didn't respond. Tozzi waited for the capo to react, but Buddha's face remained placid. Tozzi was surprised. Capos normally don't tolerate being called stupid, not from their underlings.

"Stupid," Bells repeated, his voice rising as if Buddha were passing up a great opportunity. "You're being stupid."

Tozzi furrowed his brow, his ear to the glass. Maybe Bells was higher up in the mob hierarchy than the FBI had thought. The guy definitely wasn't doing any bowing and scraping here.

Buddha cleared his throat. "The kid's a screw-up. He'll never pay it back."

Bells nodded toward the men's room and leaned over the table. "His buddy Santoro will keep him in line. He looks like he's got some sense."

Tozzi grinned.

But Buddha wasn't impressed. "And what do *you* know about Santoro? Nothing."

"What do I need to know? I've seen the place these guys got over in Union City. They're putting out five hundred videos a day. They're doing good business. I checked with Canoga Park. They know who Santoro is."

Tozzi watched for Buddha's reaction. He should've been just a little bit impressed. After all, Canoga Park, California, was the porno capital of the United States, and the Bureau had gotten a big porno distributor out there who was now cooperating with the government to vouch for Mike Santoro with the New York mob. If Santoro had friends in Canoga Park, he had to be okay. Tozzi put his ear back to the glass.

Buddha went back to clicking the salt against the pepper. Another long wait. "No," he finally croaked. "The kid'll screw up. It'll end up being messy. No one needs messy."

Bells started tapping the backpack with the side of his shoe. "He came up with this, didn't he? That doesn't make him a fuck-up. You said he couldn't borrow any more until he paid up what he already owed. Well, here it is. Thirty-two, five. I don't call that being a fuck-up." Bells stepped on the backpack and flattened it out a little.

A sickly smile uncurled under Buddha's nose. "Who do you think you're kidding, Bells? The kid didn't come up with that money. You did."

Bells laughed. "Me? Are you crazy or what? What do I look like, Santa Claus?"

The capo's smile snapped back into a short flat line, and his eyes dimmed. Buddha didn't have to say that he thought Bells was full of shit.

Bells showed his palms. "Let's start making a little sense here, okay? Why the fuck would I put up this kind of money for anybody."

Buddha shook his head. "Not for anybody. For Freshy DeFresco."

"So what's so special about Freshy DeFresco that I should go in the hole just so he can get a loan from you? It don't make sense."

The salt shaker clicked against the pepper, like a clock ticking. "Nothing special about Freshy. Except that he's got a sister named Gina."

Gina? Tozzi fumbled the glass, but he managed to catch it before it hit the floor. His face was flushed.

Bells was staring hard at Buddha, his eyes bulging. He looked the way Tozzi felt.

Buddha's sickly smile uncurled again. "You think I don't

37

know nothing. Lemme tell you something, Bells. I know a lot. I know all about you and that broad. You're like a fly around shit with her. You oughta be ashamed of yourself. That's why your wife left you. Has to be."

"What's that got to do with anything? What's that got to do with *this*?" Bells pointed down at the backpack.

"Everything. You wanna get in that broad's pants so bad, you'll do anything. Like helping out her little brother, the fuck-up. Like getting him a nice big loan that he probably can't handle. Like doing anything to be Mr. Nice Guy so you can impress the sister."

"You're crazy."

"Oh, yeah?"

"I'm telling you, you're crazy."

"So maybe I am crazy. So what? But I'm not crazy enough to give these two mooks any money. Tell 'em to go see somebody else. I don't need their business. Okay?"

"No. It's not okay."

Tozzi peered through the crack. The little capo was sitting up straight, his nostrils flared. Bells had finally pissed him off.

But Bells didn't back down. "Listen to me, my friend. No woman's snatch is worth thirty-two grand. I don't care who she is."

Buddha stared at Bells as he rolled the salt shaker between his palms. "You're a pretty weird fuck, Bells. I wouldn't put anything past you."

Bells grinned like a skull. "You're losing it, Buddha. You know that? You're losing it."

Buddha grinned back. "So why don't *you* lend it to them?"

"I don't have it."

"Bullshit, you don't."

38

Bells shrugged. "Believe what you wanna believe. I don't have cash like that to work with."

Buddha's sick grin stretched a little wider. "Go 'head, lend it to them. I give you my blessing. You don't have to cut me in or nothing."

Bells just stared at him.

"What'sa matta, Bells? You don't like that idea? How come? You can be the big cheese all by yourself. Freshy'll kiss the ground you walk on. He'll make sure his sister comes sits on your lap and tells you what she wants for Christmas."

Buddha's shoulders bounced in a quiet laugh. Bells just stared at him and said nothing. He looked like he wanted to wipe the smile off Buddha's face, and for a moment Tozzi thought he just might try it, despite Buddha's four beef boys sitting on the other side of room.

"What'sa matta, Bells? You look upset. You don't like it when I start talking about *your* money, do you? *My* money, it's okay to talk about. But when it's *your* money, it's different."

Bells didn't say anything for a minute. It was as if he weren't even listening. Then suddenly he smiled. "You do whatever makes you comfortable, Buddha. Nobody's twisting your arm. All I gotta say is that from a business perspective, you're being stupid. These two guys are clearing ten grand a week now selling porn. You give 'em the money they need, they'll buy more equipment, hire more people, expand their distribution. They say they can triple what they're making now if they can get their hands on some capital."

"Guys say a lot of things when they want money."

"I'm telling you, do what makes you comfortable. You don't wanna give it to them, don't. I just came to you first because I always do. We do good business together. But if you don't wanna do this one, I'll just go look for someone who's not afraid to make some money. No hard feelings."

The little capo's mouth snapped back to a short line. He turned his wrist over and started to punch out numbers on the calculator in his wristwatch. His delicate little fingers had no trouble with the minuscule keypad. Every time he'd get a tally, he'd stare at it for a second, then clear it and start all over again. He did this at least a half-dozen times in a row. Bells watched, grinning like he knew something Buddha didn't.

"All right," Buddha finally said, his voice soft and suddenly sleepy.

Bells nodded as if he knew all along what the outcome would be.

Buddha pointed down at the blue and yellow backpack. "I know this money came from you, Bells. I don't care what you say. If you wanna stick your neck out for this DeFresco kid, that's your business. But my business is making money. You believe in these two guys so much, fine. I'll give 'em what they want, but it's gonna be at a point and a half a week, and *you* are responsible for them. You understand me? They fall behind in the vig, *you* pay it. They screw up, they skip town, they blow it at the track, I don't give a shit. It's *your* problem. You understand? If they don't pay up, then it's *your* headache."

Bells looked him in the eye. "And who in his right mind is gonna collect from me?"

Buddha leaned into his face and stared back at him. "Don't flatter yourself, my friend. You're not the only freak in this business."

Tozzi was confused. Freak? What was that supposed to mean?

"You're hurting my feelings, Buddha."

"I don't give a fuck about your feelings. All I care about is the green. And so do you."

Bells shrugged. "Money can't buy me love." He laughed at his own statement.

Buddha stood up. "Tell your porno friends they can have the money. If I were you, though, I'd get some collateral out of them. Remember, they're your responsibility."

Bells stared up at him. "I never forget anything, Buddha. You know that."

The capo didn't answer. Instead he reached over the table and rearranged the salt and pepper shakers, putting them back where they'd been, next to the bowl full of sugar packets and the Heinz catsup bottle. He headed for the back door then, and two of his four gorillas rushed ahead to get it for him. The other two brought up the rear as the little capo walked out with the blue and yellow backpack under his arm.

Tozzi put the glass down on the sink and flushed the toilet. He ran some water and washed his hands. When he unlocked the eyehook and opened the door, Bells was slumped down in his seat, his arms laid out on the table, palms down. He was staring straight ahead, lost in thought.

Tozzi took a tentative step toward him. "You okay, Bells?"

The loan shark nodded like a robot, then suddenly stared up at Tozzi and grinned. "Yeah, I'm okay. How about you?"

Tozzi shrugged. "Fine."

Bells stared out into space again. "I got some good news for you guys."

The toilet was still running back in the men's room.

FIVE

Tozzi stared out the window at the lower Manhattan skyline across the choppy, steel-gray waters of the harbor. He could hear the shower going upstairs, Freshy singing some stupid rap song about shaking his body, shaking his body. The choppy waves reminded Tozzi of swirls of frosting on a chocolate layer cake, and that made him think about food again. He was tired, hung over, and starving, and there wasn't a solid thing to eat in this house because Freshy's parents were spending the week down in Atlantic City, and Freshy would never think of something as obvious as buying groceries. Tozzi had already packed the garbage pail with rotten moldy stuff he'd found in the refrigerator in his useless search for breakfast. The milk he'd poured down the sink was almost cottage cheese, and Tozzi was drinking his coffee black, waiting for Freshy to get out of the goddamn shower and get dressed so they could go find a diner.

Sitting at the kitchen table, he sipped from a New Jersey Devils mug and made a face. He hated his coffee black, but he needed the caffeine. He was fixated on one of those nice big Greek diners where he could have all the milk he wanted in his coffee, eggs over easy, and a pile of hash browns. Yeah, a mountain of crispy-edged home fries would really fill that hole in the

42

middle of his gut right now. And toast, too. Buttered rye toast. If friggin' Freshy would only get out of the goddamn shower.

Tozzi arched his back and rolled his head on his shoulders. He felt like a bag of shit. He'd ended up sleeping on that lumpy old couch in the living room here. Last night he'd thought about going back to his own place in Hoboken since Joey's Starlight Lounge was just on the other side of town, but that wouldn't have been smart. Mike Santoro lived down the shore, an hour away. Someone could've followed him home, his real home, and that could've led to his cover being blown. So instead of going back to his own apartment and getting eight hours of sleep so he would be rested for his black-belt test tonight, he'd left the bar as Mike Santoro and gone back to Freshy's parents' house in Bayonne, crashed on the couch for five hours, and wrecked his back. But that was okay. Better this than having Bells and Buddha know where he really lived. But as soon as he got a decent cup of coffee and that mountain of home fries so that he could carb up for the test, he intended to go home, crawl into bed, and get a few more hours. Good hours. If Freshy would only shut up about shaking his goddamn body and get out of the friggin' shower.

He rubbed the back of his neck and wished he'd taken a shower himself. He felt pretty scuzzy, and he'd do anything for a fresh pair of underwear. He looked up at the ceiling toward the sound of the running water. C'mon, goddamn it.

Unconsciously he reached for the mug of coffee and brought it to his lips, then frowned and put it back down. Without milk, it was like battery acid. He gazed out the sunny window, about to dump the rest of the cup down the sink, when suddenly he thought he heard something outside. Footsteps coming up the wooden steps that led to the kitchen entrance. Instinctively he turned in his seat so he'd have quicker access to the gun in his ankle holster. Then he remembered that he wasn't wearing his gun. He had decided not to bring a gun to the meeting last night. One of Buddha's gorillas could've frisked him, and they would've taken the gun as a sign of bad faith.

A key slipped into the lock from the outside. Through the opaque curtains on the door window, Tozzi could see that who-ever it was was carrying two grocery bags. Tozzi figured it must be Freshy's mother, back from the shore.

The door swung open and banged against the kitchen counter.

"What the hell're *you* doing here?"

It wasn't Freshy's mother. It was his sister, Gina.

Tozzi just stared at her, wondering whether that look of dis-gust on her face was for the smelly garbage or for him. He reminded himself that he was Mike Santoro, not Mike Tozzi, and the hots he had for her weren't supposed to be any different from the hots he had for every other good-looking babe he saw in the course of an average day. Except for Mike Tozzi, that wasn't the case. Gina was special. She was real. She was the Italian-American girl from the neighborhood he'd always wanted.

Gina set down the grocery bags on the counter and pushed her glasses up her nose. The glasses were round with thin purple metal rims, and on her they were sexy. She had soft brown hair that fanned out just below her shoulders, light brown eyes, and a Roman nose. She tended to look mad a lot of the time, but that was just her normal expression. She was slender, about five-five, five-six, somewhere in her early-ish thirties, and she always wore slacks. Never a dress or a skirt, from what Tozzi had seen. Today it was black slacks and black patent-leather flats with a silky banana-yellow top under a green satin bomber jacket. Tozzi thought she looked sharp, very tailored but still hip. But the one time he'd told her he thought she was very attractive, she told him he was full of shit and said she looked like John Lennon in drag, complaining that her breasts were too small and her can was too big, daring him to agree with her. Tozzi knew better than to fall for that one.

Tozzi sat there and watched her unpack the groceries. He didn't dare say anything even vaguely nice, like hello, because he knew what her reaction would be. Besides, Mike Santoro was a slime-bucket pornographer, so he couldn't be polite or anything. Anyway, he'd already tried and failed with her on their one-afternoon stand when she'd refused to believe that he thought she was attractive.

It had been one of those incredible warm but colorful fall days when the leaves have already begun to turn, but it's still sunny and lazy like the end of August, a day plucked out of time, the kind of day when you want to do something wild because you think days like this don't really exist on anybody's real-life calendar so whatever you do will be your secret.

One of Gina's cousin's kids was getting baptized that day, and Freshy had invited him to the ceremony and the party afterward. Tozzi never made it to the party because while the baby was screaming its lungs out as the priest poured holy water over its little head, he and Gina had been flirting like crazy. She didn't know he was into porn. As everyone left the church, Gina started walking back to her apartment instead of following everyone to her cousin's house for the party. Tozzi followed her, and it was like one of those wonderfully horny dreams you wish you'd never woken up from. She strolled nice and slow, zigzagging down the sidewalk, stirring the orangy yellow leaves, sneaking glances back at Tozzi. Tozzi stayed about three car lengths behind her, watching the spears of sunlight pierce the falling leaves and shine through her loose light-brown hair. When they got to her apartment building, she stopped and turned around and just looked at him, grinning a sly little grin, waiting for him to do something. He sauntered up slowly. Even though they didn't know each other that well, they both knew what they wanted, except neither one was ready to make the first move. Then he started to laugh, and she started to laugh, and pretty soon they were hysterical, out of control, howling like a couple of lunatics.

"You wanna come up for coffee?" she asked, brushing tears out of her eyes.

"Sure," he said.

"Or would you rather go back to the party?"

"No thanks."

She shook her head. "Me neither." The way her hair shushed over her shoulders made him dizzy.

Her apartment was small and functional. Bare wood floors and blinds. No curtains, no knickknacks, no flowers. Just a lot of framed black and white photographs of laughing kids on the walls. She said she'd taken them herself.

Tozzi sat down on the couch, threw his arm over the back, and watched her make coffee.

"Don't do that," she said with a self-conscious grin.

He moved his arm. "What?"

"Don't look at me. Look at something else."

Tozzi shrugged. "If it bothers you." He turned sideways and stretched out on the couch. Orange sunlight slanted in through the casement windows and encased Tozzi's feet and face in blocks of warmth. He closed his eyes and almost fell asleep. Then he thought of her.

He squinted up through the sunlight to see what she was doing and was startled to see that she was standing right over him. She kicked off her shoes and sat on his toes on the other end of the couch. The smell of the brewing coffee drifted in from the kitchenette. She shaded her eyes from the sun and looked into his.

"So what do you think?" she said.

He smiled. "I dunno."

She tucked her feet up and turned sideways to face him, leaning back against the arm of the couch. Her toes burrowed under his butt. "My feet are cold," she said.

"Uh-huh."

"Any ideas?"

"About what?"

"Getting them warm."

Tozzi grinned. "I may have a few."

"Okay."

"Okay, what?"

"Get them warm."

"Oh. Okay." He reached between his legs, pulled out one of her feet, and rubbed her toes between his hands. "How's that?"

"Good. Do the other one."

He took the other foot and rubbed that one. "Better?"

Her eyes were closed, head tilted back. "Yeah . . . that's nice." When he stopped, she opened her eyes. "I'm still cold, though." She was smiling.

"Oh. What parts are cold?"

"All of me."

"Well, where would you like me to start?"

She grabbed his forearms and pulled herself up until she was on top of him, nose to nose. "How about right here?" she said, and kissed him. And kissed him. And kissed him some more. And then he kissed her. A lot. And then they started exploring with their tongues and toes and fingers. And Tozzi started to get light-headed it was so nice, with Gina on top of him, and the sun all over the room, and her skin so white and soft, and her silky hair between his fingers, and her lips and her shoulders and her ears and her nipples and . . .

And they never got around to having that coffee.

Gina banged a can of plum tomatoes on the countertop, yanking Tozzi out of his sweet memories. He stared at her, remembering what Buddha Stanzione had said to Bells about her last night. Tozzi considered the possibility again, but the two of them seemed like such a mismatch. Except Buddha's comment wasn't the only evidence he had. There was the message he had heard on her answering machine that day while they were lying on the couch.

They'd been dozing in twilight bliss, her head nestled on his shoulder, when the phone suddenly rang. Neither of them moved to get it. Four rings, then Tozzi heard her voice on the recording telling whoever it was to leave a message after the beep. *"Gina, it's me,"* the caller said. *"Gimme a call."* Tozzi had recognized the voice right away. It was Bells.

He watched her putting vegetables away in the refrigerator now. He didn't like being ignored, so he decided to risk a question. "You bring any milk?"

She looked at him as if he were a worm. "What's the matter? You can't say hello?"

"Hello. Did you bring any milk?"

"Hello. No." She went back to unpacking the groceries, reaching into a bag and pulling out a big turkey. She opened the refrigerator again and put it on the bottom shelf.

"You didn't have to buy that," he said, nodding at the bird. "Your brother says he's got a whole bunch of turkeys."

She glared at him. "Did they fall off the truck?"

Tozzi shrugged and didn't pursue it. She was in a mood. Gina was supposedly the straight arrow of the family. She had a real job as a children's clothing buyer at Macy's in Manhattan. A couple of her relatives—an uncle and two cousins—had done time for auto theft, and her father always seemed to have something hot for sale in the trunk of his car. None of them were big-time hoods, except for her brother Freshy, who had been trying his best to work his way into the Mafia when the FBI presented him with a alternative career path. But like a lot of people whose family members have no problem breaking the law, Gina didn't want to know anything about it. She didn't participate, but she didn't preach to them either. She loved her family because they were her family, and she was devoted to her screwy little brother because he was her screwy little brother, but if they sold stolen turkeys, or they knew where to get stolen cars, or they smoked cigarettes that didn't have the federal tax stamp on the pack, she didn't want to know anything about it. That was their business, not hers.

Supposedly.

In his head, Tozzi kept hearing Bells's voice on her answering machine. *"Gina, it's me. Gimme a call."* At the time, she'd picked her head up off his shoulder, rolled her eyes, and made a face at the machine, but she didn't offer an explanation, and Tozzi didn't ask for one. But now he was starting to wonder about her and Bells.

The first thing Gina unpacked from the second grocery bag was a cellophane package of bread stuffing. Tozzi's stomach growled. It wasn't crispy-edged home fries, but it was food. He stood up and ambled over toward the counter.

She looked at him warily over her glasses, like a dog eyeing a cat coming too close to her bowl. He leaned against the counter and crossed his arms. Her eyes didn't leave him.

He glanced down at the package of stuffing. He knew this was probably for the DeFrescos' Thanksgiving dinner, but he was starving. He was dying to rip the bag open and shove a handful of the dry bread cubes into his mouth, but that wouldn't be right. Of course, he wasn't Mike Tozzi, he was Mike Santoro, and Santoro was a bad guy as far as Gina knew. So why shouldn't he open the bag and take some? It would be consistent with his character. And anyway he was hungry.

He reached for the bag and the sound of rustling cellophane invaded the quiet kitchen. The steely glint in her eye made him freeze.

"You like that hand?" she asked.

"What?"

She looked down at his hand on the bag. "You like that hand?"

"Yeah. I like it."

"Then keep it to yourself before I cut it off." There was a knife rack on the counter behind the bags of groceries.

Tozzi looked her in the eye and grinned, but she was serious. The DeFrescos were Sicilian.

"C'mon," he said. "Just lemme have a few."

"No."

"C'mon. You're not gonna use the whole bag."

"No." She pulled the bag of stuffing out from under his hand, threw it in the cupboard, and slammed the door shut.

Tozzi shrugged and gave her a helpless look. "Gina, why so mean? What'd I ever do to you?"

"You don't know?" She was weighing a can of cranberry sauce in her hand.

"Oh, c'mon, will ya? You make it sound like I forced you."

"I didn't say that."

"Well, then what *are* you saying?"

She put the can on the counter and pulled another one out of the bag. "I don't want to talk about it."

"Why not?"

She sighed, exasperated. "Why don't you just go away?"

"We had fun. It was great. Why don't you want to talk about it?"

"Because I don't."

"Well, I do."

"Then go outside and talk to yourself." She pulled out a package of walnuts, and Tozzi's stomach growled out loud.

She looked down at his gut and shook her head.

Tozzi frowned. "You know, Gina, I don't get you. I bend over backward to be nice to you, and you treat me like shit. For a while there I thought maybe we coulda had something together, but I guess I was wrong."

"You've got that right."

"See? You've always gotta be nasty. Why? I'm nice to you, but you're nasty to me. That's not right." This was Mike Santoro talking, but Tozzi was getting into it. His undercover identity gave him license to be totally Italian.

"I'm nasty with you because you're an infantile jerk who sells dirty movies for a living. Do I need any more reason to be nasty to you?" She sounded very logical and reasonable as she told him off, and for some reason that made her even more appealing to him.

"Hey, Gina, you make it sound worse than it is. It's good wholesome stuff I sell. Softcore, that's all. I've got sex therapists who buy from me. They tell me my stuff is very therapeutic. Perks their patients right up."

"Oh, shut up."

"No, I'm telling you the truth. I don't do hardcore. No snuff, no heavy bondage, no animals, and definitely no kids. Never ever would I deal kiddie porn. It turns my stomach just thinking about it."

51

His stomach gurgled.

She looked at him over her glasses.

"I'm telling you the God's honest truth, but I can see you don't believe me. You've just got it in for me, that's all. But I don't know why. I'm a nice guy." Tozzi flashed a cocky grin, thinking Santoro. "I'm very sensitive, too, and you hurt my feelings. I gave myself to you that day, and look what I get for it."

"What'd you say?"

"You heard me. I gave my heart and soul to you, and this is the thanks I get."

She picked up the package of walnuts and flung them at him. It hit his shoulder and broke open. A downpour of walnuts hit the linoleum, rattling and clicking, rolling all over the place.

"Now look you what you did," he said. "Was that necessary?"

"Pick those up," she snapped.

"You help me."

"Pick those up!"

Tozzi stooped down and picked one up, grinning up at her, being a real wiseguy. But inside he was still wondering about her and Bells, hoping it wasn't true.

"I said, help me pick those up."

"If I do, whatta'ya gonna do for me?"

"Go to hell!"

"C'mon, Gina, I'm kiddin'—Hey, where you going?"

"To the bathroom. You mind? And I want those things picked up. I'm serious."

Gibbons was listening through the headphones. He crossed his brows and looked over at Dougherty, the surveillance technician who was working the equipment. Gibbons still had the toothache, but it seemed to be in remission for the moment. He knew it was only temporary, though. Eventually the sledgehammer would start up again. They were parked down the block from the DeFresco house, sitting in the back of a dark blue FBI surveillance van with B & B PLUMBING AND HEATING painted in white and red along the sides, listening to Tozzi flirt with Freshy DeFresco's sister. Gibbons couldn't figure out what they were talking about now, what she wanted him to pick up. He shrugged at Dougherty to show his confusion.

Dougherty shrugged back. The top half of the technician's face looked concerned, but the bottom half was overjoyed. Dougherty always had a big smile on his face, no matter what, a big openmouthed smile that gave him that mad scientist look. Gibbons was beginning to think it was some kind of palsy. Either that or he was a born-again Christian. Somehow Gibbons doubted it, though. For most Irish Catholics it's bad enough the first time around. They don't need to be born again.

Gibbons slid the headphones off one ear, but kept them on his head. "Sounds like she broke a string of pearls, doesn't it?"

"I don't think so." Dougherty's eyeballs were tucked up under his lids as he listened. He pointed to a pair of VU meters on the console, their needles relatively still now that Gina was out of the room and Tozzi was by himself in the kitchen. "The sound wasn't quite right for pearls. It would've been higher in pitch, a sudden cluster of *sharp* clicks. This was much lower, and it had a rattle to it."

Gibbons shrugged. He was willing to give Dougherty the benefit of the doubt. The guy knew sound. He was one of the best surveillance techs the FBI had, and his weird balding pattern attested to his devotion to the science. A hairless path ran across the top of his head in a direct line from ear to ear. Years of wearing headphones day and night had worn his hair away.

"Where's Tozzi wearing the wire?" Gibbons asked.

"He's got a transmitter in his beeper. He's wearing it on his belt. Nice clarity, huh?" Dougherty was proud of his work.

Gibbons nodded. He didn't care so much about the sound quality. It was the content that concerned him. "What's going on with these two? I don't remember seeing anything in Tozzi's daily reports about DeFresco's sister."

Dougherty's Labrador retriever smile turned into a lurid grin. "There's a reason for that."

Gibbons's tooth started to throb. He knew it. Goddamn Tozzi, thinking with his dick again. A sharp twinge froze Gibbons's face in the middle of a wince. "He screw her yet?"

Dougherty was leering, like a *dirty* mad scientist. "C'mon, Gib. Some things are private."

"Not to you they aren't. Spill it, Dougherty. Did he do her yet?" Between the nagging pain in his tooth and his dumbshit, fuck-happy partner, he was ready to punch a hole in the wall of the van.

"Well . . ." Dougherty took off the headphones and hung them around his neck. "Yeah, he did. But just once."

"And you listened in on it?"

"Tozzi left the transmitter on. What could I do? Shut him off?"

"Yes. You could have."

"Gib, I swear to God, I didn't know where he was going at the time. I'm supposed to monitor everything he does, right? I didn't realize till things started heating up with Ms. DeFresco that he wasn't at her apartment to gather information, if you know what I mean."

"Yeah, I know what you mean." Frigging peeping Tom.

"I'm telling you, Gib. It's not what you think. Tozzi should've deactivated the transmitter if he wanted privacy. But as long as it's transmitting, I *have* to record it. Those're the rules."

54

"You have it on tape?" Gibbons rubbed his swollen jaw.

"Of course. I have to account for my time." Dougherty reached over to a plastic milk crate full of reel-to-reel tape boxes, ran his finger down the line until he found the one he wanted, then pulled it out. "Here. You wanna listen to it."

Gibbons scowled at the box. "No. But just tell me this. How long has he been boffing her?"

"As far as I know, it was just that one time. But he's been trying hard ever since. If you ask me, I think Ms. DeFresco regrets that she gave it up so quick."

"Who are you? Dr. Ruth?"

"I'm just saying."

"How exactly did it happen?"

A sheepish grin replaced the leering one on Dougherty's face. "C'mon, Gib, that's Tozzi's business. I feel funny—"

"My dumbshit partner goes to bed with the sister of a unstable flake like Freshy DeFresco, who can fuck us up royally, and I'm not supposed to know everything that's going on? What're you, crazy? Tozzi could end up eating a couple slugs the way Petersen did this morning if those guys ever find out he's a fed. What if Freshy double-crosses Tozzi? He's nuts enough to do it. What if he gets pissed off because Tozzi screwed his sister? What better way to pay him back?"

Dougherty stopped grinning. "I suppose that's always possible, but I don't think he'd do that to Tozzi. They seem to be getting along pretty well. All things considered."

"Dougherty, you don't know shit." Gibbons gritted his teeth as a new wave of agony washed over his jaw and seeped through his body.

Through the one headphone, he could hear Tozzi talking again. He quickly adjusted the set and put them on both ears.

55

"I picked up the nuts. Aren't you gonna at least say thanks?"

"Why? You made me throw them at you."

"I did not."

"Just shut up. You're annoying me."

Gibbons heard departing footsteps.

"Hey, Gina! Where ya going?"

No answer.

"Gina! Where ya going?"

No answer. A door slammed.

Gibbons moved over to the small one-way window in the side of the van. He focused on the front of the DeFresco house. A brunette with glasses came huffing down the driveway. Gibbons was surprised. Gina DeFresco wasn't what he expected. Knowing Tozzi, he'd just imagined that she'd be some kind of Jersey special, a mousse girl with hair all over the place, Dragon Lady fingernails, stacked heels, tight skirt up to her butt, and cleavage you could get lost in. But this woman was . . . normal. Actually he was even more surprised that she could be related to that scumbag Freshy. He tried to get a better look at her face as she turned onto the sidewalk. She was kind of cute.

Tozzi came trotting down the driveway after her, shrugging into a navy cashmere overcoat. *"Gina! Wait! I'll walk you to your bus."*

Gibbons walked in a crouch to the back of the van and pulled up on the door handle.

"Hey, Gib, where ya going?"

"Gotta talk to Tozzi. He doesn't know about Petersen yet."

"But, Gib, direct contact with a man in the field on an undercover is not kosher. Ivers'll ream your ass out for—"

The metal doors slammed shut. Gibbons didn't give a shit about rules and regs. Tozzi had to be warned before he got

56

himself killed, so that Gibbons could kill him later for being so goddamn stupid.

Holding his swollen jaw, Gibbons pulled down his hat and headed across the street to catch up with his skirt-chasing partner.

SIX

Tozzi followed Gina as she walked down to the bus stop on Kennedy Boulevard. "What'd I ever do to you? Huh? Except be nice to you."

She kept walking, ignoring him.

"Hey, Gina, you can't even be decent enough to talk to me now?" Tozzi was trying to sound like Mike Santoro the pornmeister, but the feelings were all his own. He wanted to connect with her somehow. At the very least he wanted to find out why she was treating him like a piece of toilet paper. After all, they had had that incredible Sunday afternoon together. They certainly had connected then, even if it was only for a few hours.

Tozzi sighed as he watched the back of her head, her brown hair whipping back and forth over huffy shoulders as she walked. Up ahead the morning rush-hour traffic was roaring by on Kennedy Boulevard. He just wished he could tell her who he really was. If she knew he wasn't really a pornographer, maybe she'd give him a shot at defrosting that cold shoulder the way he'd warmed her toes on the couch.

A bus pulled up to the curb then. The electronic sign over the windshield said PORT AUTHORITY TERMINAL. It came to a stop with a loud whoosh, and the doors unfolded. Gina climbed up the steps without looking back.

"Gina!" he called out to her, but the door slapped closed, and the crowded bus pulled away with another airy whoosh.

Tozzi held his breath until the bus exhaust dissipated, then he shoved his hands into his coat pockets and sighed, "Gina, Gina, Gina."

"Gina, my ass."

Tozzi snapped his head around, and there was Gibbons, his hat pulled down over his brow, that witch nose of his hanging down below the brim. His mouth was a downturned horseshoe of disapproval. The left side of his face was so swollen, it looked like a blowfish was attached to his cheek.

Tozzi looked left and right, trying to be subtle about it. "What the hell're you doing?"

"Shut up and listen, numbnuts. Gary Petersen was shot last night."

Tozzi's gut clenched. "Oh, shit." He didn't need to hear the reason.

"Last I heard he was in stable condition."

A young guy wearing a leather jacket and carrying a briefcase stepped into the nearby bus-stop shelter. Gibbons immediately shut up and walked back to the plate-glass window of the candy store on the corner.

Tozzi waited a few moments before he joined his partner. "Who shot him? Do we know yet?"

"He was supposed to be meeting Tony Bells at one last night."

"Bells? That fuck."

"Ivers ordered a manhunt."

"I was with Bells last night. It was after three, though. Jesus."

"You know where he is now?"

Tozzi shook his head. "I don't even know where he lives. He's a very strange guy, very secretive."

"Well, stay away from him. I don't think the press has the whole story yet, so we may be able to grab him before they tip him off. Let's hope."

"I could reach out and see if I can find him."

"No," Gibbons snapped. "You'd better not be anywhere in the vicinity when he's arrested. Buddha Stanzione and his merry men will put two and two together. Then to save your hide, we'd have to get the word out that you're a fed, and that would be the end of Shark Bite. Ivers wants to keep the operation going if we can, and for once I agree with the shithead."

"But I can—"

"No, you can't. Go to a movie, go take a ride down the shore, go get laid—just stay away from Bells until we can find him."

Tozzi frowned and thought of Gina. He wished he *could* get laid.

"By the way, Toz, what's all this shit with you and Freshy's sister? What're you, nuts?"

The blood rushed to Tozzi's face. "I don't know what you're talking about."

"The fuck you don't. Listen to me, asshole. For once in your life, I'd like to see you keep it in your pants while you're on the job. Why do you always have to get involved with the wrong women?"

"There's nothing wrong with Gina DeFresco. She has nothing to do with her brother or the mob. She's an innocent civilian."

"Don't try to bullshit me, Tozzi. She's a blood relative of a connected guy ratting on his friends to help us out. I'd say that makes her pretty involved."

"You know, I resent you saying that. You don't know—"

"I know enough. Just leave her alone, *capisce?*"

Tozzi didn't answer. He wanted to know how the hell Gibbons knew about him and Gina. Then he suddenly remembered the transmitter on his belt. Dougherty. That deceitful mother—

Gibbons started to go into the candy store.

"What happened to your face?" Tozzi asked only to stop him. He was still smarting from his partner's remark about Gina being a wrong woman, and he wanted the last word.

"Abscessed tooth. Hurts like a bitch."

"Why don't you go to the dentist?"

Gibbons glared at him. "When do I have friggin' time to go to the dentist?"

Tozzi glared back. "Why not have 'em all pulled and get dentures? Then you can just send them out when you have trouble."

Gibbons looked him in the eye, puckered his lips, and suddenly four of his upper teeth were hanging out of his mouth. Tozzi stepped back, startled by the sight. He never knew Gibbons had bridgework. It reminded him of something he'd seen on one of those nature shows on TV. A shark's jaws work independently of the head. The teeth chomp, and the mouth catches up a split second later. He stared at Gibbons's snaggle-toothed mouth in disgust. He'd always thought of Gibbons as having a crocodile smile. Son of a gun.

The teeth slipped back into Gibbons's mouth, but the mean bastard still looked like he was ready to bite. "I gotta go call your cousin," he grumbled.

Tozzi wondered if his cousin Lorraine had done something to piss Gibbons off. Over the years, Tozzi had noticed that Gibbons usually referred to his wife as "your cousin" whenever they were fighting about something.

Gibbons had his hand on the doorknob of the candy store. "Maybe she can get the goddamn dentist to give her a prescription for some pain-killers. In the meantime, you get lost and make yourself scarce until we find Tony Bells. And call in to the office before Ivers wets his pants." Gibbons went into the store, holding his swollen face.

Through the plate-glass window, Tozzi watched his partner lumber to the pay phone at the back of the store. What a grouch. Tozzi wondered how Lorraine could stand him sometimes.

Tozzi headed around the corner back toward Freshy's house. He'd have to tell Freshy something, make up some kind of bogus excuse so he could disappear for a while. He couldn't risk telling Freshy the real reason. Freshy might get cute and try to win some brownie points by tipping off Bells to the manhunt.

But just as he rounded the corner, he heard two short toots on a car horn. He looked up and saw a silver four-door BMW 735 double-parked at the curb.

"Hey, Mike. Mike!" Freshy was in the back, the tinted window rolled down. "We were looking for you. C'mon. Get in." His hair was still wet from the shower.

Tozzi didn't recognize the car. He crossed the street and leaned down to see who was inside, trying to hide his suspicion. Bells was in the front passenger seat, a copy of the *Daily News* open on his lap. Behind the wheel was Stanley, the Tazmanian Devil.

Bells lowered his window halfway. "Get in," he said with a smile. "I gotta show you guys something."

"Right now?" Tozzi looked at his watch for effect. "I told this guy I'd meet him at ten in Brooklyn—"

Bells shook his head. "Forget about your meeting. This is more important."

"But I—"

"You want the loan?"

"Yeah, of course I do, but—"

"Then get in." Bells went back to his paper. He was reading the gossip column. He seemed pretty low-key, but the anxiety on Freshy's face made Tozzi anxious. He did not want to get in with them, but if he didn't, Bells would get suspicious. He didn't know Mike Santoro from a hole in the ground, and if he was as paranoid as Tozzi figured, he might start thinking Mike Santoro was an undercover cop. If he did, Bells would flee, sure as shit, and they might lose him for good. He'd get away with the attempted murder of a federal agent—murder one if Petersen died. Tozzi balled his fists in his coat pockets. He had to make a decision and make it fast.

Bells kept his head in the paper. Stanley had his head bent, looking up at Tozzi from under heavy brows, waiting for him to get in. His underbite looked lethal.

Freshy's eyes were pleading. "C'mon, Mike. Get in. It won't take long, will it, Bells?"

Bells didn't answer, and when Tozzi didn't make a move to get in, Bells turned to Stanley. "C'mon, let's go. This guy doesn't wanna do business."

Stanley was reaching to put the car into gear when Tozzi suddenly made up his mind. "Hang on. Lemme call the guy I'm supposed to meet and tell him I can't make it. I'll be right with you." He figured he could go into the candy store and quickly tell Gibbons what was going on.

But Bells rolled his head back and looked up at him, no expression. "Who's more important to you, Mike? This guy or me?"

It wasn't a question. Tozzi had no choice.

He opened the back door and got in next to Freshy. "All right, all right, let's go."

Stanley put the car in gear and pulled up to the intersection, where the traffic light was red. He signaled to turn right, but there was too much traffic to turn on the red. He had to wait for the green light.

As they waited, Tozzi noticed Gibbons coming out of the candy store, scowling and holding his swollen face. Tozzi made eye contact with Freshy, who knew Gibbons and had spotted him, too. Freshy's face was long, cheeks sunken, eyes wide. He was so obvious, Tozzi wanted to smack him.

Bells turned a page. "Hey, Mike, who was that old guy you were talking to before?"

Tozzi shot a quick glance at Freshy. Had he said something to Bells and Stanley about Gibbons? If he had, what did he say?

"Which guy you talking about?"

"That guy right over there. On the corner."

"You mean that guy? The one whose face is all swollen up?"

"Yeah, that guy. What'd you do, smack him?"

Stanley started to laugh, but it turned into a raspy cigarette cough. Freshy looked like he was ready to jump out of his skin.

Tozzi started laughing, too. "Nah, I didn't touch the guy. What a nut, though. He told me he had a toothache, and it was driving him crazy. He wanted to know if there was a dentist somewhere around here he could go to. I told him I couldn't help him, I didn't live around here. But the guy wouldn't leave me alone. He kept asking me what he should do, he was in agony. I couldn't get rid of the old bastard. Finally I told him to go look up dentists in the Yellow Pages and leave me the fuck alone."

No one said anything, and Tozzi's heart stopped. He looked at Freshy, convinced that he'd told Bells who Gibbons really was. But as the moment stretched and nothing happened, something else occurred to him. If Bells saw him on the corner with Gibbons, did he also see him out there with Gina? He remembered that phone message Bells had left on her answering machine, and the high-octane paranoia that only a guy in deep cover can experience began to creep through his gut and barberpole up his spine as he considered the possibility that maybe Bells and Gina really did have something going together. And Bells was definitely the jealous kind. Tozzi's pulse was in overdrive.

Bells ruffled the newspaper. "You should've smacked the guy," he mumbled.

Stanley laughed, then coughed into his fist. The light changed, and he made the turn onto Kennedy Boulevard, heading north toward Jersey City. They made the next two lights but caught the third one and had to stop. A butcher shop called Meat City was on the left-hand corner.

"So where we going?" Tozzi asked, trying to sound curious but not alarmed.

No one answered. Bells folded the paper over. Freshy's eyes were so wide, they would've fallen out if he looked down.

"What is it, a secret?" Tozzi said with an annoyed laugh. "Where we going?"

Stanley looked at him in the rearview mirror. "You'll see," he whispered. He was almost reverent, the way he sounded.

Bells didn't lift his head from the paper.

SEVEN

"Coffee break," Stanley shouted as they filed into the garage through the muffler shop's waiting room. "Go get some coffee. Hurry up. Go."

The two dark-skinned black guys in green coveralls didn't pay any attention. They continued to work on the cars that were up on the lifts. One was putting new brake pads on a maroon Buick Century; the other was using a pneumatic drill to loosen the bolts on a fire-engine red Celica's rusted-out muffler. Years' worth of caked rust and road dirt rained down on his goggled face, but he didn't flinch.

Freshy and his buddy Mikey stood off to the side, small mouths and big eyes, waiting to see what they were here for.

Bells watched them, amused by their uncertain state in an uncertain situation. He turned his head slowly and let his gaze settle on the two mechanics as they worked. He knew they were both from the islands, and that the guy doing the brake job was from Haiti and only spoke French. He scanned the garage bays. The floor under his feet was soft with oily grime. Open tool carts stood against the wall like openmouthed monsters waiting for Holy Communion, showing off neat rows of hanging open-end and box wrenches, like teeth. Rubber belts hung from the ceiling like nooses. Muffler parts hung from the ceiling, too, like spare body parts. Pinned to the back wall was a soiled yellow satin banner with the muffler shop's name and slogan printed in black: MAXXIMUM MUFFLER—MAXXIMUM QUALITY, MAXXIMUM SERVICE, MAXXIMUM VALUE.

This was one of those minor-league franchises that looked and sounded a little too much like Midas Muffler. Bells had gotten an empty feeling in the pit of his stomach as soon as they'd walked in here. He hated cheap substitutes. He liked essentials, basics, real things. If you needed a muffler, get a good one and then don't think about it anymore. He didn't like having cheap crap. Owning stuff like that distracted him. It was like wearing a shirt with a stain. You couldn't stop thinking about the stain even when you weren't looking at it. People who borrowed money and then fell behind in their payments were just like stains. They forced him to waste his time thinking about them. People like that were faulty goods and had to be fixed, replaced, or eliminated so that he could unclutter his mind.

Stanley walked under the Celica. "Did you hear what I said, man? I said go take a coffee break."

The man working on the rusted muffler pushed his goggles up onto his forehead. There were dark circles around his bloodshot eyes where the ochre-colored dust hadn't lightened his skin. "Boss not here, mon," he said. "Can'na leave now." His lips were pouty, his expression sullen, and he looked off into the space next to Stanley as he spoke to him.

"Give 'em some money," Bells said, a little annoyed with all this dickering. Stanley should know better. You want a guy to get lost for a while, you make it worth his while.

Stanley dug a five out of his pocket and gave it the guy. He took it, but still wouldn't look at Stanley. He was looking at his buddy, the French nigger from Haiti, who was just standing there holding a wrench in each hand, his eyes bugging out of his head.

"Go 'head, go. *Cafe* time. Whatta'ya, stupid?"

The guy didn't move. He was petrified.

Stanley looked to Bells for advice.

Bells walked over toward the French guy. "Get going, Frère Jacques," he said. "And hurry up before I call the *tonton macoutes.*"

The French guy's head snapped up at the mention of the Haitian secret police. Freshy looked confused, as usual, but Mikey Santoro seemed surprised. Bells was insulted. What'sa matter, he didn't think a guy like him would know about stuff like the *tonton macoutes?* Asshole. The first time he'd met Santoro, Bells had figured him for someone who thought his shit didn't stink, one of these guys who thinks he's a little bit better than everybody else. What'd he think, just because a guy's a shylock from Jersey, he's ignorant, he's some kind of dees-dems-and-dose bum who only reads *The Racing Form?* Yeah, Bells had known guys like Santoro before, guys who thought they were God's gift to something. He knew one thing for sure: Mikey-boy thought he was God's gift to Gina DeFresco.

Yeah, he knew all about Mikey-boy making a big play for Gina. What Freshy hadn't told him, he'd pretty much pieced together himself. It wasn't hard to figure. Santoro was trying to use all his Mr. Clean charms to sweep Gina right off her feet and right into his bed. See, he thinks he's better than everybody else. He thinks just like her. She thinks she's better than her upbringing. But in her case, that was okay. He liked the fact that she had a backbone, that she told people to go to hell all the time, and that she said she wanted nothing to do with wiseguys. That was okay.

But on Santoro, this attitude wasn't so becoming. It just

showed him up for what he really was, a snot-nosed shitass. He needed to be taken down a few pegs, and Bells was just the guy to do it. That's what he gets for messing around with Gina. That was the only reason he'd gone head to head with Buddha over getting these two mamelukes their loan. Sure, they were gonna get their money, and he was gonna encourage them to use it on their business right away, all of it. He was gonna lead them down the garden path because he wanted them to fuck up. And they *would* fuck up, he'd make sure of that. And when they did, they'd have to deal with their good ole shy, who was gonna be right there to wipe that smile off Santoro's face. First off, Bells was gonna have to take over their porn business and run it himself to satisfy the loan. He'd keep Freshy around to run the day-to-day stuff, out of the goodness of his heart, of course. But Mikey-boy would have to go. And Gina, if she was brought up right, which Bells knew she basically was, would thank him from the bottom of her heart for saving her little fuck-up brother's ass. In fact, he *knew* she would thank him, even though she might not make a big show of it, because he knew she was devoted to the little jerkoff and worried all the time about Freshy getting his head blown off or being sent to jail or something. She'd told him.

The two black guys were moving slow toward the door, the one with the dirty face still holding the fin in his fingers like a retard who didn't know enough to put it in his pocket. Then the boss showed up. Finally.

"Hey, Bells, Stanley, what's happening?"

Randy Slipowitz was a skinny guy with black black hair, thick eyebrows, and a honker like a sailboat sticking out of his face. He sort of looked like that guy on *M*A*S*H* who was always wearing women's clothes to get himself booted out of the army. Slipowitz smoked like a chimney and always wore dress shirts and dark dress pants, which were always covered with hair. He had this problem. A sickness, really. He had this nutty thing for animals. His house was full of strays he'd picked up here and there. Two dozen dogs and who knows how many cats. It wasn't unusual for him to have a couple in the car with him, and right this minute he was holding this little cat, a sleepy little orange tabby, bigger than a kitten but not quite a teenage cat. Slipowitz scratched its head with a lit cigarette between his fingers even though the thing was already sacked out in the crook of his elbow with its little head upside down and its paws up in the air.

But Randy Slipowitz's animal problem went beyond stray cats and dogs. He had a thing for the ponies, too. Without fail, he'd spend every afternoon at the track, winning some, losing more, just like every other schmuck who lives for the ponies. He'd borrowed a hundred and seventy-five grand from Buddha to buy this Maxximum Muffler franchise, but he wasn't here enough to make the place work for him. He must've thought the place would run itself, that it would somehow turn into some kind of magic money machine. But that wasn't how you ran a business. You didn't leave the help in charge day after day on a regular basis. Bells could see disaster coming down the road. Slipowitz hadn't fallen behind in his payments—not yet—but Bells knew the signs, and it was definitely coming. The franchise itself was worth shit as far as he could tell. If the Slip defaulted, Buddha didn't want the shop and neither did Bells. So that was why Bells was here today. To give ole Randy a little financial advice and get him back on track *before* he got off track.

Slipowitz sucked on his cigarette. "What's up, Bells?" His eyes darted from Bells to Freshy to Mikey-boy and then back again. He avoided looking at Stanley. He didn't even want to acknowledge that Stanley was there. No one liked seeing Stanley.

Bells walked up to him with a smile and scratched the little cat's lazy head. "This is a cute one, Randy. What's his name?"

"I call him Pancho. 'Cause it's always siesta time with this one." Slipowitz took a long drag off his cigarette, his eyes still darting all over the place.

Bells took the cat from him and cradled it in one arm. He explored the fur on its belly with his fingers. "Hey, Randy, this cat has teats. How can it be Pancho? It's a girl."

"I know, I know. It's just that she looks like a Pancho to me. You know what I mean?"

Bells smiled. "Yeah. I do."

"So what brings you around here, Bells? Need a new muffler?"

Bells shook his head and scratched the little cat under the chin. She squeezed her eyes shut and stretched, lounging in the lap of luxury.

"So, ah . . . so what's up, Bells?"

Tozzi noticed that Slipowitz's hand was shaking. The guy was scared shitless, and he kept flicking ashes on the floor with his thumb even after there were no more ashes to flick.

Bells looked down at the little cat as he scratched its chin. "So how're the ponies running these days, Randy? You making out?"

Slipowitz shrugged. "I dunno. You know how it is, Bells. You got good days—and you got not-so-good days, too . . . sometimes. You know?"

Tozzi couldn't tell if little Pancho was all the way asleep or not, but she sure looked it.

Bells kept scratching her chin. "Tell me something, Randy. How's business?"

"Business?"

71

"Yeah. How many mufflers you sell in an average day? About."

"Whole mufflers?"

"Yeah."

"Well, see, you don't sell a whole system all that often. Usually it's just pieces that people need. Pipes, condensers, the actual muffler itself, that kind of thing. Very unusual for someone to need a complete exhaust system replaced."

"Interesting. So how many cars you work on a day? About."

Slipowitz glanced out the Plexiglas panels in the garage door. Except for Bells's BMW and his own Pontiac, there were no other cars out front in the lot, which meant they didn't have a whole lot of business today. He held the cigarette butt carefully as he took the very last drag, then dropped it on the floor and stepped on it. "Well, that all depends, Bells. Every day is different. See, it's a little slow now, but that's to be expected this time of year. Once it snows and the weather gets shitty, this place'll be hopping. You know the way they salt the roads around here. That really speeds up metal corrosion. Then there's the slush that builds up in the wheel wells and freezes. You're driving along and this big chunk of frozen slush breaks off—it can get caught on the muffler. Maybe you drag it for a couple hundred feet. You don't realize how much damage that can do."

Bells was grinning down at the cat, so calm and contented. "Frozen slush, huh? Is this what they taught you out at Maxximum Muffler School? Where was it? Kansas?"

"No, Omaha."

Bells stared at Slipowitz and nodded. "So when did you open up this place? Last April, wasn't it?"

"Yeah, April."

"So you haven't actually been through a winter in the muffler business yet, have you?"

"Well, no, but—"

"And how long did you go to that muffler school down there?"

"Five days."

Bells nodded. "And not counting what you did down there, how many mufflers have you personally put in, Randy?"

"Oh, I done quite a few, Bells. One of the guys calls in sick, I fill in. Oh, yeah. I do."

"How many mufflers, Randy?" Bells kept staring at him.

Slipowitz couldn't look at him. "Gee, Bells, offhand? I dunno. If you want a number, I'd have to look it up."

"Ah-huh."

Tozzi didn't like the way this was going. He didn't know what the story was with Slipowitz, but it seemed like Bells was here to collect on a late payment. Stanley was standing between Slipowitz and the door, his big head tilted back on a bull neck, eyes half-closed with attitude.

The lazy little tabby was nearly comatose, laid out across Bells's forearm like a fur pelt. Bells walked it like he was walking a baby, jiggling it, stroking its chin, cooing to it. As he walked around in circles, he found his way under the Celica up on the lift. He stopped and stared up at the underside of the car as if he were gazing up at the stars.

"Randy," he said, "lemme tell you something you should know. A team is only as good as its coach. An army is only as good as its general. And a business is the same thing. It's only as good as its boss."

"I agree with you, Bells."

Bells looked over his shoulder at Freshy and Tozzi and raised his eyebrows. "Listen to this, you two. This applies to you guys, too." He went back to gazing up at the rusty underside of the car. "Now you said you agreed with me, right, Randy?"

"Absolutely."

"Then I guess you don't practice what you preach."

"Wha-wha-whatta'ya mean, Bells?" Slipowitz had an unlit cigarette wedged between his lips.

"What I mean is, we both know that you don't pay a whole lot of hands-on attention to this place, Randy, and I consider that a breach of contract."

"I don't know what you're talking about, Bells. I been paying you on time. I haven't made you wait once."

"That's not the point, Randy. The point is, you have other things on your mind that interfere with your muffler business here. Things like playing the ponies and picking up strays, like little Pancho Villa here, and worrying about all the mangy mutts and cats you got living at your house."

"You don't understand, Bells—"

Bells shook his head, and Slipowitz shut right up. "No, *you* don't understand, Randy. When I lent you the money you needed to buy the franchise, I became like your partner in this place. If this place goes under, I'm affected, too, right? So that's why I'm here, to give you a little business advice *before* it's too late. Sort of like as an extra service that I offer. You know what I mean?"

"Yeah. I guess. I dunno."

Bells looked over his shoulder and stared at Tozzi.

Tozzi stared back but didn't say a thing. This was all for his benefit, his and Freshy's. Bells wanted them to see what it was like doing business with him.

Bells stepped out from under the car, still stroking the lethargic cat. He looked down and found the metal lever on the floor that controlled the lift. With his toe, he flipped the lever out of the lock position and activated the release. The car started to descend, a slow loud hiss emanating from the greasy metal column that held the car up.

Tozzi's gut clenched. He watched Slipowitz, who was shaking like a chihuahua.

"You see, Randy, it's like this." Bells hunkered down next to one of the depressions in the floor where the car's back wheels would settle. "I could yell and scream and make all kinds of threats against you and your family and all your pets, but that's not me. I'm not like that. I'd rather help you out *now*, *before* you have a problem. 'Cause no one likes problems. Right, Mikey?"

"Sure. Right."

"What'sa matter, Mikey? You look worried."

"Me? Why should I be worried?"

"I dunno, but your face is as tight as a fist. Relax."

"I said I'm not worried."

"Oh. Good." Bells was grinning at him.

Tozzi wanted to kick the bastard's head off.

The red Celica was about three feet off the floor now. Bells stroked the cat and grinned up at Slipowitz.

"What I want, Randy, is for you to take a little more personal interest in this place. Those two black guys you got may be excellent muffler technicians or whatever the hell you call them, but they are not management material. I want you to spend less time at the track and more time here. Otherwise . . ."

Bells leaned forward and gently laid the sleeping tabby in the tire gully. The Celica was less than two feet from the ground.

Tozzi's heart started to pound.

The cigarette fell out of Slipowitz's mouth. "Don't, Bells, please. Don't." He stepped forward to rescue the cat, but the Tazmanian Devil stepped in front of him, and he backed right off. No one wanted to get too close to Stanley.

Slipowitz pleaded from a distance. "C'mon, Bells. Please. Don't."

Bells had to peer around the descending tire to see him. He stroked the little cat's head until it realized that it was in danger. It tried to turn over and move, but the son of a bitch already had his hand around its neck, pinning it down. It struggled and fought, scratching like crazy with its back paws, but the pain apparently didn't bother Bells. Tozzi couldn't believe what he was seeing. Buddha was right: Bells *was* a freak. He tilted his head and smiled down benevolently at the frantic little cat in his bloody hand, then he looked up at Tozzi.

"What'sa matter, Mikey? You look upset. Don't worry. Scratches heal."

Tozzi shrugged. "It's your hand, Bells." You goddamn freak you.

Bells turned back to Slipowitz. "From now on, Randy, what I'd like to see is you coming in every morning *before* the help, taking some pride in this place, wearing the Maxximum Muffler coveralls, the whole bit. I want you to make this place really take off."

The poor little cat was howling. The tire was right on top of it. Bells carefully slid his hand out just in time, so that he still had it by the neck as the tire pinned its body to the floor. Tozzi had to force himself to stay put.

Randy tried to get to the cat again, but Stanley blocked his way. "Okay, Bells, okay. Whatever you say. Anything. I'll even wear the overalls. Anything."

"Don't bullshit me, Randy."

The cat screamed.

Tozzi wanted to save the poor animal, but he couldn't risk blowing his cover for a cat. Mike Santoro wouldn't dare get in Bells's way, not now, not with a big loan pending.

Slipowitz was in a real state, practically on the verge of tears. "I swear, Bells! Whatever you want."

"Really?"

"Really! I swear! I promise!"

"Fine."

Bells yanked the cat out just as it was about to be crushed. The tire spun for a few rotations, then squeaked to a stop as it touched ground. He swung the cat by the scruff of the neck, but instead of letting it go, he forced it back into his arms, cradling it, stroking it, shushing it, scratching its head with his scratched bloody hand until the cat finally settled down and relaxed, tipping its head back and accepting the attention just the way it had before. It wasn't long before the little tabby was nearly comatose again, stretched out and totally limp.

The black guy from Haiti dropped his cup of coffee, and it splattered in a sunburst on the grimy floor. He and his buddy had been watching quietly from the doorway between the office and the garage. *"Mon Dieu,"* he breathed, staring with big yellowish eyes at the sleepy little cat.

"Did you see that?" Freshy whispered to Tozzi.

"I saw."

"Mon Dieu! Mon Dieu!"

Bells cradled the cat and laughed out loud. He opened his eyes wide and stared back at the guy from Haiti. "It's voodoo, baby."

Freshy's mouth hung open. He looked just like the guy from Haiti.

"What'sa matter, Mikey? You still look all upset over there."

"I'm not upset, Bells. I told you."

"Oh, yeah, right. You did tell me." Bells was still laughing.

Tozzi just looked at him. This son of a bitch wasn't just a freak. He was a freak and a half.

EIGHT

From the backseat of the BMW, Tozzi watched Stanley as he carried a big white paper bag and a small brown paper bag back to the car. Tozzi was still brooding over what had happened back at the muffler shop. He kept thinking: What if it had been Randy Slipowitz's head under that tire? In that case, Tozzi couldn't have just stood around and watched. He would have had to do something to stop it, and that would've blown his cover. Then what? Bells and Stanley might've tried to flatten *his* head under the car, that's what. Bells was that crazy. Tozzi wished he could stop thinking like this, but Bells had really gotten under his skin, and this fixation wasn't healthy. It was too close to fear, and once you showed fear, forget about it. But Tozzi knew he would never admit to himself that he was ever afraid, and *that* worried him, too. Too much ego clouds your judgment, and for a guy working undercover, that could be fatal. He stared at the back of Bells's head as the freak calmly read his newspaper up front in the passenger seat. Asshole.

Stanley got into the car and handed the brown bag to Bells, then reached into the white one and pulled out what everyone else had ordered. Tozzi got the large coffee—milk, no sugar. Freshy got the light and sweet coffee and the buttered roll. Stanley got a coffee and a cheese Danish for himself. Bells opened

78

his bag and pulled out a white cardboard container, a foam cup, and a pair of wooden chopsticks. He was having shrimp fried rice and tea. From the backseat, Tozzi watched him break the chopsticks apart and pry the lid off the cup of tea.

They were parked in the lot of a strip mall somewhere off Route 46, past Paterson, that had a discount baby furniture store, a cosmetics outlet, a luncheonette, a Chinese take-out place, a cheap women's shoe store, and a jewelry store. Bells turned and sat sideways in his seat as he started to shovel fried rice into his mouth, holding the carton close to his face. He seemed to be ravenous.

When he finally stopped to chew, he looked over the seat back at Tozzi. "Rice," he said, pausing to swallow. "Best thing for you. It's true."

"Oh, yeah?" Tozzi sipped his coffee, immediately on his guard and angry that he was.

"That's right. Chinese people are the healthiest people in the world, and rice is like eighty percent of their diet. It's the best carbohydrate you can put in your body. And that's what you need. Carbs." He picked out a shrimp with his chopsticks and studied it while he chewed. "You wanna be healthy, eat like a peasant. People should live more like peasants. They'd be better off." Bells popped the shrimp into his mouth.

Tozzi couldn't tell if Bells was busting his balls or what. Stanley wasn't snickering behind his coffee cup, so maybe Bells really did believe this. But not for himself. Bells didn't see himself as a peasant, that was for sure. He was more like the guy in the castle the peasants revolted against.

Bells reached for his tea on the dash. "This is how I eat every day. Ask Stanley."

Stanley nodded, his mouth full of Danish.

"I always eat a lot of rice, pasta, stuff like that. For energy.

'Cause you never know when you're gonna need it. This is good advice for you, Mikey: Always keep your tanks full. Very important. The other thing is, I never eat unless I'm hungry. And it's very rare that I'm hungry at regular mealtimes. I think you should use up what you've got, then fill up the tanks again. That's how the body was meant to run. I really believe that." Bells blew over the surface of his steaming tea, looking Tozzi in the eye.

Tozzi was grinding his teeth. He hated this guy's guts, and he hated the fact that the guy got to him like this. But he still wasn't sure if Bells was trying to bust his balls with this health rap of his. Bells was about five-ten, five-eleven, average build, but he didn't look particularly fit. Actually it was hard to tell how he was built since he always wore dark loose-fitting suits that hid his shape. The real odd thing about him was the way he moved. He wasn't fast and he wasn't slow, but he was always moving, always constant, like when he was walking that cat around the muffler shop. He never stopped. He even ate that way—not fast, not slow, but constant. Maybe it was the chopsticks that made Tozzi think of this, but he suddenly remembered an old tai chi master he'd seen a couple of years ago at a demonstration who moved the same way, with purpose but not deliberate. No intention. Tozzi wondered if Bells had ever had any martial arts training.

Tozzi thought about his own training. In aikido, you react to an attack; you never initiate anything. But with that old tai chi master, it would be hard to tell what was an attack and what was just normal movement because you could never tell when he was moving away from his opponent and when he was moving toward him. It was all the same. Just like Bells. He never seemed menacing until it was too late. Tozzi couldn't help wondering how he would handle him if it ever came down to a one-on-one confrontation.

He gulped his coffee and frowned behind his cup. It was stupid to speculate about a showdown with Bells because it wasn't going to happen. As soon as Tozzi could get away from these guys, he was going to call in to the field office and give Ivers their location so that a squad of agents could grab Bells. He wasn't going to be anywhere near the takedown. If he was lucky, he'd be in his own bed when it happened, resting up for his black-belt test tonight.

Bells put the fried rice carton on the dashboard and reached into the brown paper bag on the floor. He pulled out a cellophane packet with two fortune cookies inside, ripped it open, and handed one over the seat to Tozzi. "Here. You didn't get anything to eat."

Tozzi took the fortune cookie warily. "Thanks." He set his coffee down on the floor so he could break it open.

"Wait, Mikey, before you open it—do you know how to read these things?"

Tozzi crossed his brows. "Whatta'ya mean?"

"You're supposed to add 'in bed' to the end of your fortune. That's how you find out what it really means. Go 'head. Try it."

Tozzi raised one eyebrow and looked at Freshy, who only shrugged and chewed, his mouth full. Tozzi broke open the cookie, uncurled the slip of paper, and read it out loud. " 'Your first love and last love is self-love.' "

"In bed," Bells added, raising his eyebrows.

Stanley nearly spit out his coffee.

"I don't get it," Freshy said.

Stanley struggled to talk through his coughing. "Sounds like Mikey's got a thing for his hand."

81

"In bed." Bells sipped his tea, his eyebrows arched over the rim of the cup.

"Oh." Freshy shrugged. "I still don't get it."

Tozzi did and he wasn't amused.

Bells cracked his cookie open and examined his fortune. " 'The current year will bring you great happiness.' In bed." He rocked his head from side to side as he considered his fortune, but he didn't smile. "Hmmm . . . Not bad, I guess." He left it on the console between the seats.

"Here. You want mine." Tozzi held out his slip of paper.

Bells shook his head. "Keep it. Secondhand fortunes are like used rubbers. They only work for the first guy."

Tozzi stared down at Bells's fortune. Great happiness in bed. With Gina maybe? He wondered if Bells was thinking about her right now; then he remembered her answering machine. *"Gina, it's me. Gimme a call."*

Freshy wiped his mouth with a paper napkin, balled it up, and dropped it in his empty coffee cup. "So what's the deal, Bells? You gonna take us home now or what?"

Bells sipped his tea. "One more stop." He looked over the seat at Tozzi. "You don't mind, do you, Mikey?"

"No. No problem." As if he had a choice.

"Good. 'Cause like I was telling you guys before, when I make a loan, I want everybody to go into it with their eyes open. That's why I'm taking you around today, to open your eyes. Now, I'm not saying any of this will ever happen to you. As God is my witness, I hope to Christ with all my heart that you guys have success beyond your wildest dreams and your vig never becomes a problem for you. But you should still be aware of what *can* happen if success doesn't come right up and bite you in the ass in the beginning. Just so you know what you're getting into. Okay?"

Freshy nodded and looked at Tozzi. "Yeah, sure. We understand. You just want us to know what *could* happen."

Tozzi nodded in agreement, looking at Freshy to make sure his stupid face didn't give them away. Of course that Woody Allen, high-anxiety wince was his normal expression. Tozzi had no idea what kind of face would be abnormal for Freshy. He hoped Bells didn't know either.

"Okay. Let's go see my friend Mr. Blake. C'mon." Bells got out of the BMW and headed for one of the stores, Park Avenue Fine Jewelers. He walked alone while Stanley hung back and waited for Tozzi and Freshy to follow.

Tozzi got out of the car and closed his door, staring at Bells's walk. It was so weird the way he moved. Purpose without intention. Like that old tai chi master. Like a friggin' ghost.

By the time Tozzi walked through the door, the old guy behind the counter was looking at Bells as if he were seeing a ghost. Tozzi assumed this was Mr. Blake. The man must've been in his early seventies, but he was tall and fit, good-looking with a forceful jaw and a pretty respectable head of white hair. Mr. Blake wasn't trembling, and his eyes weren't popping out of his head—he seemed to have too much dignity for that—but he was frozen, staring at Bells as if he were the Grim Reaper.

Tozzi could see that Bells had something in his hand, and he was startled when Bells suddenly unraveled a length of thin green string. His first thought was that Bells intended to strangle the guy with fishing tackle, but when Bells started to wrap the ends around his index fingers, he realized that this wasn't fishing tackle. It was dental floss. Mint-flavored dental floss. Tozzi was only slightly relieved.

Bells started to saw the floss through his bottom front teeth. "So?"

Mr. Blake didn't say a thing. He just stared at Bells, a condemned man ready for the firing squad. Stanley was leaning on the glass case closest to Mr. Blake, looking to Bells, waiting for the go-ahead. His tongue wasn't hanging out, and he wasn't slavering, but he definitely had that Tazmanian Devil look.

Tozzi and Freshy stayed out of the way. Freshy's head was bouncing, and he kept shifting his weight from one foot to the other, but nothing seemed to make him comfortable. Tozzi wasn't very comfortable either. He glanced around the store, hoping the old guy had a cat.

"So what's it gonna be?" Bells sawed the floss between his eye teeth, staring at Mr. Blake, mocking the old guy with his eyes.

"You know my situation, Bells." Mr. Blake wasn't cowering. Tozzi was impressed, but under the circumstances he didn't think it was very smart. A little cowering might not be so bad right about now.

Bells shook his head as he pulled the floss through his molars. "You're wasting your money, Mr. Blake. She's gonna die anyway."

The old man didn't answer.

"Whatta'ya want? *Two* sets of hospital bills? What's that gonna prove?"

Tozzi didn't know what Bells was talking about.

Stanley looked at Tozzi and Freshy and explained. "Mr. Blake's daughter's got the AIDS. Skin and bones, the poor thing, just barely hanging in there. He's spending everything he's got on her." Stanley turned to the old man. "But he thinks just 'cause his daughter is dying, that gives him some kind of moral right to forget about his obligation to us."

Blake was glaring at Stanley. He was furious, but he wasn't going to say anything. He had too much dignity to discuss his daughter with a bunch of hoods. Tozzi felt for the guy.

Bells opened his mouth wide and did the molars way in the back. When he was finished, he unwound the floss from his fingers, leaned over the counter looking for the wastepaper basket, and got rid of it. Tozzi wondered if the labs in Washington could do a DNA analysis from the saliva on the floss. If they worked over Mr. Blake, the saliva on the floss could put Bells at the scene of the crime, and—

But Tozzi wouldn't let it come down to that. He couldn't stand by and watch while Stanley beat the shit out of Mr. Blake. The guy was old; they might end up killing him. But if Tozzi got in the middle of this, Bells would definitely get suspicious. If Bells got real hinky, he might flee and escape the manhunt. But he'd probably want some payback from "Mikey-boy" the rat before he left.

Tozzi tried to imagine what would happen if Bells and Stanley went after him as a tag team. He had a feeling his aikido skills might not be enough. No martial art that he knew of taught you how to defend yourself against a hail of bullets coming from across the room.

Bells shoved his hands into his jacket pockets and lowered his chin. He nodded toward the glass case between him and Mr. Blake. "I could save myself a lot of trouble by just taking what you owe me in jewelry. Looks like you got enough to bring you up to date. But . . ." He gave the word some hang time. "But I don't wanna do that."

Mr. Blake just stared at him, his chin sticking out like Burt Lancaster.

"You know why I don't wanna do that? Because I don't like you. Plain as that. You got a shitty attitude, my friend. You think you're special, just because your daughter slept with some fag who had AIDS. Well, that's not my problem. This is business. Your personal life, I don't give a shit. Business is business."

85

Tozzi had a feeling Bells had given this speech before. It flowed too easily. He noticed that while Bells was talking, Stanley had put on a pair of black leather driving gloves. Tight ones. To keep from splitting a knuckle when he started throwing punches.

Stanley started to move around the counter, stalking Mr. Blake. The old guy still didn't say anything, but the wet gleam of fear suddenly showed in his eyes.

Tozzi wet his lips. He had to do something.

Except he wasn't carrying a weapon, he couldn't depend on Freshy to help him out, and Bells just might go ballistic if he tried to interfere with "business." He touched the beeper clipped to his belt. Gibbons hadn't seen him getting into Bells's car back in Bayonne. If he had, he and Dougherty would've followed them in the surveillance van, and they'd be hearing all this right now. They'd have plenty of backups with them, who'd barge in and save Mr. Blake. But Gibbons hadn't seen him getting into the car, so no one was listening now. Shit.

Stanley was behind the counter, closing in on his prey, and Bells was moving on the the balls of his feet, stepping in a box pattern with a look of glee on his face. Tozzi wondered if this was some kind of tribal dance he was doing. Or just something he did when he was enjoying himself.

The Tazmanian Devil was smoothing the leather on the backs of his hands, moving in for the kill.

Bells was doing his little witch-doctor dance. It could've been the fluorescent lights in there, but Tozzi swore the bastard's eyes were glowing.

Tozzi had to do something quick, but what? He was gonna have to reveal himself, say he was an FBI agent, and hope they'd back off. He was gonna have to blow his cover.

Mr. Blake was backing around the counter, but there was no getting away from Stanley, and he knew it.

Tozzi's heart was thumping. Maybe there was another way. He looked at the floor, looked all around him, not knowing what the hell he thought he'd find that could help Mr. Blake now. Then something caught his eye. A purple sparkle in the glass case behind Bells.

He walked over and quickly pointed to it, a silver bracelet with tiny dangling purple gems cut like tear drops. The silver was dark and antique-looking, and the settings were like little silver petunias. A chain of glittering little eggplants jammed into petunia horns. The color of the stones reminded him of the color of Gina's glasses.

"Stanley, excuse me," Tozzi said. "Before you do anything, I'd just like to ask Mr. Blake something." Tozzi was making this up as he went along. "Mr. Blake, how much for the bracelet with the purple stones? This one, right here." Tozzi pointed through the glass.

Bells stared down at the bracelet in the case. He looked a little baffled, but more amused. "Whatever it costs, it won't be enough to begin to cover what he owes me." He shifted his gaze to Mr. Blake. "Go 'head. Show Mikey what he wants to see." He leaned over the counter then and whispered to the old man, "Hey, maybe you can make bundle off this guy, and everybody'll end up happy. See, I'm a very fair person. I never believe in interfering with a man's business. Especially a man who owes me money."

Mr. Blake kept his eye on Stanley as he moved around the counter to the bracelet with the purple stones. He unlocked the case and pulled it out, handing it to Tozzi. His hand was shaking. "They're amethysts," he said, but he seemed reluctant to name a price. Obviously he must've owed Bells a lot more than the bracelet was worth. Naming a ridiculous price to save his ass would be playing Bells's game, and Mr. Blake had too much self-respect for that. But with the Tazmanian Devil hovering over his shoulder, he also knew he had run out of alternatives.

"How much, Mr. Blake? Go 'head. Give him a price." Bells was eating this up.

Tozzi held the bracelet up to the light. "Hey, Freshy, you think she'd like this?"

Bells's head snapped around. "Who you talking about?"

Freshy looked like he was gonna piss his pants. "I, ah, I . . ."

Tozzi kept his eyes on the glittering stones. "She really loves purple. I think she'd like this. What do you think, Fresh?" Tozzi didn't look at Bells, and he didn't mention Gina's name. It was a gamble, but Bells was too clever to be led by the nose. He had to fill in the blanks for himself.

"So how much you want?" Tozzi asked Mr. Blake.

The bracelet was suddenly snatched out of Tozzi's hand. Bells held it up, tilting his head back to examine it. Then he furrowed his brow at Tozzi. "Forget it. It's sold," he said.

"What?"

"*I* want it," he said, and slipped it into his pants pocket.

"But you just said—"

"Tough shit. It's mine."

Tozzi shrugged and turned to Mr. Blake. "You got another one like that? This girl would *really* love that bracelet."

The old man shook his head. "It's handmade. One of a kind."

"Too bad, Mikey-boy." Bells was grinning like a skull.

Tozzi shrugged, then turned to Freshy. "Too bad. She would've liked it. If you decide you don't want it, Bells, lemme know. I'll buy it off you."

The skull's grin dissolved. He didn't answer. Bells went into another trance, staring into one of the glass cases, thinking hard.

Suddenly he checked his watch, then waved Stanley out from behind the counter. The Tazmanian Devil looked very disappointed.

Bells regained his composure. "Tell you what, Mr. Blake. This is what I'm gonna do for you." He held up his index finger. "One week. That's what I'm gonna give you because I'm a nice guy, and I got someplace to go right now. One week. Next Wednesday I'll be back, and I want the money, up to date, everything you owe so far. If not, we'll pick up right where we left off today."

Stanley was taking off his gloves, but he smiled when he heard that.

Bells backstepped toward the door. "C'mon. Let's go." He seemed to be in a hurry all of a sudden.

"What about the bracelet?" Mr. Blake asked.

"You're giving it to me. For my trouble."

"But—"

"You want to argue about it?"

Mr. Blake shut up.

Bells was at the door, holding it open. "C'mon. Let's go, I said." He looked at his watch again.

Freshy was paler than usual. "You gonna take us home now?"

"Nope. Gotta make a stop in the city. C'mon now. Hurry up."

As they filed out of the store, Tozzi caught Bells staring at him. There was mischief in his eyes. Or malice. Tozzi wasn't sure which.

NINE

"So where is she?" Bells hovered over the edge of the desk, polite but insistent.

Gina's secretary shrugged, the phone cradled on her shoulder as she called around the department store looking for her boss. She was a black girl in her twenties with one of those Buckwheat hairdos. She had an attitude when they first walked in, but the presence of four grown men with bad grammar and no place else to be in the middle of a weekday was making her a little uneasy. She was having a hard time looking Bells in the eye.

The top floor of Macy's humongous flagship store on Thirty-fourth Street in Manhattan didn't look like the rest of the store. It was full of offices and pretty drab ones at that, just like a regular old office building. Gina shared an office with another buyer, but neither of them was in right now. The secretary's desk was out in the hallway.

Tozzi, Freshy, and Stanley hung back as Bells did the talking. He stood there with his hands clasped behind his back, shifting his weight from one foot to the other, staring down at the secretary, always moving.

The secretary dialed yet another extension and asked if Gina was there. She kept her eyes down, staring at her blotter, playing with her hair. Bells watched her like a cruel headmaster. He knew he was making her nervous, and Tozzi could tell from his face that he was enjoying it.

"Is Ms. DeFresco down there?" she asked one more time. She glanced up at Bells, shook her head, and looked down again. "Have you seen her? . . . No? . . . Okay, thanks."

"No luck?" Bells tucked his chin in and puckered his lips.

She spoke fast, not wanting to disappoint the creep. "No one's seen her. Maybe she left for Hoboken already."

"Hoboken?"

"Yeah. That's where they make the floats for the parade. The Macy's Thanksgiving Day Parade? You know, with all those big balloons? The cartoon characters? The store has a big warehouse somewhere over in Hoboken."

Bells kept shifting his weight, back and forth. "Why would she be going over there?"

"Well, she wasn't supposed to leave until after lunch, but she's got all these kids with her. They're going to be in the parade tomorrow, on Santa's float. Gina is supposed to take them over and show them what they're supposed to do."

"So who are these kids?"

She lowered her voice and rolled her eyes. "The bosses' kids. Getting your kids on Santa's float is one of the big perks around here."

"But if Gina isn't supposed to go over to see the floats until after lunch, where the hell could she be with all these kids?"

"Wherever they want to be. They're the bosses' kids." She looked at her watch. "It's almost lunchtime. Gina could be feeding them, either upstairs in the cafeteria or down in the Cellar. Or they could be somewhere on five in kids' clothes. Or toys on eight. Maybe electronics on seven. I dunno. It's a big store. And these kids get whatever the hell they want when they're here."

"No kidding." Bells's voice softened. He sounded genuinely concerned about the young woman's grievance.

"Santa's treat," she said with a smirk. "Like they don't have enough." She didn't seem so intimidated now that he was listening to her complaints.

Bells crinkled his eyes and nodded at the phone. "Make a few more calls, would'ja? I'll bet they're still here."

The secretary shrugged. "All right." But she didn't sound hopeful. She pounded out another extension and asked if Gina was there.

Tozzi noticed that Bells kept his hand in his jacket pocket. He was jingling that bracelet he took from Mr. Blake, the jeweler. Tozzi got the impression from the way he kept playing with it that he was anxious to give it to Gina. Tozzi hadn't even been sure Bells had something going with Gina when he made believe he wanted to buy it for someone who loved purple, but now it seemed that he was right on the money about them. From what Tozzi could see, Bells had it pretty bad for Gina, and that was really pissing him off. Bells's voice on her answering machine kept replaying through his head. He wondered if Gina felt as strongly for Bells, though. Maybe it was just a one-way thing. But maybe all that stuff she'd told Tozzi about not wanting anything to do with her brother's wiseguy friends was a load. Maybe it was just her way of giving him the brush-off because she was already taken.

The secretary nodded, said thanks, and hung up the phone. "Gina was in kids' shoes on five about ten minutes ago, but she's not there now. The kids are with her. You want me to have her paged? Is this an emergency or something?"

Bells shook his head. "No, no, don't have her paged. I don't want to get her upset." He glanced over his shoulder at Freshy. "Maybe she'll think someone died." He laughed, but no one joined in. That didn't bother him. He turned back to the secretary and smiled at her. "If she's in the store, we'll find her. Thanks for your help."

Bells turned and spread his arms like a big bird of prey, ushering them all back down to the end of the hall to the bank of elevators. An oil portrait of old man Macy was on the opposite wall to greet people as they got off the elevator.

Stanley looked at his watch. "Whatta'ya wanna do, Bells?"

"We'll split up and look for her. She's in the store. She should be easy to spot if she's baby-sitting a bunch of kids."

Tozzi and Freshy shrugged and said okay. They didn't have much choice. It wasn't like he was asking them to break some deadbeat's leg. But in this instance, Tozzi might've rather done that than help Bells give Gina a gift that he had picked out because he'd genuinely thought she might like it.

"What is it, a little after noon?" Bells asked.

Stanley looked at his watch again. "Yup."

"Okay. Stanley, you come with me. We'll start on the top floor and work down. Mikey, you and Freshy go down to the basement and work up. We'll meet back here in what? Half an hour, forty-five minutes?"

They all shrugged and nodded. Tozzi planned to get to a phone and call in to the field office as soon as he could. Maybe they could take Bells down in the store.

Bells grinned at Tozzi. "Now, if you guys find her first, you just tell her I got a surprise for her and bring her back here, okay?"

"Sure." Tozzi nodded. Bells was really busting his balls now, but Tozzi didn't want to give him the satisfaction of letting him think he was jealous. Even though he was.

Bells pressed the down-button for the elevator. He was still grinning at Tozzi. "And don't tell her what it is. Gina likes surprises."

Tozzi held his tongue and just nodded. How about you, Bells? he thought. You like surprises?

"See? I told you she'd be here. She eats here all the time." Freshy bounced as he cut through the circular racks of dresses and blouses on the fourth floor. Tucked away in a corner, there was a little snack bar done up like an ice cream parlor from the fifties. The girl who worked the counter wore a pink and black poodle skirt, and her blond hair was tied back in a high, tight ponytail. Gina was sitting in a booth with a bunch of kids—nine- and ten-year-olds, Tozzi guessed. They took up the only two booths in the snack bar.

Tozzi followed Freshy through the racks. "If you knew your sister would be here, why didn't you tell Bells?"

Freshy gave him a look. "Would you want that friggin' freak hanging around *your* sister?"

The answer was obvious, but Tozzi pondered Freshy's statement. Was Freshy implying that Bells had been hanging around with Gina? As in the past?

Tozzi stopped and watched Gina and the kids from behind a rack of iridescent green parkas. They were flipping through the selections on the jukebox in the booth, arguing over what they wanted to hear. He didn't like what he saw. He'd just made a quick call in to the field office and told them that Bells was in Macy's and that he'd try to keep him here until an arrest team could get there. But if Bells found Gina and these kids, making an arrest would be too risky. Bells had to be isolated somehow. As Tozzi walked over toward the snack bar, he wondered how the hell he could do that. He'd have to go off and search the store for Bells. But he didn't want to leave Gina and the kids alone.

As he moved closer to the snack bar, he saw that Gina had her finger in one boy's face. "Jason, if you play Guns 'N Roses one more time, I'm gonna break your hand."

"Not if you like your job you won't." The kid had a face like a choirboy, but he wore a small gold hoop in one ear and a black wool baseball cap and had the kind of sneer that started fights.

The older kids egged them on, congratulating Jason on "dissing Gina good." Tozzi had to smile. He got a kick out of hearing middle-class white kids talking black. He'd love to leave someone like this Jason kid on 125th and St. Nicholas Avenue some night and see if he could communicate his way back to Scarsdale before he got his ass kicked good by the real brothers.

The kid reached over and dropped a few quarters in the slot, then punched out his selections without even looking. The other kids started to hoot for Jason's victory. The music started, and Axl Rose let out the pig squeal from hell. Jason leaned over the counter and sneered in Gina's face. "Deal with it, babe."

Gina met his gaze with the Sicilian look of death. She glanced over at the poodle-skirt blonde, raised her arm, and pointed down at the jukebox. A moment later Axl was cut off in mid-squeal as the blonde pulled the plug and the jukebox went dead.

She sneered into Jason's face. "Deal with *that*, mega-turd."

The kids hooted louder. She'd dissed him better. Jason maintained his sneer, but he knew she'd got him and got him good. Little Bart Simpson was going down in flames. Tozzi grinned.

"Hey, Gina, Gina." Freshy walked up to the booth. "Where you been? We been looking for you?"

One eyebrow rose over Gina's purple glasses. She didn't look too happy to see her little brother.

"What're *you* doing here?" When she noticed Tozzi, she

glanced over at the innocent-looking girl with the long blond Alice-in-Wonderland hair sitting at the end of the booth, then smirked up at him. "You getting into kiddie porn now?"

Tozzi just stared at her. He imagined her with Bells on her living-room couch. He wasn't sure if he liked her so much anymore.

"Bells is looking for you," Freshy said. "C'mon. He's got something for you." Freshy sounded annoyed but resigned to his duty. He didn't know the troops were on the way. He'd been in the bathroom when Tozzi had made the call.

Gina's eyes narrowed. "Bells is here?"

She didn't sound particularly upset. Of course, she didn't sound very happy either. At least Tozzi didn't think so.

Freshy nodded like a horse. "Yeah. He's here, he's here. Why the hell else would we be here? To go shopping, for chrissake? Jeez."

Young Jason looked Freshy up and down. "Wouldn't be a bad idea." Freshy was wearing a shiny electric blue suit under his bone-white brushed wool topcoat.

Freshy scowled and started to give the kid the finger when Gina caught his eye and changed his mind. The aborted gesture just ended up looking retarded with Freshy pulling on his ponytail in a lame attempt to save face. The kids all laughed.

Gina laughed with them. She laughed like a little kid, with her eyes. She wasn't laughing at Freshy so much as she was laughing *with* the kids, and in that instant Tozzi changed his mind about her again.

Freshy waved his arms as if he were helping a truck back up. "C'mon, Gina, c'mon. Bells is gonna be waiting up by your office. Let him give you the thing so we can get outta here. Okay? C'mon."

Gina frowned. She held up her palms and looked at all the kids around her. "How? How can I leave?"

"Mike'll watch 'em. C'mon."

She glared up at Tozzi. "Like hell, he will."

Tozzi flashed his wiseguy grin. He was glad to see she wasn't jumping to go get her surprise. He was also glad that she was staying put here with the kids so he could watch them. He'd decided it would be better to let the arrest team find Bells. They'd be armed.

Bells breezed through the electronics department, scanning the area for a brunette with a bunch of kids. The computer department was supposed to be down this way someplace. Kids like computers. Maybe they were down here. He kept jingling the bracelet with the purple stones in his pocket like a pair of dice. Mikey-boy was right—she did like purple. He knew that.

"You looking, Stanley, or what?" he asked, but he was talking to himself. When he realized that Stanley wasn't with him, he stopped and looked over his shoulder. Stanley was back by the TV sets. The friggin' guy was watching TV.

"Hey, Stanley, what the hell're you doing?" Bells went back to get his man, who was in a trance, his brow all wrinkled as he stared at the rows of TV sets lined up on the wall. He was watching the goddamn news.

Bells stopped to see what was so interesting. Just a bunch of cops hanging around this white car, yellow police tape all around. There was a close-up of some blood on the front seat, but you could barely make it out. The reporter was saying something about this being "off the New Jersey Turnpike in Ridgefield, New Jersey."

Bells furrowed his brow as he watched the broadcast on a fifty-four-inch projection television. He listened carefully to the reporter's voice-over as the camera panned some of the cops hanging around the white car. *"Local police and federal authorities have joined forces to apprehend the prime suspect in the attempted murder of FBI Special Agent Gary Petersen. Right now they are focusing their efforts on this man: Anthony Bellavita, who police say is also known as 'Tony Bells.' "*

"Bells! Did you hear that?"

"Shut up." Bells stared at the giant television. His picture was on the set. A black-and-white shot of him walking down the street in a short-sleeve shirt. A friggin' surveillance photo.

In his pocket, Bells fingered through the stones on the brace-let as if they were rosary beads.

"Law-enforcement personnel are always particularly upset when one of their own is shot in the line of duty, and FBI agents are no different, as you can see from the angry response one FBI official had to the presence of our camera crew."

"Move on. Now. Or I'll blow your bleep-*ing eyes out."*

On the screen, some ugly old guy was pointing his gun right into the camera lens. You could hear the film crew arguing with him.

The purple stones were flying through Bells's fingers. His mind was fixed on that picture of himself he'd just seen on TV.

He stared blankly at the old grouch on the screen, then suddenly noticed that the guy's face was all swollen on one side. Bells stepped closer and focused on the guy's face. That was the old guy that Mikey Santoro had been talking to on the corner this morning in Bayonne. The old guy who was supposedly looking for a dentist.

Dentist my ass.

Bells looked up from the big television and saw that swollen face on every other set in the store. Three long rows of the ugly mother filled the whole wall, floor to ceiling, five inches to thirty-two inches. Son of a bitch. Son of a *fucking* bitch.

That surveillance photo came back on, Bells walking down the street in black and white times a hundred.

"Authorities are asking for any information that will lead to the arrest of this man, Anthony 'Tony Bells' Bellavita. If you have any information, please call the number you see at the bottom of your screen."

Bells ground the bracelet in his fingers.

Stanley was hopping around like a flea. "Bells? Bells? We better get outta here. Jesus Christ! C'mon!"

But he didn't hear Stanley. He didn't hear anything. His mind was fixed on Mikey-boy Santoro, or whoever the fuck he really was. He was either a cop working undercover or some punk the cops had flipped. Whichever he was, it didn't matter because what he really was was a rat. A big fuckin' rat.

Bells pulled the bracelet out of his pocket and stared at it in his palm. Yeah. A big fuckin' rat with big fuckin' ideas. Too big. He put the bracelet back in his pocket and started to walk toward the escalators, nice and easy, not running, wondering just how the hell Mikey the rat knew she liked purple. How?

"Bells? Bells? Whatta'ya doing? We gotta get outta here."

Stanley trailed behind, but Bells didn't pay any attention to him. He kept walking, not fast, not slow. He was looking for a fuckin' rat and his Minnie Mouse. And he was gonna find them. Oh, yes. He was gonna find them.

Bells was walking fast now, shaking that bracelet in his pocket like a maraca, scanning the departments, the racks of clothes, the shoe departments, the shirt departments, the furniture, the luggage, the towels, the curtains, everything. He looked at everything, but he didn't see any of it because he only had one thing on his mind. Finding Gina and Mikey-boy.

He was aware of Stanley trailing behind, trying to keep up, squawking that they should get outta there fast. Well, they *were* gonna get outta there. He had every intention of getting outta there. He just couldn't put anything into words right now because he was like a guided missile. He only had one function: Finding them.

As he hopped on another escalator and loped down the moving steps two at a time, slipping around shoppers and leaving Stanley behind, his mind was a blur. He had no plan. He wasn't sure what he thought about those two just yet. All he knew was that someone was fucking with him, and that had to be dealt with.

Bells leaped off the last three steps of the escalator and picked up his pace, scanning the faces of the women in the teens' department, scanning and rejecting, one face after another, searching for the purple glasses. Then suddenly he heard kids laughing, and he turned his head and saw them, in a little snack bar, her sitting at the end of the booth full of kids, looking up at Mikey-boy, those purple glasses looking right up at her Mikey-boy.

Bells stopped and stared at them, and in his mind they gradually became one and the same because they were both guilty of the same thing: Disloyalty to him.

Mikey-boy was working with that ugly old grouch from the FBI. For all Bells knew, Mikey-boy could *be* FBI. But in Bells's mind, being a fed was no excuse for what Mikey-boy had done. The bastard had worked his way into Bells's confidence, had even gotten Bells to vouch for him with Buddha Stanzione. And all the while the guy intended to rat on him, to fuck him over. Mikey-boy was the lowest, the worst of the worst. He was a traitor, and if there was one thing that Bells could not stand, it was a traitor. To him, there was nothing more important in the world than loyalty. Without it, people were no better than animals. And if a man couldn't be trusted, he deserved to be shot like an animal, a diseased animal.

As for Gina, she was no better. She'd betrayed him, too. With Mikey-boy. Bells could see from the way she was looking at him that she was all wet in the pants for him. Besides, why else would the bastard want to buy her a bracelet? With purple fucking stones.

The jingling bracelet was a little rattlesnake in his pocket.

Stanley came up behind him, huffing and puffing. "What the fuck're you doing, Bells? Forget that broad. Let's get outta here."

But Bells didn't hear. He was moving now, moving toward those two. He didn't know what he was going to do to them, but he was going to do something. He'd figure it out when he got there.

Without thinking he reached into his coat and pulled out his gun, a .25 Raven automatic. He swooped into the snack bar, and Gina's face changed to shock and horror, like the Creature from the Black Lagoon had just arrived. He held the automatic in his palm like a rock.

Mikey-boy was surprised to see him, too. "Hey, Bells, there you are—"

Bells bashed him over the head with the gun. The kids screamed. Mikey-boy clutched his head and stumbled back, stunned. Bells hit him again, hard, then again. He collapsed to the floor, flat on his face. Bells gazed down at him. Mikey-boy was moving a little, but not much. Bells watched him as if he were a squished bug that hadn't died yet.

"Holy shit!" When Freshy saw the gun, he backstepped out of the snack bar and ducked down behind a rack of red coats.

"What the hell did you do that for?" Gina was on her feet, screaming in Bells's face. "Oh, my God! Are you crazy or what?"

He ignored her. He was waiting to see if Mikey-boy would get up. He hoped he would.

The kids were squealing and yelling. Gina told them to quiet down and stay put. She was down on her knees now, seeing if her Mikey-boy was okay.

"Bells, c'mon—" Stanley took him by the arm, but Bells shrugged him off.

"Hey! What's going on here?"

Bells whipped around to see who the intruder was. A security guard. A greasy old guy with a Latino mustache and a big beer belly hanging out of his maroon Macy's blazer.

"Hold it right there, pal. What've you got in your—?"

Bells smashed him over the head, too. Quick and hard, one shot. The guard crumpled, out cold, flat on his back. Blood started to show below his greasy hairline. Bells wanted to stomp on his big belly and squish him, too, but then he spotted a square brown leather case on the guard's belt. Handcuffs. Bells unbuttoned the case and pulled them out. He stared at the cuffs dangling in his hand, the same hand with the gun, mesmerized by the glint of the light on the shiny metal.

The kids were still screaming, the boys jumping over the sides of the booths to get away.

"What in the hell is wrong with you?" Gina screamed. She was still down on her knees with her poor Mikey-boy. "What the hell you gonna do with those, you sick son of a bitch?"

Bells stared down at her. Mikey-boy was rolling his head on the floor, trying to get it together.

Bells squeezed the bracelet in his pocket and realized that he'd been holding it the whole time. He let go of it and switched the gun to that hand. He knew what he was going to do now.

"I've got a little present for you, Gina."

TEN

Gibbons pushed his way through Macy's revolving doors, jostled a pack of slow-moving, white-haired old bags weighed down with too many shopping bags, and fought his way into the store. When he got inside the inner doors, he scanned the huge main floor and scowled. The place was overwhelming —overwhelmingly female. There were pocketbook counters to the right of him, jewelry to the left of him, cosmetics up ahead. The whole place thrummed with women. He hated these kinds of department stores, and he hated going shopping. Better to walk through a minefield than set foot in any kind of women's department. But right now it wasn't the store and all these buy-happy women that made him want to strangle someone; it was his tooth. It still hurt like a bitch, and he'd specifically told Lorraine to meet him outside Macy's at the Thirty-fourth Street entrance near Broadway, right next to the subway stop. He'd told her to look for the dark blue van with B & B PLUMBING AND HEATING painted on the side and to bring the pills. He'd told her the van would be parked illegally at the curb, which it was. He'd also told her they'd be there at noon. It was almost one now. She knew he was dying with this goddamn tooth. So where the hell was she? Shopping? She and her goddamn cousin Tozzi were two of a kind.

Gibbons winced as he scanned the aisles. His tooth was doing an S&M rumba in his mouth. He knew Tozzi was somewhere in here doing something stupid because he'd heard a lot of yelling and crap come through Tozzi's transmitter as he and Dougherty, the surveillance techie, sat in the van waiting for goddamn Lorraine to show up.

After Gibbons had lost track of his partner back in Bayonne earlier that morning, he'd told Dougherty to go park by the busy entrance to the Lincoln Tunnel, figuring that if stupid Tozzi came by that way, they'd pick up his signal. Gibbons didn't trust him to go disappear the way he'd told him to. If he knew Tozzi, Tozzi would be out hunting for Bells—by himself.

Gibbons's hunch paid off around eleven-thirty when they picked up a strong transmission and spotted the silver BMW with Tozzi in the backseat headed for Manhattan. They followed Tozzi's signal here to Macy's department store and listened to see if they could figure out who he was with. When Gibbons and Dougherty agreed that Bells was in there with him, they called in to the field office for a backup team. That was about fifteen minutes ago. But as they waited in the van, listening to Tozzi's transmissions, Gibbons and Dougherty couldn't figure out what the hell was going on now. All of a sudden there'd been a lot of hollering and screaming. Gina DeFresco was all excited about something, but Bells sounded real calm and even. Especially when he'd said "I've got a little present for you, Gina."

The weird thing was that they hadn't heard Tozzi's voice in any of this after the commotion started, and Gibbons was afraid something had gone wrong. Ms. DeFresco hadn't screamed as much as bitched, and they hadn't heard any gunshots, but Tozzi could still be in trouble. All Gibbons could think was that Bells had stuck a shiv in Tozzi's side or slit his throat or something gruesome like that, and Ms. DeFresco, the Mafia princess, didn't know how to cry and scream and react like a normal female who's just seen a guy get stabbed. All she knew how to do was bitch and complain. Probably got blood on her shoes or something like that.

Gibbons marched up the center aisle past all the makeup counters where the saleswomen stared at him and his swollen face, all of them made up like hookers. The whole place reeked of perfume, something else he hated. To him, all perfume smelled like dead old ladies laid out in flower print dresses. He looked all around him, hoping to spot Tozzi and the gang, but the first floor of Macy's was bigger than a gym, for chrissake. The whole store was gigantic, ten floors on an entire city block. How the hell was he supposed to find Tozzi in here? As he headed for the escalators, he figured he'd start from the top and work his way down. He had a feeling that if Bells was making trouble, he was doing it in private, away from the crowds, maybe in a dressing room or something.

But as Gibbons approached the escalators, he spotted something that made him slow down. There was a girl in tails and nylons spraying guys with perfume as they got on the escalator. Free samples of some new men's cologne. Gibbons hated perfume on men worse than he hated it on women. It reminded him of asskissers like his boss Brant Ivers, who left his scent on every piece of paper he touched like a dog marking his territory.

If that perfume broad even came near him with that spray bottle, he swore to God he'd deck her. Gibbons stopped walking and looked around the walls. There had to be elevators here someplace.

"Gibbons!"

He whipped his head around, ready to cold-cock anyone who got too close.

"Gibbons! Over here."

He squinted against the pain in his tooth and saw his wife coming down the aisle from where he'd been. She was wearing one of her schoolmarm outfits: white blouse, plain black skirt, low-heeled black pumps. The string tie with the turquoise clasp and the black Persian lamb jacket with the big shoulders dressed it up a little, but she had her dark hair tied back the way she always did when she was going to work. Lorraine didn't think it was proper for a fifty-three-year-old tenured professor of medieval history at Princeton to wear her hair loose. Gibbons disagreed. She kept it long, down to the middle of her back, and when she did wear it down with a mother-of-pearl comb over one ear, she looked like a tall and stately lady of Spain. The silver hairs picked up the light when she wore it down, which made her even more intriguing. But only when she wore it down. The rest of the time she was a schoolmarm.

"How do you feel?" She sounded more exasperated than concerned.

"I'm ready to shoot myself with this tooth, I got three and a half hours of sleep last night, and I can't find that numbskull cousin of yours—how do you think I feel?"

"You don't have to bite my head off. I'm just concerned about you." She was wearing her schoolmarm attitude, too.

"Did you get me the pills?"

"Yes, I got you the pills." She opened her purse and pulled out a brown plastic prescription bottle.

Gibbons snatched it out of her hand and popped the top. "How many am I supposed to take?"

"Can't you read the label?"

He glared at her. "Yeah, I can read it, but I'm asking *you*."

"How am I supposed to know? I'm not a pharmacist."

"Yeah, I can see that." He shook out a few of the round white tablets and read the label.

"I know you're in pain, Gibbons, but the sarcasm is uncalled for."

He put all the pills back in the bottle but one, then tossed it back into his mouth, swallowing it dry. He looked at the label again. Percodan. He hoped they worked quick.

Suddenly she snatched the bottle away from him. "Why do you have to be such an ass? Would it hurt to say 'thank you'?"

He gave her an evil look and held out his hand. "Thank you."

"Look, I've got to catch a train to Princeton. Dr. Lewis said he could fit you in at two forty-five."

"I can't go then—"

"Then suffer. I can't go to the dentist for you, too." She looked like she wanted to strangle him.

"Call him and tell him I can't make it."

"*You* call him! I'm not your secretary."

"Look, Lorraine, I can't. I gotta find—"

"Oh, my God!" Lorraine's dark eyes rose, and she bit her bottom lip.

The cosmetic hookers and all their customers were looking up, too, their lipstick mouths hanging wide open. Gibbons turned around, expecting to see a flasher with his pants down around his ankles. But he was wrong.

"Jesus Christ," he murmured.

The four of them were gliding down the escalator like they were coming down from heaven. Tozzi was shaking his head and blinking his eyes, leaning heavily on the railing for support. Next to him was a red-faced Gina DeFresco looking mad as hell, but looking pretty scared, too. Behind them, a step higher, was Tony Bells, and behind Bells was his legbreaker Stanley. Gibbons didn't like the look of this. Then he noticed the shiny metal cuff on Gina's wrist down by her side right next to the sleeve of Tozzi's coat, and he realized that they were handcuffed together.

"Shit," he grumbled, grabbing Lorraine's arm and pulling her out of the aisle. But she whipped her arm away, still angry at him.

"Lorraine," he growled under his breath. "Come over here."

She ignored him. "That's Michael," she said out loud. "Don't you see him? He's not well. He looks awful." She started to walk toward the escalators to help her cousin.

"Lorraine, come back—"

"Hey, Gib, what the hell're you doing here?"

Gibbons turned toward the whispering voice. It was Freshy DeFresco, stooped and cowering behind a counter, looking like he'd just run out of a haunted house.

"Bells is somewhere around here, Gib, and he's lost it, man. The guy's in hyperspace. I just took off when I saw it starting, man. I'm getting outta here. I'm sorry. I'm goin'."

But Gibbons wasn't listening. He was watching his stupid wife walking straight toward her dumbass cousin, putting herself in the middle of a very dangerous situation. "Lorraine!" he hissed. "Get over here." He rushed up behind her and gripped her arm, pulling her away.

But as he glanced up quickly at the four on the escalator, he suddenly made eye contact with Tony Bells, who was staring right at him, staring like he knew who he was, staring like he intended to do something about it. Gibbons felt his insides drop out. This was all wrong. Bells wasn't supposed to know who he was.

Bells's arm came up over Gina's head, and Gibbons saw it happening as if it were in slow motion. Bells had a gun. Instinctively Gibbons reached into his jacket for his gun, Excalibur, got it out of the holster, and was just about to yell "Freeze!" when the perfume girl in the tails screamed and dropped her spray bottle. It smashed to the floor at the same moment that the gunshot rang out, and Gibbons saw the automatic jump in Bells's hand just as he felt the impact of the bullet somewhere on his chest.

That friggin' perfume is gonna stink up the whole place, he thought as he fell backward, and he hoped he wouldn't get any on him.

That was the last thing he thought just before everything went fuzzy . . . then black.

Lorraine turned and saw Gibbons skidding across the floor on his back. She thought he was trying to sneak away, and this seemed like a peculiar way to do it. But then she felt the whoosh of someone running past her, the man who was on the escalator standing behind her cousin Michael, the gaunt-faced but good-looking man. He moved like a dancer, she thought, or a dancer imitating a ghost. A smooth, continuous flowing motion. The man swooped up to Gibbons, and before she realized what the man was really doing, the crack of a gunshot roused the crowd again. His arm was extended like a matador's sword over the downed bull. He'd fired into Gibbons's body, which bounced off the floor as if there were no life in it. Immediately she wondered why she thought of Gibbons's body as an "it," as an object and not a person, not "her husband."

"Gib!" It was a croak more than a shout, the voice of a far-off spirit coming to take Gibbons away. But it was Michael, her cousin, coming off the escalator now, reaching out to his partner.

"Get back." The handsome ghost dancer spun around and pointed his gun at Tozzi. "Move," he ordered. "Go." And without warning, the man grabbed the woman beside Tozzi by the hair, the woman with the purple glasses, and he dragged her off in his wake. And for some reason that Lorraine couldn't understand, her cousin Michael followed, stumbling behind as if he were under a spell and unable to control his own body.

The ghost dancer whipped Michael and the woman ahead of him as if they were weightless and held the gun to Michael's neck. "Run," he said. "Run!" And they ran, like horses pulling a sleigh, down the next aisle, disappearing behind the counters of hanging scarves and handbags.

Shoppers ran for their lives. Women in heels slipped and fell, scrambling on their knees to escape. The hard faces of the saleswomen melted in screaming panic. People pushed and shoved on both escalators, desperate to get upstairs.

Lorraine was the calm at the center of the cyclone. Her feet were bolted to the floor. She twisted her body to see her husband lying on the polished floor, his arm tangled in the high chrome stool of the Revlon counter.

A thick squat man was standing over Gibbons, shaking his head, saying "Jesus H. fucking Christ," saying it over and over again. Another man, a pale, skinny, frightened man was there, too. They were the only ones not running for cover. They were both holding guns down at their sides, but the skinny man didn't seem comfortable holding his. They both seemed confused and upset.

People were yelling and shouting, some screaming, all of them fleeing down the other aisles, but Lorraine couldn't move. She managed to loosen her feet and inch closer to her husband, but she couldn't get to him. She was made of lead, and she could only look at him. She couldn't cry or wail or weep. She'd done all that before, in her nightmares, in her daymares. The fear that this would happen someday used to ambush her at idle moments, gripping her soul, hanging on, and refusing to let go.

111

She'd always fend off the attacks, eventually convincing herself that this would never happen to *her* husband, but before it was over she'd always end up crying for him in her mind, crying and crying and crying. She'd cried so much, it seemed pointless to cry now. There were no more tears left in her. The inevitable had finally happened, and the only surprise was that she wasn't really surprised because she'd rehearsed this so many times before.

Now, finally, she was the widow, the one who wears the black veil, the one who gets to keep the flag they'll drape over his coffin, folded into a neat, forbidding triangle. Like Jackie Kennedy so many years ago. Just like the wives of all the slain cops she'd ever seen on television. Except now it would be *her* at the cemetery, not someone else. Gibbons had finally done what she'd cursed him for so many times in the past whenever she'd wake in the middle of the night with a pounding panic in her chest. He'd made her a cliché. He'd made her the mourning widow.

She stared at his arm tangled in the chrome rungs of the stool. *Damn* you, Gibbons.

ELEVEN

1:01 P.M.

"Aren't you dead?"

Gibbons heard the voice, but the words didn't make any sense to him. He kept blinking his eyes, trying to get them to focus. He could sense that there was a lot going on around him—yelling in the distance, yammering up front, running feet—but he couldn't tell exactly what was going on because he couldn't keep his eyes open. His chest felt like someone had just tried to poke a hole through it with a telephone pole. His stomach didn't feel so great either. Queasy. But it wasn't as bad as he thought it would be—as if that were any consolation. He could still feel the reverberations of the impact, but there really wasn't that much pain. He squeezed his eyes closed to stop the room from spinning, and without thinking he probed his bad tooth with his tongue. Surprisingly that didn't hurt either. Then he remembered that he'd just taken that pill, the pain-killer Lorraine had brought.

"You're not dead."

He opened his eyes, finally recognizing Lorraine's voice.

"I thought you had died," she said. She seemed sad and disappointed.

He just stared at her, struggling to keep both eyes open. He couldn't read her at all. She was kneeling by his side, but she

113

didn't seem very happy that he wasn't dead. He sat up. "I was wearing a vest. Standard procedure for a manhunt." He unbuttoned a shirt button and showed her a tan patch of the bulletproof vest. "You see any blood?"

She sat back on her heels and looked him up and down, then scooted backward on her knees and checked his legs. She shook her head. "I don't see anything."

Gibbons nodded, but he still couldn't figure her out. She was acting weird. She should've been glad that he wasn't dead. What the hell was wrong with her?

He probed his chest and side through the vest, trying to figure out exactly where he'd been hit. He figured he had to have fractured a few ribs. As he felt the bones along his side, his hand found the empty holster, and suddenly he thought of Excalibur. He looked around on the floor, remembering that he'd pulled his weapon just before he was shot. It couldn't have gone far. But where the hell was it?

"Lorraine, did you see my gun?"

"*I've* got it."

Freshy DeFresco was standing a few feet behind Lorraine, and Excalibur was in his hand, aimed at Gibbons's head. Gibbons couldn't believe it. Friggin' Freshy DeFresco, this little piece of shit, was holding his gun, the gun he'd used his entire career as an FBI agent. Talk about nerve. He couldn't fucking believe it.

"Give me my gun," he said. If the punk had been within reach, Gibbons would've ripped his face off.

Freshy laughed. "Get real, man."

Gibbons furrowed his brows.

All of a sudden, Freshy was trying to be a tough guy, but it was a pathetic attempt. The little shit kept hunching his shoulders and twitching his head to one side, and he couldn't look

114

Gibbons in the eye. He was acting weirder than Lorraine. Gibbons wondered if maybe he had died and this was hell: one big mental ward that looked like Macy's.

"I said, give me my gun, you little piece of—"

"Can it!" Tony Bells's legbreaker, the guy with the big jaw and the dumb look in his eyes, was standing over Gibbons from behind. He had a gun, too.

Gibbons just looked at him. Shit, this had to be hell.

Lorraine glanced from one gun to the other, not particularly concerned. Gibbons couldn't figure her out. Either she was pretending these two clowns weren't there, or that she wasn't there. Or was she just resigned to the fact that she and her beloved husband were gonna get blown away by these two? Gibbons didn't get her at all.

Freshy was bouncing like a ball, twitching all over the place. "Stanley, let's get outta here. C'mon."

"What about my cousin?" Lorraine asked without emotion. "What about Michael?"

"What about him?" Freshy shot back, almost offended by the question. "C'mon, Stanley. Let's go."

Lorraine stared up at him and made him look away. "They'll find your friend, the man who took Michael. They will."

Stanley the legbreaker squinted. "Who? Who's gonna find 'my friend'?"

Lorraine was defiant. "The FBI, that's who. Michael's a special agent. They'll track your friend down to find Michael."

"Fuck." Stanley started muttering to himself. "I told him not to handcuff them. You do federal time for kidnapping. I told him that. I told him I didn't want no part of no kidnapping. I *told* him I wasn't gonna come if he handcuffed them."

Gibbons was about to scream at Lorraine for blowing Tozzi's

115

cover, but then he realized that it was obviously already blown. Why else would they have Tozzi in handcuffs?

"Stanley, don't listen to her. C'mon, let's go before the cops come." Freshy was jumping out of his skin.

"Shut up, will ya? I'm thinking."

Stanley must've been thinking very hard because his face was bending and twisting like chocolate swirling into vanilla. His brain must've been the one muscle he hardly ever used.

Lorraine got to her feet, and Freshy backed away from her. She looked mean. "They'll find your friend. They're tracking them right now. You wait."

"Lorraine!" Gibbons could've killed her.

"Michael is wearing some kind of device on his body, a microphone or something. They can hear everything with this little gizmo. That's how they're going to track down your friend."

"Lorraine!"

She ignored him and continued to rip into Stanley and Freshy. "They've got all kinds of state-of-the-art equipment. Don't worry. They'll find your friend." She wasn't asking for their help; she was gloating over Tony Bells's eventual defeat. She was trying to get back at someone, anyone, for the kidnapping of her cousin.

Gibbons sat up. He was gonna murder her.

"You wait," she said. "They'll find your friend. The FBI will—"

Gibbons decided to cut her off before she could say any more. "Lorraine, just shut up."

"No, *you* shut up." Her eyes flashed as she turned on him and screeched. "I want them to know that their friend has no hope, that the van outside is tracking Michael right now as we speak, that they should tell us where they've gone and help us find

Michael before it gets any worse. *Tell* them what will happen."
She was all over the road, lashing out at everyone.

Gibbons struggled to get to his feet, but only managed to get
to his knees. Lorraine had snapped. She was yelling at *him* for all
this, and he was the one who'd just been shot, for chrissake. He
was in nutball hell, he had to be. He gritted his teeth as he tried
to get to his feet again. "Don't say any more, Lorraine. What
the hell is wrong with you?"

"Everything! At least according to you."

"What?"

"Nothing I do is ever right. I can't even deliver pills the right
way. I couldn't have your toothache for you, which is what you
really would've wanted. And I couldn't even be a good widow.
Well, I'm sorry, but that's the way I am. You ought to just get rid
of me."

"What the hell're you talking about, Lorraine? Have you lost
it or what?"

"I don't know. Maybe I have."

Gibbons grunted and strained and finally got to his feet. "In
case you missed it, I just got shot, Lorraine. I could've been
dead. I don't need this shit."

She was waving her arms like a real honest-to-goodness nut.
"So shoot me! Then you won't have me around to aggravate you
anymore."

He stared at her, then pointed at Freshy. "I can't. He's got
my gun."

She turned on Freshy and startled him. "Give him his goddamn precious gun back so he can shoot me. I'm sick of living
with him."

Those words hit Gibbons harder than the bullets had. He
didn't understand what had gotten into her. Sure, he'd been
grouchy and nasty when she'd gotten there with the pills, but so

117

what? He was always grouchy and nasty. "Lorraine, you don't really mean that."

She snapped her head around and glared at him. "Don't tell me what I mean and don't mean. Goddamn it, I can think for myself."

Stanley shouted over her. "Shut up, the both of youse. I can't think."

"*You* shut up," Lorraine screeched.

Gibbons scowled at him. "Yeah, shut the fuck up and mind your own business."

Stanley's face expanded with anger. "Don't tell me to shut the fuck up. *You* shut the fuck up."

Freshy was hopping around like a first-time firewalker. "C'mon, Stanley. Let's go!"

"You shut up, too. I'm trying to think." Stanley's eyes were confused little pinpoints. He pointed at Lorraine with his gun. "You said something about a surveillance van being outside?"

"Yes! Don't you listen?"

Gibbons couldn't believe her. Why the hell was she telling this asshole anything? Why couldn't she just shut up?

The gears started turning in Stanley's head, and his gaze returned from the ozone. He panned his gun toward Gibbons as he snatched Lorraine's upper arm. "Let's go. Move. I want to see this van."

"Fuck you," Gibbons said.

Excalibur's cold metal barrel was suddenly pressed to his scalp. "You heard the man," Freshy said. "Move!"

The little shit had grown balls all of a sudden. Gibbons would've bitten his hand off at the wrist if Stanley weren't there holding a gun on Lorraine.

"Move!"

Gibbons raised his hands in surrender and looked over his

shoulder at Lorraine. She had a smug expression as if she had everything under control. Maybe in *her* mind. He couldn't imagine what she thought would happen when these guys saw the van. Half of him hoped Dougherty had moved the thing; the other half hoped he hadn't. No telling what this dumb leg-breaker might do if he didn't find it. Never promise an attack dog a bone unless you know you've got one.

The main aisle was deserted as they moved in a pack toward the exit. Unarmed security guards watched from behind counters, biting their lips and pissing their pants, wishing the cops would show up already. Freshy and Excalibur escorted Gibbons out onto Thirty-fourth Street. Stanley backed through the glass doors, dragging Lorraine with him.

"Where is it?" Stanley grunted, looking up and down the crowded street.

Lorraine pointed with her head. "Right there. The blue plumbing truck." She sounded annoyed.

He dug his gun into her back. "Go."

Freshy jammed Excalibur into Gibbons's spine, but Gibbons moved as slowly as he could get away with. Dougherty was a surveillance technician, not a street agent. He wasn't required to carry a weapon, though it was possible that he kept one inside the van. If he was smart, he'd just take off as soon as he saw them coming. *If* he saw them coming. Knowing Dougherty, he was probably in the back with the headphones on, fiddling with his dials and knobs, trying to pick up whatever he could from Tozzi's transmitter.

"You," Stanley said as they came up to the van. He let go of Lorraine and shoved her ahead. "Open the door."

Lorraine stumbled forward and hesitated.

"Do it," Stanley barked, rushing up behind her and jamming the gun in her back.

Finally she looked scared. Gibbons was almost relieved.

"Hurry up." Stanley pushed her again.

Reluctantly she knocked on the sliding door.

No response.

"Try the handle," Stanley ordered.

She tried it, expecting the door to be locked, but it flew open with her jerk.

"Mrs. Gibbons!"

Dougherty was shocked to see her. He was leaning forward on one of the stools, wearing his headphones of course, but he was also holding a .38 down by his side. Gibbons could see right away that Dougherty didn't know shit about using a gun. Stanley could see that, too. He shouldered Lorraine out of his way and backhanded Dougherty with his heavy automatic. Dougherty buried his face in his lap, and Stanley clobbered him over the head. The surveillance tech poured out of the van and landed on the sidewalk in a heap, out cold. His forehead was scraped and bleeding.

"In." Stanley motioned with his gun, looking all around at the passing pedestrians, but no one had noticed Dougherty lying on the curb yet. "Everybody in."

Lorraine obeyed right away, which really pissed Gibbons off. She never hopped to it like that when he told her to do something. 'Course he never held a gun on her either.

"Get in."

Gibbons ignored him and hunkered down next to Dougherty. He knew Freshy didn't have the balls to shoot him. Stanley stuck his gun in Gibbons's ear and repeated the order, but Gibbons didn't give a shit. He went ahead and checked Dougherty's pulse. The guy had one, which was good enough for Gibbons. He'd be all right.

"Get up!" Freshy said, his voice rising.

Gibbons ignored him and looked up at Stanley, nodding at Dougherty's revolver on the curb. "Take his gun," Gibbons said. "Some punk may pick it up."

"What?"

"I said, take his gun. There are enough guns out on the street."

"Oh." Stanley turned to Freshy. "Pick it up."

Freshy did as he was told, but he didn't look happy about it. Taking orders for menial tasks didn't make him much of a tough guy. Gibbons smiled with his teeth.

"Now get in," Stanley ordered.

When Gibbons took his time doing it, one of them shoved him from behind, and he landed on top of one of the stools, banging his chest. A dull pain like an old bruise radiated through the entire left side of his chest. He had a feeling that if he hadn't taken that pain-killer, he'd be in tears right now. He hauled himself up with some difficulty and sat down on the stool. Stanley was reeling in the coiled wire of Dougherty's headphones, yanking them off the poor guy's bloody head.

Freshy shut the sliding doors. "Drive," Stanley said to him. The little shit stuck Excalibur in his coat pocket, climbed behind the wheel, started the engine, and screeched out into traffic.

"Where'm I going, Stanley?"

"Pass by the parking lot. See if Bells got the car. We gotta find him."

"Right. Good idea."

Stanley gazed at all the high-tech surveillance equipment jammed into the back of the van. He looked like a chimp sitting in a space shuttle. He pursed his lips and frowned as he tentatively pulled the headphone jack out of its plug. A speaker mounted on one of the walls suddenly crackled to life with an

121

erratic wash of static. Stanley held out the headphones to Gibbons. "How's this stuff work?"

Gibbons laughed. "Don't ask me, pal." He jerked his thumb over his shoulder. "The guy you left back at the curb is the one who knows how to run this stuff, not me."

Stanley glared at Lorraine. "I thought you said they could track them. Huh?"

Lorraine set her jaw, then threw an accusing look at Gibbons. "I thought you *could* track them with this equipment."

Gibbons shook his head. "You two watch too many James Bond movies. That transmitter Tozzi's wearing is very fluky. You gotta be within a quarter mile to pick up a signal. And if he's in a steel-frame building or there's one between the transmitter and the receiver, forget about it."

Lorraine protested, "But you heard him inside the store, didn't you?"

Gibbons shrugged. "It's an old building. I dunno. Ask Dougherty."

"This is giving me a friggin' headache," Stanley grumbled at the speaker, and he went to put the headphone jack back in to silence the static.

"Why don't we leave it?" Lorraine blurted. "In case something comes through."

Gibbons stared at her. He was gonna kill her. No question.

She stared back at him, defiant and angry. "Leave it on. I want to know if Michael's all right."

"Yeah," Freshy piped up from the driver's seat. "I want to know if my sister's okay, too. That freakin' nut Bells is liable to do anything."

"Shut up!" Stanley yelled.

Gibbons reached over to the volume control and turned it down.

Lorraine was glaring at him. For some reason she really had it in for him, but he couldn't believe it was just because he was grouchy before.

"Hey, Stanley, look. The car's still there." Freshy was pointing through the windshield at a parking lot on Thirty-fourth Street past Ninth Avenue. The silver BMW was parked out front, facing out. There was no one in it.

Two NYPD patrol cars sped down Thirty-fourth in the opposite direction, lights flashing, sirens whooping. No one said anything. No one had to. It wasn't hard to guess where the cops were going.

"Take this right," Stanley said.

Freshy turned in where a big green sign said LINCOLN TUNNEL. "But this goes back to Jersey, Stanley." Even though he was already on a one-way access road to the tunnel and he couldn't turn around, he wasn't so sure about this. "What about Bells . . . and Gina?"

"Don't worry. I know Bells. I know where he's gonna go." Stanley sounded grave.

"You do? How do you know that?" Freshy was obviously worried about his sister.

"Everybody's out looking for him. His face is on TV and everything. I know how he is. He's going nuts thinking about it." Stanley looked at Gibbons. "He probably thinks he killed a fed, too. You are a fed, right?"

Gibbons nodded. He was tempted to say something about Bells shooting Special Agent Petersen, but he decided not to get Stanley riled. If Stanley was in the mood to talk, let him talk.

"If I know Bells," Stanley said, "he's gonna go where he feels safe, and there's only one place. He's pretty good at keeping his cool, but I've seen him lose it. Gotta find him before he does. Gotta get him outta here before he gets pinched." Stanley was mumbling to himself, gazing down at the gun in his hand, imagining something.

"Whatta'ya mean? What happens when he loses it?" Gibbons wished he could see into Stanley's head.

Stanley looked up with basset hound eyes, but he didn't answer the question.

Freshy glanced back over the bucket seat. "So where's he gonna go, Stanley?"

"You know."

"No. Not there."

Stanley didn't answer.

"Shit! Shit, shit, shit!" Freshy was suddenly very upset.

Gibbons was confused. He didn't like the sound of any of this.

As the van slipped into the artificial light of the tunnel, the soft crackle of the static began to fade. Lorraine stared at the speaker, then threw her head back and sighed. "Oh, God."

TWELVE

"Just walk. Keep walking. Just keep on walking."

Tozzi wanted to kill the bastard. He and Gina were walking, holding hands and climbing the subway steps like a nice couple, just the way Bells wanted, but the son of a bitch kept giving them orders anyway. He was right behind them, holding his gun on them in the pocket of his overcoat, talking nonstop in that singsong wiseguy drone of his, telling them to keep walking. Tozzi swore to God he was gonna kill this bastard. For Gibbons.

The image of Gibbons lying on the floor—one leg crooked back, lifeless arms up over his head—was driving Tozzi crazy. He wanted to rip Bells's fucking heart out. *Gibbons*. He'd killed *Gibbons*. The bastard should suffer, suffer a lot. Tozzi wanted to get a piece of Bells so bad, his hands were shaking.

When they reached the top of the stairs and walked out into the sunlight on the corner of Sixth Avenue and Spring Street, on the edge of SoHo, Tozzi glared at Bells sideways.

Bells was grinning like a lizard. "You like this, don'cha, Mikey-boy? Holding hands with Gina, strolling down the street. Maybe we should go check out some art galleries while we're here. That's your kind of thing, isn't it, Gina?"

"Go fuck yourself, Bells."

125

Bells laughed. "You got some fresh mouth, Gina. I don't know why they call your brother Freshy."

Tozzi tried to smother his fury. "Where we going, Bells?"

"Whatta you care, Mikey? You got the girl. Just enjoy it."

"Yeah, right."

"You telling me you're not enjoying it? C'mon, Mikey, be honest now. You been dying to get Gina in the sack. Or who knows, maybe you done her already. Is that it, Mikey? You had her a couple of times, and now you don't want no part of her no more? Is that it? What'sa matter? She snores?"

Tozzi slid his eyes toward Gina, but she kept her eyes straight ahead. He wasn't sure if Bells was just guessing about them. Maybe he knew about that afternoon at her apartment.

"Tell me. Is she nice, Mikey?"

Gina's glasses flashed as she whipped her head around. "Get off it, will ya, Bells? You're not funny."

"Oh, no? You used to think I was funny."

Tozzi tried to catch her eye, but she was looking straight ahead again.

They passed an old-fashioned barber shop and a jewelry repair shop as they headed east toward West Broadway, where the expensive shops and galleries were. And the crowds. Tozzi had been shitting bricks on the subway, worrying about Bells with that gun in his pocket while they were jammed in shoulder-to-shoulder with dozens of citizens. Tozzi was afraid something might set him off, and he'd start shooting again the way he did in Macy's. Luckily, nothing happened on the subway, but Tozzi knew he had to keep him away from crowds.

Tozzi's head started to throb again from the pistol-whipping. He thought about his black-belt test scheduled for that night, and suddenly he wanted to bite something, he was so mad. Not because he was going to miss it again. That didn't matter anymore, not after what had happened to Gibbons. What pissed him off was that he'd come all this way, studied aikido for five and a half years, and what good did it do him? Here he was at the mercy of some jerk who had no formal training in anything, just some scumbag lowlife with a gun. He remembered what they always said at aikido practice. A guy comes at you with a gun, just give him what he wants. No martial art in the world can help you against a bullet from across the room. And even though Bells was up close and the gun was in his pocket, which could've given Tozzi some leverage, he was handcuffed to Gina, so he couldn't risk it. He felt totally helpless handcuffed this way. The only thing to do was to just stay calm and relax. Be aware of everything that's going on all around. Maintain the basic principles of aikido. And hope for a miracle.

Tozzi sighed. Why bother studying any martial art when all you have to do is plunk down a couple hundred bucks for a handgun, and you've bought yourself total control? It wasn't fair. Sure, he knew aikido training was supposed to be a constant ongoing thing, something you did for life. You were always a student, no matter how long you'd been doing it, and no one ever "mastered" it, not even the masters. Besides, aikido was supposed to be *life* training, not combat training. There was a lot more to it than just fighting. Tozzi knew all that, but it wasn't very reassuring right now. All he knew was that he was almost a black belt, and Bells, who only wore a belt to keep his pants up, had the upper hand. And all he had was a goddamn gun. Christ.

Tozzi's temper started to simmer down. Getting mad never helped anything. He felt Gina's fingers in his hand. They were cold. She was gonna catch pneumonia. It was pretty chilly out, and she was only wearing slacks and a blouse, but she wasn't complaining, not about that. The wind blew her hair across her face and into her glasses. He wondered what she was thinking.

He wondered what was really going on between her and Bells. She was too quiet, angry but not outraged. Sure, she was tough, but wouldn't someone being kidnapped at gunpoint be a little more hysterical? Maybe she felt guilty about something she'd done to Bells. Maybe she thought she deserved this. Why wasn't she putting up more of a fuss? Why didn't she seem scared?

But that got Tozzi thinking about how *he* looked. Was he reacting like Mike Santoro the pornographer or Mike Tozzi the FBI agent? Maybe *he* should be a little more hysterical. Maybe he should try to weasel his way out of this, the way Mike Santoro would, profess shock and innocence at what was going on, grovel a little. Maybe he was being too stoic for the greaseball he was supposed to be.

Yeah, but what if Bells already knew that he was an undercover agent? Freshy could've told him. Tozzi wouldn't put it past that little shit. If Bells knew, maybe he was thinking he could use Tozzi as a bargaining chip to negotiate his way to freedom. The problem was, he didn't know what Bells knew, and Bells wasn't saying anything. Obviously Bells knew Gibbons was the law, or he wouldn't have shot him. But how much else did he know? Tozzi glanced over his shoulder at Bells's face. It was disturbingly placid under the circumstances, almost as if he were meditating. You could never tell what this guy was thinking, what set him off. Tozzi had to get him talking.

"Why me, Bells? What'd I do to you? I don't get it."

Bells didn't answer. They were walking together at a nice clip, but Bells was in his own world now.

"Talk to me, Bells. Lemme help you. We'll figure something out."

Bells started to laugh. It started as a private little hiss, but it soon snowballed into near-hysterical belly laughs.

Gina parted the hair out of her face and looked back at him. "You're sick. You know that?"

"C'mon, Bells. Listen to me. Lemme help you out here. Take the cuffs off. C'mon."

Gina smirked. "How's he gonna do that? He doesn't have the key."

She was right. Bells hadn't taken the security guard's keys when he knocked the guy out. Still, Tozzi had to keep up the chatter. He had to get Bells talking. Bells had to realize his hostages were people, not props.

"Bells, you're not listening to me. I wanna help you out."

Bells slowed down their pace. He was laughing so hard, he was in tears. "Help me out? How're you gonna help me out? You're a fucking rat, Mikey. You don't wanna help me. You wanna screw me."

The word hit Tozzi like a dagger in a tree trunk. *Rat.* Bells did know.

"Whatta'ya talking about, Bells? Whatta'ya mean, 'rat'?"

Bells was out of control, laughing like he was on laughing gas. "You're a rat, Mikey-boy, a big fucking rat. That old guy I shot at Macy's? The one with the swollen face? You met him out in front of the candy store in Bayonne this morning. You told me he was just some guy looking for a dentist or some shit. Well, I saw him on TV, Mikey. He's a fucking fed, my friend."

Was a fed, Tozzi thought.

"You've been working with the feds, Mikey-boy. That ain't nice." Bells wasn't laughing anymore.

Tozzi's gut turned to concrete. He was afraid to deny it. Bells might go berserk. But if he admitted that Bells was right, Bells would kill him for sure.

"Is that true?" Gina glared at him.

"What?"

129

"That you're working with the government. You were trying to get my brother in trouble, weren't you?"

"No."

"Liar."

"Gina, I'm telling you the truth. I didn't rat on anybody."

Bells was hysterical again, getting a real charge out of their arguing, but Tozzi was shitting bricks. He never liked being on the defensive, having to make excuses. It made you sound like a liar even if you weren't. He had to give her a direct answer, and denial was his only choice.

She let go of his hand and tried to pull it away, forgetting that they were cuffed. "You're a real jerk, you know that? You sweet-talked me and fed me all that bullshit about liking me, when all you really wanted was information about my brother. You came up to my apartment that day just to see if you could get some-thing on my brother. You didn't give a shit about me. I can't believe this." There was venom in her eyes.

The sweat was dripping down Tozzi's back. Oh, shit . . .

Bells stopped laughing. His mouth was a straight line, his eyes were dull and flat. Tozzi could feel his motor revving. "You screwed her?"

"Bells, listen to me—"

He looked at Gina. "You slept with this guy?"

She turned her face away and didn't answer.

Bells was nodding. His face was like a dark house. "This is nice. You're sleeping with this rat, and he's trying to fuck me over. Very nice, Gina. I like this."

"It was only once," she snapped.

But Bells wasn't listening. He was talking to himself, running it down out loud. "They got my face on TV, and a million cops are out there looking for me, and you went to bed with this guy. Wonderful."

The back of Tozzi's shirt was drenched under his coat. "You're jumping to conclusions, Bells. It's not what you think. Talk to me."

But Bells didn't hear. His face was empty; he was in another world. Tozzi followed his gaze to a Korean grocery store on the corner across the street. A truck driver was unloading crates of lettuce from the back of an open panel truck.

"Hey!" Gina yelped as Bells suddenly grabbed a fistful of her hair and pushed her across the street. His gun hand was still in his pocket, and Tozzi could see the bulge of the barrel through the fabric. They moved toward the cab of the truck like a dysfunctional conga line. Keeping his grip on Gina's hair, Bells stepped up on the running board, glanced inside, then stepped down all in one motion.

"Leggo," Gina yelled, but he shoved her toward the back of the truck, dragging Tozzi along with them.

Tozzi didn't resist. The gun was pointed at Gina's back, and he knew that Bells wasn't shy about shooting in public.

The Korean man unloading vegetables glanced up when he heard Gina's complaining. The automatic flew out of Bells's pocket and was in the man's face, making him cross-eyed.

"Keys," Bells ordered.

The man sputtered in Korean.

"Keys to the truck."

The man shrugged and jabbered. He didn't understand English.

Bells backhanded him across the temple with the gun barrel. The man staggered back, and suddenly another Korean in a white apron rushed out of the store with a sawed-off shotgun in his hand. Bells let go of Gina and moved right into his face, jamming the automatic into his throat and beating him to the

131

punch. The trembling man raised his arms in surrender, and Bells slapped the shotgun out of his hand.

"Keys. I want the truck keys."

"Yeah, yeah, okay, okay, okay," the Korean grocer said. His accent was thick, but he understood what Bells wanted. "In pocket." He pointed to the stunned truck driver who was sitting on the sidewalk, tendering his head. "In pocket."

Bells tipped the grocer's chin up with the gun barrel. "Get them. Get the keys."

"Okay, okay, okay. I get for you. I get." The grocer hunkered down and fished the keys out of the driver's jacket. He dangled them in his fingers, holding them up at arm's length, straining his neck muscles against the muzzle digging into his throat. "You want money, I get money. No shoot me. Please. I get money for you."

Bells ignored the offer and knocked the squatting grocer to the ground with a bump of his hip. He turned the gun on Tozzi and Gina. "In," he said, nodding into the back of the truck.

Tozzi couldn't believe what he'd just seen. It had flashed by him as if it were on a movie screen. The way Bells had moved was unreal. His focus and execution were extraordinary. There was no emotion or hesitation in his attack. Bells didn't think, he just acted. It was the kind of spirit Tozzi had seen only in the very best aikido practitioners, the real masters. The whole incident had taken fifteen, twenty seconds tops, but it wasn't until it was over and Bells was ordering them into the back of the truck that Tozzi realized that he'd been mesmerized by the spectacle. If he'd had the presence of mind to act, he might have been able to do something to get Bells's gun away from him while he was threatening the Koreans. But Tozzi hadn't done a thing. He'd just watched. It gradually materialized in Tozzi's mind, like a Polaroid developing as he watched, that despite all his FBI training and all his aikido training, he was probably no match for Bells.

"In." Bells pointed into the back of the truck with the gun.

Gina looked totally put out, but she started climbing in, crawling onto the edge on her knees. She jerked Tozzi's handcuffed wrist. "C'mon!" Her voice was like new chalk on a blackboard.

"Go 'head, Mikey. Get in." Bells was smiling again, back under control. Dr. Jekyll and Mr. Hyde.

Reluctantly Tozzi climbed up onto the tailgate. He jerked Gina's arm without meaning to, and Gina jerked back, tit for tat. They stood up together and looked down at Bells, Tozzi feeling stupid and helpless.

"Have fun," Bells said as he grabbed the hanging strap and pulled the overhead gate down with a rattle and a crash.

Standing there in the dark, they could hear the clatter of Bells padlocking the gate.

Tozzi looked around as his eyes adjusted to the darkness. A sliver of sunlight penetrated the emptiness from a crack in the seam of one of the side walls. It was uncomfortably cool and damp back there, and there was a faint smell like something about to go bad.

"Shit," Gina said. "This is all your fault."

"Mine?"

"Yes, yours. You got him mad."

"*I* got him mad?"

The truck engine turned over then, and Tozzi heard the parking brake being released. The truck took off with a jerk, and they both were thrown back.

"Sit down," Tozzi said, squatting down and feeling around for something to sit on.

"Don't tell me what to—"

The truck suddenly braked hard, and Gina was thrown forward, nearly yanking Tozzi's arm out of its socket.

"Sit down!" he repeated, annoyed with her hard head.

"Don't tell me what to do." She settled down without his help and found a place for herself, keeping as far from him as possible. "Now what?"

"Whatta'ya mean, 'now what'?"

"Now what? That's what I mean."

"I don't know."

"Great."

They didn't say anything. Only the sound of gears grinding and whining filled the gloom. Tozzi was thinking about what Bells had done to those two Koreans back there, how smooth and efficient his movements were, how detached and unemotional he was when he was hurting someone. It was terrifying.

"God*damn* it!" Gina suddenly yanked his arm again as she tried to get up. "Yuck!"

"What's wrong?"

"I'm sitting in tomatoes, dammit."

"Oh."

As she shifted her position, Tozzi felt around to see what he was sitting on.

Potatoes.

THIRTEEN

1:34 P.M.

Lorraine stared at the speaker, lulled by the soft hiss of the static. The interior of the van was dim and solemn. Traffic was backed up inside the Lincoln Tunnel, heading toward New Jersey. Craning her neck, she could see through the windshield. The taillights of the cars up ahead reflected off the tile walls, like long unfurling neon-red streamers. It made her think of Chinese New Year.

Traffic slowed, and brake lights flashed on, one after the other. The red glow gave Freshy's pale face some color. He looked anxious, but Lorraine suspected that this might be his standard expression.

Gibbons was leaning against the wall in the rear of the van, his head tipped back, face shrouded in shadow. His eyes shimmered through the dark. He was staring at Stanley.

Half of Stanley's face was shaded, the other half tinged with red. His huge jaw made him look like the Tin Man, only stouter and more menacing. His eyes shimmered, too, under half-closed lids as he stared back at Gibbons. He held his gun on the flat of his thigh.

No one had said anything since they'd slipped into the tunnel. The strange light and shadow had hushed them. Even the static coming out of the speaker seemed more subdued.

Lorraine looked at Gibbons, hoping to catch his eye, but he kept his stare leveled on Stanley as he rubbed his chest in slow rhythmic circles. She wished he'd look at her, acknowledge her, acknowledge that he wasn't angry with her, even though it infuriated her that she was feeling guilty like this. He was the one who had been acting like an ass, using his toothache as an excuse for being Attila the Hun. But she did feel guilty, and she couldn't help feeling that way because after he'd been shot and he was lying there and she thought he was dead, *she did not cry.* She wasn't distraught; she wasn't sad. She was simply resigned and, in her heart of hearts, maybe even relieved. Not happy that he was dead, but relieved that something she'd been secretly dreading had finally happened, and now she could let her breath out and get on with the next phase, whatever that was. Widow? Widowed professor? Old schoolmarm widow? Fifty-ish white widow, Ph.D., seeking stimulating companion for chess, Chaucer, long walks on the beach, fine wine, and low-fat cheese at sunset. Smokers and men likely to be shot to death in the line of duty need not respond.

Lorraine thought back to when she was kneeling over him on the polished floor in Macy's between the cosmetics counters. Had she really filed him away like an obituary cut out of the newspaper, right on the spot? It was humiliating to have to admit to herself that she'd actually thought about "the next one."

She could feel her face getting hot. Christ, if Gibbons had really died, she could've hopped up on a stool and had one of the counter girls do a makeover on her. After all, she would have to start "dating" again, as those old gaudy divorcees always say on the TV talk shows. The thought of a postmenopausal woman using the word *dating* had always seemed idiotic and embarrassing to her, but now she was ashamed to admit that she'd secretly believed all along that someday she'd be "dating" again herself.

Because deep down she believed that her husband would inevitably be killed in the line of duty.

She stared at Gibbons's hand rubbing circles into his shirt. She didn't want to apologize to him. Feeling what you feel isn't a crime, and besides, he didn't deserve an apology. But she did want to connect with him, talk to him, figure out what was going wrong between them. Of course, she knew what he'd say if she tried to discuss her feelings. "What is this, a support group, Lorraine?" He always avoided real emotion with his snide humor. But this she had to get off her chest. She had to know why she was so ready to accept his death, why she couldn't cry when she saw him lying there. Maybe that said something about their relationship, something neither of them was willing to face. She needed to talk to him about this, but the evil Tin Man was sitting right there, and moonfaced Freshy was up front in the driver's seat. And Gibbons was furious with the whole situation, she could tell. He was definitely in no mood to talk. As if he ever were.

The van suddenly jolted, and everyone lurched forward as Freshy hit the brakes hard.

"Hey!" Stanley shouted. "Whatta'ya doing, jerkoff?"

"Sorry."

"You're driving like an idiot. What'sa matta with you?"

Freshy turned around and gave Stanley a dirty look. "What'sa matta with *me*? Bells has my sister in fucking handcuffs, and he's taking her back to his place. That's what'sa matta with me. He's fucking crazy, that guy."

Stanley glared at him, like an unamused largemouth bass ready to swallow something whole, just out of spite. He clearly didn't like anyone saying anything bad about Bells.

"Watch out!" Stanley yelled.

Freshy turned back to the road and slammed on the brakes.

137

Tires screeched as the van came up fast on the car ahead. They stopped inches from the car's bumper.

"Will you watch what the fuck you're doing? You're gonna have an accident."

"I'm nervous," Freshy shouted back. "You guys got me all nervous."

Lorraine glanced at Gibbons. Her heart was pounding. She was certain he would've taken advantage of the diversion to pounce on Stanley. But he didn't. He just sat there, not moving, staring out of the shadows, his eyes glimmering. Her heart pounded harder. She couldn't help thinking that his anger was all directed at her, not Stanley or Freshy, at her. For not crying. But that was ridiculous. She was being absurd. He wouldn't want her to cry. He hated it when she got emotional.

She looked away to avoid Gibbons's accusing stare. "I don't think you really have to worry about your sister," she said to Freshy, hoping to break the tension. "Wiseguys don't hurt women, do they? La Cosa Nostra rules of honor forbid it, no? Especially an innocent woman."

The largemouth bass coughed up a laugh. "An innocent woman . . . I like that."

"Shut up!" Freshy snapped.

Lorraine wrinkled her brow. She was confused.

Gibbons's voice came out of the shadows, like the oracle of doom. "Nobody's innocent, not with these people."

Freshy was pouting and scowling at the windshield.

Lorraine looked at Stanley. "Did Freshy's sister do something wrong? Why did you say that?"

The big jaw grinned. "Lemme put it this way. Bells has this thing about loyalty. To him, it's like the most important thing there is. He's loyal to his people, no matter what."

"What people?" Gibbons asked.

The jaw grinned again. Stanley wasn't going to mention any names. "Bells expects the people he deals with to be as loyal to him as he is to them. You follow?"

Lorraine frowned. "No. I'm afraid I don't."

Stanley sighed and rolled his eyes. "Listen. As long as I've known Bells, he always says the same thing to me: 'Trust, Stanley, trust. It's the most important thing there is in the world. If people can't trust each other, they may as well be animals. It's the only thing that makes people human.' I've heard him say this a million times. Now if he trusts you and you turn around and fuck him over, you deserve the worst, the way he figures. 'There's nothing worse than a traitor,' he always says. 'Nothing.'"

"What's that got to do with my sister?" Freshy grumbled.

"Just shut up and watch the road."

Lorraine's brow was still furrowed. "Are you saying he'd even hurt a woman if he thought she betrayed him?"

Stanley shrugged and gave her the fish face, but Freshy cut in. "His wife paid the price for—"

"Shut up!" Stanley exploded. He glared at Freshy, then at Gibbons, who just sat there, taking it all in, like an owl in the dark.

A sudden chill ran through Lorraine's bones. She was still confused, but also frightened, because she sensed a bond between Stanley and Gibbons that excluded her. It was Gibbons's silence that frightened her. From the way Stanley talked, it seemed that punishing an unfaithful woman needed no comment. It was automatic and deserved no appeal. But was Gibbons's silence his unspoken agreement with this male code of justice? Is that what he felt she deserved for not being a good wife, for not crying and howling at the moon in utter grief for him?

But that was ridiculous. Gibbons had been unconscious, and when he came to, he was disoriented. How would he know what she had done, or how she had reacted? He wasn't a mind-reader; he didn't know how she felt.

But she still felt that she was being accused, that she had done something fundamentally wrong. A crime against a man.

Her gaze bounced from one face to the other—red-faced Freshy, the largemouth bass, Gibbons in the dark. One cop and two criminals, but to her they had more in common with each other than she had with any of them. They were men and she wasn't. And she hadn't cried when her man had been shot.

She glanced up at the softly hissing speaker. If Michael were here, would it be four against one? she wondered.

FOURTEEN

The slit of light beaming through the black shifted whenever the truck made a turn. Tozzi watched it creep up Gina's arm, then settle across her body, like a sash from her hip to her shoulder, continuing into a crate of red onions by her head. She got fidgety when the light didn't move off her right away, but with the handcuffs on, she couldn't get away from it. The diagonal line crossed her hair, and Tozzi's eye was drawn to the soft brown strands shimmering on a field of black nothing. Under this kind of scrutiny, the color seemed lighter than he remembered it, almost a blondish brown. He wished the light would move up to her face so he could see her eyes and mouth. He wanted to see her expression to get some inkling of what she was thinking. He couldn't figure her out for shit.

He couldn't stop thinking about Bells's voice on her answering machine that day. *"Gina, it's me. Gimme a call."*

Supposedly she wanted nothing to do with the mob, wouldn't give any of her brother's hoodlum friends the right time of day. So why was Bells calling her? Why was he so jealous? What was he, the exception to her rule? Why?

And another thing: Why did she admit to Bells that she'd slept with Tozzi that one time? Why didn't she tell him to mind

141

his own business and go to hell? Why did she feel she had to confess to him?

From the way Bells had reacted—going nuts with those two Koreans and hijacking this truck and all—it certainly looked like these two had some serious history together. But if Bells went rip-shit because Tozzi had slept with Gina, why didn't he take it out on Tozzi directly? Was it because he knew Tozzi was a fed, and he didn't want to kill another one and make it worse for himself? Not likely. Bells didn't think like that. Kill one, kill two, kill three—what's the difference? But why didn't he even pistol-whip them to get it out of his system? Why wait?

Maybe because he had something else in mind, something worse than a beating. Why else would he be keeping them captive like this?

Shit.

The truck changed direction, and the golden sliver of light moved up Gina's cheek, slicing the corner of her purple glasses, illuminating her eye from the side. It was like looking through amber. Unfortunately he couldn't see her eyebrow, so the eye had no expression, no attitude. Was she sulking? Was she mad? Was she afraid? What did she think Bells was going to do to her? She'd say something if she were afraid, wouldn't she? Even if she hated Tozzi, she would say something, wouldn't she? She was stubborn, though, the type who'd rather stay pissed off than show her real feelings and let on that she might be human, like the rest of the world. And they say guys are bad.

It was getting colder back there with the vegetables. Cold like a basement. Gina had to be freezing.

"You want my coat?" he asked.

She didn't answer right away. "How? What about the handcuffs?" Sarcastic.

"You wear it inside out. I can get it over the cuffs."

142

"Keep it."

Her drop-dead response reminded him of Gibbons. That was just the way he talked. Or used to talk. It was hard to think of Gibbons as being dead. . . .

"I changed my mind." Her voice flew out of the dark.

"About what?"

"The coat. I'm cold." She said it just like Gibbons would've, making it sound like it was his fault that she was cold.

"Sit up and I'll pass it to you."

They both sat up and Tozzi shrugged out of the coat, then turned it inside out as he passed it over his arm. She grabbed his wrist, and he felt a little tingle at her touch. Then he realized that she was only trying to make it easier to get the coat off his arm and onto hers. As she struggled and wriggled into the inside-out overcoat, the satiny blue lining appeared in the slit of light. The shine was regal.

"I'll give it back as soon as I warm up."

"That's all right. Keep it. I've got a sport jacket on."

Silence. Not even a thank you.

After a few moments, her voice came out of the dark again. "Who was that guy back at the store?"

"The one Bells killed?" He knew she meant Gibbons, but he asked anyway.

"Yeah, him."

Tozzi didn't answer right away. "He was my partner. His name is Gibbons."

"Your partner? I thought my brother was your partner."

"My FBI partner. I'm an agent, too."

She turned over to face him, but he had no idea how she was reacting to this. All he could see was a slice of her hair shining in the light. Maybe she wasn't surprised. Maybe she'd figured as much. Maybe she was sympathetic.

143

"Gibbons was a good man. We put in a lot of years together, he and I . . . a lot of cases."

"You were undercover. You were trying to frame my brother." There was scorn and accusation in her voice. She didn't give a shit about Gibbons.

"Freshy wasn't our target. Actually your brother was helping us. We flipped him."

"What the hell does that mean?"

"It means we got him to work for us. We knew he was associated with certain organized crime figures that we were interested in—"

"Who?"

He didn't answer.

"*Who?*"

"Bells. Buddha Stanzione." Normally Tozzi wouldn't name names, but it was pretty obvious now. "Your brother agreed to introduce me to his mob associates in exchange for dropped charges and our promise of witness protection afterward."

"Witness protection? We'll never see him again. My mother will die!" She sounded genuinely upset, almost vulnerable.

"Family visits are permitted. They do it all the time. Your mother can go into witness protection with him if she wants. It can be arranged."

"That'll kill her for sure."

Silence seeped into the black like a vapor. The truck made a sharp turn, and Tozzi rolled back. Gina started to roll, too, but she put her free hand on his hip to brace herself. She took her hand off right away. The slit of light was on him now, slicing across his chest.

"Sorry," she muttered.

"No problem." He listened to her breathing. Her face was closer to his now. "Can I ask you something?"

"What?"

He wasn't sure how to put this. "Are you . . . ? Why is Bells so jealous? About you, I mean."

"He's nuts."

"I know that. But why is he so jealous? Are you two . . . ?" He let it trail off, hoping he wouldn't have to say it.

"Are we what?"

"You know, involved. Romantically."

The truck turned again, but not so sharply. They both braced themselves for this one and weren't thrown. The light shifted over to her face. He could see her mouth now. She had a very sexy mouth. He'd never really noticed it before. It was pouty, very French.

"So? Are you involved with him?"

"You ask the stupidest questions." The upper lip curled with impatience.

"It's not a stupid question. The guy goes berserk in a department store, knocks out a security guard, kidnaps two people, and kills another one, all because he wants to give you a stupid bracelet but he finds you talking to me instead? I'd say those are some pretty serious feelings. Certainly looks like something's going on between you two."

"Well, you're wrong."

Tozzi could feel the blood rush to his face. "No, I'm not wrong. You're lying."

"Where the hell do you get off calling *me* a liar? How many goddamn lies have *you* told? Or are you excused because you're an undercover cop?"

He wasn't about to debate her on that one. He'd heard plenty of righteous defense attorneys lambaste the ethics of taking a false identity for the purpose of nailing a known bad guy. Unfortunately, whenever Tozzi got on the stand, he wasn't allowed to bring up the ethics of lawyers who take dirty money from these same bad guys, their clients, for services rendered.

"And who were you supposed to be the day you came up to my apartment?" she continued. "What, was I supposed to be your *goomata*? Was that gonna be part of your cover?"

The slit of light moved to her eyebrow. It was vicious.

"You've got it all wrong. I did not consider myself undercover that afternoon."

"Yeah, right."

"I spent that time with you because I wanted to. Because . . . because I really felt something for you."

"You've got a hell of a lot of nerve saying that to me. Do you really expect me to believe that? How could you feel anything for me? You were undercover. It was the perfect male fantasy. You could sleep with me and not be responsible because you were really someone else. Men have wet dreams over stuff like that. Love 'em and leave 'em. Right?"

"That's not the way it was." Tozzi hated it when women used that line of reasoning, blaming him for something "all men do." He wasn't personally responsible for every high crime and misdemeanor committed by the entire male race, for chrissake.

"So how was it then? Tell me. You didn't even tell me your real name. How genuine could your 'feelings' for me have been if you couldn't tell me who you really are?"

"You know my real name. It's Mike."

"Is your last name Santoro?"

He stared at the line of light on her brow for a moment. "No."

"Then what is it?"

He sighed. "I can't tell you that."

"Why not?"

"I can't. It goes against policy." He cringed at the way that

146

sounded, but she was a loose cannon with that big mouth of hers. Giving her his real name would be stupid, worse than stupid.

"Wonderful," she said. "You have all these deep feelings for me, but you can't tell me who you are. What is this, *Beauty and the Beast*?"

Tozzi couldn't hold it in any longer. "And what about Bells? What about that call you got on your answering machine? The one from him. Tell me about *your* deep feelings for Bells, and I'll tell you my name."

"Oh, here we go. He sleeps with me once and now he wants to own me. What is it with men? It must be the hormones. They can't borrow, they have to own."

Tozzi kneaded his own thigh to keep his hand busy. If she were a guy, he'd strangle her. Except a guy wouldn't say stupid shit like this, and a guy wouldn't tell it to the air as if he weren't even there, a guy would say it to him directly.

The truck took another sharp turn, but neither of them had a chance to brace for this one. Gina muttered something under her breath as she rolled into Tozzi and immediately pushed herself away again. He could just imagine what she'd said. She scooted away from him, stretching out both their arms to get as far away as possible. That's when he noticed something shimmering in the slit of light, something he hadn't noticed before. She was on her back, and in the light that crossed her blouse, he saw the necklace she was wearing. Hanging from a thin gold chain was a gold ring with delicate carving on it. Tozzi wasn't sure, but when he squinted, he thought the carving looked like an ivy vine that twined around the sides of the ring. He wondered if it was a wedding band.

But why would she be wearing a wedding band around her neck? Did Bells give it to her? What were they, going steady?

147

Or since it was a wedding band, maybe it was like being engaged? But if that were the case, Bells would buy her a rock, a real engagement ring. Of course, Gina was strange. She seemed to do everything against the grain. She'd never wear a rock. He could just imagine what she'd have to say about something like that. Mousse girls wear rocks, not her. Anyway, she liked antique-looking things. Wearing an antique wedding band around her neck as an engagement ring? Sure, that would be something she'd do.

But who gave her the damn ring? Bells? She wasn't gonna tell him if he asked. Not a chance.

But Tozzi couldn't help staring at the ring. It was the only thing to look at, except for some loose apples rolling around on the floor near her shoulder. He couldn't stop thinking about her and Bells. Then as he went over the day in his mind, it all started to add up. Bells getting upset at the jewelry store because Tozzi wanted the bracelet with the purple stones for Gina. Bells flying off the handle at Macy's when he found them together. Gina not being totally hysterical when Bells kidnapped them. (Was she thinking maybe she could reason with her fiancé?) Gina refusing to tell Tozzi anything about her relationship with Bells. And then there was the call on her answering machine. *"Gina, it's me. Gimme a call."* His voice casual and familiar, like he called there all the time—so familiar he didn't have to be lovey-dovey on her answering machine. Couples that tight don't make a big show of it. They're cool about it. *"Gina, it's me. Gimme a call."*

The more he thought about it, the angrier he became. Here he was thinking that Bells had gone ballistic because he'd figured out that he was the target of an undercover operation when in fact it was his jealousy that drove him over the edge. Christ Almighty, it was just a lovers' quarrel gone haywire. Gibbons died because of a fucking lovers' quarrel. Tozzi couldn't believe it.

"Why'd he have to kill my partner?"

"What?"

"Bells. Why did he have to kill my partner?" Tozzi's jaw was tight. He was struggling not to shout.

"How should I know why he does anything?"

"Gibbons was the best fucking street agent the FBI ever had, *the best*. He was good. Even wiseguys knew he was good. That's why they hated his guts. A shitass like Bells isn't fit to shine Gibbons's shoes. Gibbons was the best. The absolute fucking best! And what'd he die for? Nothing! That's what he died for."

"Take it easy," she said.

Tozzi was yelling, and he didn't care. There were tears in his eyes. It was sinking in: Gibbons was dead!

"It's not right," Tozzi shouted. "It's not right. Gibbons was the best. He shouldn't have died that way. He . . . he shouldn't . . ." Tozzi couldn't finish his thought. He was too choked up, and he didn't want to break down in front of her. She didn't deserve it.

"Hey," she said softly, turning over on her side to face him. "Take it easy, will ya? Take some deep breaths. Calm down. You're gonna make yourself sick." She put her hand on his shoulder.

Suddenly everything was turned upside-down. His skin tingled under her touch, and her sudden concern made him doubt all his suspicions about her.

"Just breathe," she said. "Slow breaths."

He nodded. "All right, all right, I'm okay, I'm fine."

"Good. You were acting like a real wuss for a minute there. You can't be a real cop."

Her hand turned into a cockroach on his shoulder.

"Just keep breathing, in and out, nice and slow." She patted his shoulder. "Don't worry. It's gonna be all right."

He bit a knuckle on his free hand to keep from yelling. Bitch!

FIFTEEN

"Shhhhhh!" Lorraine leaned toward the speaker.

"What?" Stanley turned his ear toward the speaker, his gun hand dangling between his knees. "You heard something?"

"Is it them?" Freshy strained to hear from behind the wheel of the van.

"Be quiet," Lorraine snapped. "I'm trying to listen."

The quality of the static was changing, raising in pitch. Lorraine thought she could hear very faint voices fighting to get through. She glanced at Gibbons. He was leaning forward, elbows on his knees, looking up at the speaker, still as grouchy as an old hermit crab. Lorraine didn't even want to look at him.

Freshy was driving up Kennedy Boulevard, the main thoroughfare in Jersey City, passing huge old Victorians and wood-frame rowhouses set high up off the street. They were heading for the Heights now. They'd swept through the brownstone streets of Hoboken after getting out of the tunnel, then went straight to Bayonne where the DeFrescos lived and cruised the avenues, hoping to pick up a transmission. Bells hung out in Bayonne sometimes, and he had a brother who lived there. Stanley thought maybe he would've gone there, but so far they'd gotten nothing but static. High-pitched static, low-pitched static, screaming and fuzzy static, but just static.

151

Freshy zoomed through a yellow light. "I didn't know Bells hung out on the Heights. He got a place up here?"

Stanley just ignored the question. "Take a right."

"Where?" Freshy asked.

"Anywhere. Right here. Turn here."

Freshy did what he was told, veering into the right lane, then making a sharp turn that made everyone in the back hold on to something. "So where'm I going, Stanley?"

"You know Ogden Avenue?"

"No."

"You know Palisades Avenue?"

"Yeah."

"Odgen is one block over. It's the street where you can see New York real good. It overlooks the bluffs. Hoboken's right below."

"But, Stanley, we already tried Hoboken."

"Just shut up and go where I tell you."

Lorraine was confused. Why did Stanley want to go where there was a good view? She looked to Gibbons, but the crab's face was paralyzed in condemnation. The man of stone. To hell with him.

As the van wove through the back streets of the Heights, Lorraine could hear the quality of the static changing again. Now it was like a conversation between two different statics. She strained to make out words, but it was impossible.

A sudden wash of interference startled her. Instantly she despaired that Michael was lost again, maybe forever. But then as Freshy turned the van onto a larger cross street, the conversing static returned. But it was clearer now.

"I hear something," Freshy yelped. "I hear something."

"Shut up!" Stanley barked. "Go over to Ogden."

Out of the sea of static, two faint voices floated to the surface.

"You didn't know him. To really understand, you had to know Gibbons. I'm gonna really miss him."

"Take some deep breaths. You're gonna hyperventilate. I'm telling you."

"Forget about the deep breaths, will ya? I need my partner back. Don't you understand? He's the only guy I could ever work with. I don't know what I'm gonna do now."

"Will you please listen to me? Take some deep breaths. You're getting hysterical."

Stanley looked shocked. "What is he, crying?"

Lorraine kept her eyes on the speaker. She had a lump in her throat. Michael could cry for Gibbons. Why couldn't she?

"You think you're so tough. You don't know what it's like to lose someone that close to you."

"For your information, I do know what it's like to lose somebody close to me. You act like you're the only one in the world who's ever had this happen. You're so typical. Men think when something happens to them, it's like the first time it's ever happened."

"Do you really believe that crap? Do you know you do this all the time, with these stupid generalizations of yours? 'Men always do this and men always do that.' You sound like Jacques Cousteau talking about friggin' fish."

"But am I wrong?"

"There's no use talking to you. I might as well talk to the potatoes. You don't want to understand anything."

Silence.

"I do want to understand."

Static drowned out the woman's voice.

Freshy pulled over to the curb and slammed the transmission into park. "That phoney-baloney son of a bitch! Did you hear that crap? He's putting the moves on my sister, goddammit.

153

That smooth goddamn son of a bitch. He's trying to make her feel sorry for him."

Stanley waved him away. "Shut up, Freshy. You don't know what you're talking about."

"The hell I don't. He's trying to get into my sister's pants, that's what he's doing. He's giving her a big sob story about this guy being dead." He pointed back at Gibbons. "What a son of a bitch, I swear to Christ. You suck, Mike. You suck!" he yelled at the speaker. "Don't listen to him, Gina."

Stanley shook his fist at him. "Shut the fuck up before I smack the shit out of you. I'm trying to listen."

Lorraine wrinkled her face, straining to hear her cousin and this woman Gina. She tried to imagine where they were. It had to be someplace private. Michael wouldn't be so open with her otherwise. But if they were in private, where was Bells? She glanced over at Gibbons's stony face and wondered what he was thinking. Michael could confess his feelings for Gibbons to Gina DeFresco. So why couldn't Lorraine express hers?

She strained to see out the passenger window in the cab. From where she was sitting, she got a glimpse of the uptown end of the Manhattan skyline. The sun was shimmering off the slanted top of the Citicorp Center. The apartment buildings on the West Side were beginning to cast long afternoon shadows. On the Jersey side of the river, the streets of well-kept brownstones gradually gave way to warehouses, factories, and stark brick projects below the palisades on the poor side of Hoboken. Where in God's name could Michael and Gina be? Were they safe?

Lorraine sighed and dropped her head to her chest. Gibbons's black wingtips shone in the dark, and she stared at them, stewing in her own guilt. She could fret so easily for Michael. Why not for Gibbons?

The speaker crackled, and the conversing statics returned. Lorraine leaned into it, waiting for the voices to emerge, but the only thing she could make out was her cousin's voice saying ". . . *a good man* . . ." Then a snowstorm of interference buried him again.

"Drive," Stanley ordered. "They must be near here."

Freshy put the van into gear and pulled away from the curb. No one said a word as they listened for another clear transmission. Lorraine looked at her husband, wondering what they'd do if they found Michael, Gina, and Bells. But then she glanced at the gun resting on Stanley's thigh, and it dawned on her that there was very little they could do because they weren't the hunters here.

Gibbons was pissed and he was in pain. His head felt like it was wrapped in cotton. His chest was throbbing, and now it was really beginning to hurt. The pain-killer was wearing off, but he still felt dopey from the side effects. He tried to sit as still as possible so he wouldn't keel over, but Freshy's cuckoo driving didn't make it easy. Lorraine making cow eyes at him didn't help much either. What the hell was her problem? Things were fucked up enough without him having to worry about her feelings.

A rain cloud of dizziness passed over him. He closed his eyes and put his hand against the wall of the van until it passed. When he opened his eyes again, Lorraine was giving him the cow eyes again. Jesus. This had to be the most fucked-up day of his entire life.

First it was his goddamn tooth and the fact that it kept him up all night. Then there was Gary Petersen's shooting, and having to put up with Ivers and those snotty film guys at the crime scene. Then Tony Bells shoots him in the chest and leaves him for dead in Macy's. Then friggin' Stanley here hijacks the surveillance van and makes him and Lorraine come along for the ride while this goddamn little piece of shit Freshy has his gun Excalibur. And on top of everything else there's Tozzi, who usually manages to fuck things up even when he isn't doing anything. But today he's really outdone himself, getting kidnapped by Tony Bells, handcuffed to Freshy's sister, and now he's trying to make time with her. What a piece of work! Freshy was right on the money about that. Tozzi was working on her sympathies, trying to wear her down. Would serve him right if she yanked his crank right off, the stupid bastard.

Gibbons didn't appreciate the bullshit eulogy either. If Tozzi was really sincere about missing him and all that weepy crap, then he was a sap. But if he was just saying it to get into Gina's pants, then he was a friggin' dirtbag. Either way, Gibbons didn't like being talked about that way. When you die, you die. One day you're breathing, the next day you're fertilizer. Just put the stiff in the ground and move on. But from the way Lorraine had been looking at him all day, he knew she wasn't gonna see it that way when he kicked the bucket. She was gonna blubber and cry and carry on, just like all her other goddamn Italian relatives. You can always count on guineas to turn a funeral into a circus. They love it when people die. Gives 'em an excuse to act up.

Then something suddenly occurred to Gibbons. Why do people always assume that the husband will go before the wife? He wasn't *that* much older than Lorraine.

"*Whatta'ya doing?*" Tozzi's voice suddenly crackled through the speaker. "*Leave it on.*"

"*No. I don't want it,*" Gina said.

"*Don't be stupid. Leave it on.*"

"*I don't like it. It makes me itch.*"

"*Leave it on. You have to wear it. You'll get sick.*"

"I'm not gonna—"

Freshy slammed on the brakes and whipped around in his seat. "I can't believe this. My own sister! My mother would die if she ever heard this. What the fuck're you doin', Gina?" He shook his hands at the sky.

Stanley scowled. "What're you talking about?"

"What'm I talking about? Can't you fucking hear? He's wearing a rubber, and she's taking it off 'cause she says it itches. She's so stupid, that sister of mine. No fucking brains. None."

Stanley wasn't paying any attention to Freshy. He was staring out the window and pulling on his lower lip. Gibbons wondered what the hell he was doing, taking in the view? Stanley turned around then, his mouth a long flat line across that big jaw of his. "Freshy," he said. "Go to the Belfry."

Freshy whipped around in his seat again. He looked like someone had just told him his mother had died. "The Belfry! Why there? Bells wouldn't go there unless—"

"Shut up." Stanley cut him short.

"But, Stanley—"

"Drive. We'll just cruise by and see if they're there."

Freshy turned back around and gave it some gas. "Bells wouldn't take them there," he fretted under his breath. "Not there." He sounded like he was trying to convince himself.

Gibbons's voice croaked from nonuse. "What's the Belfry?"

Lorraine and Stanley looked at him as if he'd just risen from the dead. Freshy was going bug-eyed in the rearview mirror.

"Freshy, what's the Belfry?"

Stanley answered. "It's nothin'."

"Gibbons, are you all right?" Lorraine asked.

"I'm fine. Freshy, what's the Belfry?"

Freshy's googly eyes were rolling all over the mirror. "Ah . . . it's, ah . . . nothing really."

Gibbons wished the little shit would watch the goddamn road. Freshy made a sharp turn onto an old cobblestone road with a steep decline, and the tires thumped like crazy on the cobblestones. They were heading down into Hoboken. When the street leveled out and the pavement went back to blacktop, Freshy hung a left onto one of the narrow one-way streets that make up Hoboken's grid. They sailed past run-down tenements and burnt-out brick buildings, seedy-looking corner bodegas, dangerous-looking bars, and car repair shops housed in cramped little garages where half the work was done out on the curb. This was the other side of Hoboken, not the gentrified part near the river, where all the brownstones had been renovated and the kids from the suburbs had fistfights with the locals on Saturday nights for parking spaces near the rock clubs and upscale gin mills. This was the tough part of town, the real part of town, the part where the guy who steals your Lexus goes to find a chop shop so he can score some crack.

Tozzi lived in Hoboken, right on the borderline between the two sections. That figured. The guy never could make up his mind about where he belonged. Gibbons knew where he belonged, though. A padded cell, that's where.

As Freshy headed north, he passed a housing project where young mothers watched their preschoolers in a fenced-off playground while young bums hung out in the asphalt courtyard looking for trouble. Gibbons noticed that the hissing had stopped coming out of the speaker. He knew it hadn't gone dead, though. The static would've been deafening if it had. Nobody was saying anything. Tozzi and Gina were being quiet, as hard as that was to believe.

"*C'mon, don't take it off. Leave it on,*" Tozzi said. The transmission was very clear now.

"*I don't want it. I told you, it itches,*" Gina said. "*You wear it.*"

158

"What the—?" Freshy caught Gibbons's eye in the rearview mirror.

"Wear it, I'm telling you. You've got a hard head just like your brother."

"Screw you, Tozzi!"

"Shhh." Lorraine scowled at Freshy.

"Don't talk about my brother. You used him. You took advantage of my brother."

"That's right. You tell him, Gina."

"Shut up!" Stanley yelled.

"No, no, no, no, no. You've got it all wrong. Freshy's the one who takes advantage. Freshy watches out for Freshy first. That's why he decided to work with us in the first place."

"I don't believe that."

"We gave him a choice. Either he could help us catch his friends, or he could face charges and probably end up serving some serious time. Freshy decided to save his own ass."

Stanley was glaring at Freshy. He looked like he was going to eat him.

Freshy kept glancing in the rearview mirror as he drove. "That's not exactly true, Stanley. You don't understand. They forced me. Tell him, Gib. I didn't have a choice."

Gibbons smiled like a crocodile. Frig him. Freshy could take care of his own problems.

"C'mon, Gib. Tell him."

"Will you please shut up," Lorraine yelled. "I can't hear what they're saying."

Stanley roared. "The both of youse shut up."

Gibbons just smiled.

"I don't want your goddamn coat. Take it back."

"No. Don't be stupid. Wear it."

"Did she say 'coat'?" Lorraine looked puzzled.

159

"What're they talking about?" Freshy took his foot off the accelerator, and the van slowed down.

Stanley's big jaw was tight. "I told you to go to the Belfry, didn't I?"

"Yeah, but, Stanley, lemme explain something to you—"

Stanley aimed the gun at Freshy's head. "Go. Hurry up."

"I'm going, I'm going, I'm going."

Freshy stepped on it, and they started whizzing down the blocks. The rundown tenements gave way to factories and block-long warehouses. The streets were fairly deserted up here, and half the cars on the street were abandoned wrecks. Gibbons had to brace himself for the ride as Freshy gunned the engine and jolted through the intersections, speeding toward this place they called the Belfry. Gibbons lowered his head so he could see out the windshield, wanting to know exactly what street they were on. But as they came up to the next intersection, a long black Lincoln Continental suddenly backed out of the side street, spinning its tires.

Freshy hit the brakes. Then the sound of someone else's screeching tires came from behind. "What the—?" He was looking into the side mirror.

Gibbons got off his seat and squinted into a peephole in the rear of the van. A smoke-gray Lincoln was blocking the way from behind, parked diagonally in the middle of the street. Three doors swung open almost simultaneously, and two double-knit bruisers jumped out, followed by a small man wearing a yellow cardigan sweater under a camel hair overcoat. The little guy was Buddha Stanzione. Gibbons expected steam to be coming out of his ears, but instead he just looked bored.

"You got company," Gibbons said.

Stanley's eyes were bulging. "Who?"

"You'll see."

More wiseguys poured out of the black Lincoln up ahead, and they all converged on the cab of the van.

Buddha's face appeared in the driver's window. He was so short, the doorframe cut him off at the neck and made him look like a severed head.

His eyes roamed around the inside of the van. "Where the fuck is Bells?"

The speaker crackled. *"Will you leave the friggin' coat on, for chrissake?"*

The head's eyebrows furrowed. "What's that?"

SIXTEEN

Gibbons crossed his arms and leaned his head back against the wall of the van. His tooth was beginning to throb again, but that didn't matter. He was enjoying this.

Buddha Stanzione had one eyebrow cocked as he peered into the van. "I said, where the fuck is Bells?" He looked like a bored little monkey who couldn't care less, but that was what made him so scary. His four double-knit gorillas were staring in through the windshield, waiting for the nod from the bored little monkey to attack, and Buddha was the type who'd set them loose just for the hell of it.

Freshy was shitting his pants behind the wheel. "H-how, did you know it was us, Mr. Stanzione?"

Buddha glared at him for a moment, then nodded at the closest gorilla. "Big Dom spotted you barrel-assing down the street."

Big Dom put his big face up to the windshield, and Freshy leaned back.

Gibbons glanced at Stanley, who was wearing that blank, washed-out expression that people put on when they're trying to figure out how big a lie they can get away with. He was always amazed to see tough guys like Stanley bowing and scraping in front of scumbags like Stanzione. Of course, this was a very

162

awkward situation for Stanley. According to Mafia protocol, he would never be talking directly to a capo. Associates only deal with the soldiers they answer to, and in Stanley's case, that was Bells. But Buddha wanted Bells's head on a platter, and now Stanley's loyalties were divided. After the boss of the family, Stanley's ultimate allegiance should be to the capo of the crew he worked for, Buddha, but Stanley must've been thinking about what that psycho Bells would do to him if he ever found out that he'd been betrayed by one of his own people. Gibbons couldn't wait to hear how Stanley was gonna try to worm his way out of this one.

Buddha cocked the other eyebrow and looked at Lorraine. "Whatta'ya doing over there?"

"Me?" Lorraine pulled her hand back and put it in her lap. She'd been reaching over to turn down the volume on the speaker. "I'm not doing anything."

The monkey glared at her. Gibbons flared his nostrils and tucked his feet under, ready to spring. Go 'head, try something. Gorillas or no gorillas, if any of them so much as looked at Lorraine cross-eyed, he'd rip the guy's spine out and beat him to death with it.

Buddha seemed baffled by her presence. "Who are you? What're you doing here?"

But before Lorraine could answer, Stanley cut in. "She's with him." He pointed to Gibbons.

"And who the hell is he?"

"He's, ah—"

"Special Agent Gibbons, FBI." Gibbons dared Stanley to deal with that revelation.

Buddha just stared at Stanley. He was waiting for an explanation. The apes on the other side of the glass were waiting, too.

Stanley wet his lips. "He's helping us find Bells, Mr. Stanzione."

Then Freshy chimed in. "Yeah, he's helping us, Mr. Stanzione." Stupidity times two.

Buddha looked at him as if he were a bug. The balding gorilla who was standing right behind the capo shook his head at Freshy. "You do not talk to Mr. Stanzione. You understand? You do not exist."

Freshy nodded. "You're right, you're right. I do not exist."

The speaker crackled to life again.

"Don't touch me!"

"Will you leave the goddamn coat on, Gina? You're gonna catch pneumonia."

"Leave me alone."

Lorraine was as pale as a clam.

Buddha glared at Freshy. "Gina? Is that your sister Gina?"

Freshy shrugged and wouldn't look at the capo. He did not exist.

Buddha nodded at the speaker. "Is that Bells with this guy's sister?"

Stanley answered. "No, Mr. Stanzione. That's some other guy. But yes, yes, that is Freshy's sister."

"So is that the other FBI guy with her?"

Stanley looked like the deer caught in the headlights. "Excuse me, Mr. Stanzione?"

"Cut the shit. It's all over the news. Bells shot some undercover guy last night, then he shot another one in Macy's this morning and took Gina DeFresco and a third FBI guy hostage. He's really working overtime, this guy."

One of the gorillas started to chuckle, but the bored little monkey's stare silenced him.

"So what's the story?"

Stanley cleared his throat. "Well, you see, Mr. Stanzione, it's like this. That other FBI guy? The one Bells kidnapped with Gina? He's wearing this thing, this, ah—" He looked to Gibbons. "What's it called?"

"A transmitter."

"Yeah, a transmitter. It's like a wire, but it doesn't have a tape recorder. It's more like a radio, you know? We're listening to them from in here, trying to figure out where they are."

"Did you check the Belfry?"

Stanley glanced at Gibbons. "We just checked there, but they ain't there." He glanced at Gibbons again.

Gibbons knew Stanley was shitting bricks, praying that nobody would contradict him and tell Buddha the truth. The gorillas were getting itchy to break some heads.

Buddha cocked his eyebrow again. "So where were you going now?"

"There's this bar up on the Heights that Bells goes to sometimes, Mr. Stanzione. We were gonna go check over there." Stanley glanced at Gibbons again, begging him to keep his mouth shut.

"Did you look down in Bayonne? This Gina girl's got him crazy. Maybe they went down to her place."

Freshy shifted in his seat, bristling at the suggestion that his sister and Bells were an item, but he didn't say a word. He did not exist.

"Yeah, Bayonne," Stanley said. "We haven't looked down there yet. That's a good idea, though." Stanley was being a stand-up guy, lying through his teeth to a capo to protect his man. Either that, or he was more scared of Bells than Buddha.

"Whatta'ya looking for him for, Mr. Stanzione?"

Buddha just stared at Stanley and let the stupidity of his question sink in. "Are you supposed to be funny or what?"

165

"No, Mr. Stanzione. I only— I just thought if we found him and you wanted me to tell him something . . . you know. I could give him a message."

Buddha nodded slowly. "Okay. You tell him to make out his will. Fast. That's the message. Okay?" He kept nodding.

Stanley's eyes were bugging out of his head again. "Seriously, Mr. Stanzione?"

"You think I'm kidding? After all the shit he pulled today, tell me he doesn't deserve a"—Buddha looked at Gibbons—"a serious accident. Tell me."

"Well, gee, I dunno, Mr. Stanzione."

"You dunno, huh? Well, if you don't know, I'm gonna tell you." The little monkey stuck out his thumb. "For one thing, the stupid fuck shot that FBI guy up on the Turnpike last night. You never kill a cop. Never. It makes things very messy.

"Reason number two." He stuck out his index finger. "He got on TV. We don't need that kind of publicity. We get enough without even trying.

"Number three." The middle finger sprang up. "He kidnapped another FBI guy. That made things twice as messy as they already were.

"And reason number four." The ring finger joined the others. "He thinks he can screw me. But he can't. You know why? 'Cause I'm not gonna let him."

Stanley furrowed his brows. He was the confused baboon in this ape house. "I don't understand, Mr. Stanzione."

"Your friend Bells gave me thirty-two G's this morning to pay off what this guy owed me." Buddha nodded at Freshy, who kept his eyes straight ahead because he didn't exist. "That money was counterfeit. All of it. Pretty funny, huh?"

Gibbons was rubbing his jaw. The tooth was twitching, but he started to laugh anyway, quietly, to himself at first, but then he couldn't control himself. His eyes were tearing, and his fingers were clamped on his temples, his shoulders bouncing up and down.

Buddha was not amused. "What the fuck is so funny over there?"

Gibbons wiped the corner of his eye with his finger. "That was *our* money, the Bureau's. It was seized in another operation down in Virginia."

"What?"

"The agent Bells shot last night? He was carrying counterfeit bills. Bells ripped him off, but what he got was funny money. Serves the bastard right." Gibbons started laughing again. He knew he shouldn't be laughing because for all he knew Gary Petersen could be near death, but this part was funny. Justice comes in strange ways sometimes, and this was precious. Who would've guessed that Bells would sign his own death warrant by paying off his capo with phony bills? Once in a while, life *is* fair.

Buddha ignored Gibbons and turned his gaze to Freshy, who was keeping his eyes straight ahead, not existing. "This wasn't your idea, was it?"

Freshy shook his head, but he wouldn't look at Buddha.

"You sure?"

"I swear to God, I didn't know nothing about that money. I swear."

"He was paying off *your* loan."

"I didn't know nothing about it. I swear."

"But it was *your loan.*"

Freshy winced as if he expected to get smacked. "I'm telling you the truth. I am. I swear. Really."

"Then why do you think Bells would give me bullshit money?"

"I dunno, Mr. Stanzione. I don't."

"Take a guess."

"I don't—"

"Take a guess."

Freshy squirmed in his seat. He wished he didn't exist. "I dunno. Really. I dunno, maybe . . . maybe he did it for my sister."

"Oh, yeah? Why would he screw *me* for your sister? I don't get it."

"He likes my sister, everybody knows that. But she's—well, you know how broads are. They just try to make you crazy. First it's yes, then it's no. You never know where you stand with Gina. And that's how she is with Bells. I think."

The monkey frowned. "What the fuck has she got to do with my money?"

"Well, see, Bells probably figured he could get on Gina's good side by helping me out. We're really close, her and me. Brother and sister, you know? She, like, worries about me. She knew I was into you for a big piece, and she wasn't happy about that, so maybe Bells figured he'd be a good guy and pay it off for me. Not for nothing, I mean. I guess I'd have to pay him back. If the money was real, that is. But, you know, maybe Bells figured Gina would be so grateful, she'd straighten out and stop dicking him around, tell him what he wanted to hear. I dunno. They're both nuts. Anything's possible." Freshy was still too frightened to look at Buddha.

Buddha didn't say a thing. He just stared at Freshy, making him uncomfortable. "Are you lying to me?"

The speaker interrupted. *"I told you, don't touch me. I don't want your goddamn coat."*

"Fine. Then freeze. No use trying to be nice to you. You just end up getting your head bit off."

"Stop talking. You're giving me a headache."

"Shhh. I think we're stopping."

"Like I care."

"Shut up!"

"Don't tell me to shut up."

Tozzi didn't answer her.

A faint whining, clanking sound came out of the speaker. It sounded like a truck transmission going in reverse. Buddha stared at the speaker. One eyebrow went up as the other one went down. The monkey was taking this all in.

Buddha eyed all the equipment, then looked at Gibbons. "So where are they?"

Gibbons shrugged. Buddha could drop dead.

Stanley jumped in, afraid to leave the capo's question unanswered. "It's not like radar, Mr. Stanzione. We can't, like, pinpoint them. But they must be around here somewhere. And Bells must be with them, or else they wouldn't still be together. Seeing how much these two like each other." Stanley looked around for someone to back him up, but as far as Gibbons was concerned, he could go to hell. And Lorraine, like Freshy, was too scared to even move.

The monkey wiggled his eyebrows and thought this over, then he gestured with his head toward Gibbons and Lorraine. "Get rid of them."

Stanley looked confused. "You mean whack 'em?"

"No. Just get rid of them. Lose 'em."

Stanley waved his gun at Gibbons. "Get out. Both of youse."

Gibbons was reluctant to get out. Buddha's primates weren't that far up on the evolutionary chain. They might interpret Buddha's order as including a beating. Gibbons wasn't worried about himself. It was Lorraine. The friggin' boneheads better not touch her.

As he started to get off his seat, the side door of the van slid

169

open. Two of the gorillas were waiting to escort them out. He stepped out and turned his back on them to help Lorraine out, ready to throw an elbow into anyone who came too close. Lorraine looked scared, but Gibbons was going to protect her. A jackhammer was working on his tooth now, so a little more pain wouldn't make much difference. Besides, he was feeling ornery enough to take on all five of them at once, *plus* the monkey.

"Shut the door," Buddha ordered as he walked around the front of the van. He walked up to Gibbons and was about eye level with Gibbons's chin. He stayed away from Lorraine. She was a little taller than Gibbons, almost a full head taller than Buddha.

"Tell your people over at the FBI that they don't have to worry about Bells. We'll take care of him."

"Not if we get him first."

"You won't." Buddha walked past Gibbons and got back into the smoke-gray Lincoln blocking the road behind the van. Two of his gorillas followed him. Two got into the black Lincoln, and the last ape took Freshy's place behind the wheel of the van. Three engines started up, one right after the other, and the wiseguy caravan took off, the surveillance van sandwiched in between the two luxury cars. They turned left at the next corner and disappeared.

"Fuck you, too," Gibbons grumbled at their exhaust.

Lorraine clutched his bicep. "They're going to kill Michael, aren't they?" She seemed more resigned than alarmed.

"They won't kill him now that they know he's an agent. But Bells . . . I dunno."

She let out a shuddering sigh that was so sad, Gibbons forgot about his aching tooth.

"You okay?" he asked.

She shook her head no, slow and sad. The loose hair around her face swayed like a hula dancer's skirt.

"Are you hurt?" he asked. "I didn't even think to ask. That pill made me so dopey."

She tilted her head and gave him a weird look. It surprised him. It was the look she wore whenever he was in trouble. But what the hell did he do now? He'd had a feeling she had a bug up her ass about something ever since Macy's, but he figured she was just scared and worried sick about her cousin. But now she had this real end-of-the-world look, like she was standing on the edge of a cliff looking out at a stinky black void, and it was all *his* fault. He decided not to make an issue out of it. Maybe her problem would just clear up on its own.

"You got any more of those pills, Lorraine? My tooth is kicking up again."

She shook her head. "I lost my purse back at Macy's. I'm sorry."

"That's okay. It's not your fault."

She wasn't listening, though. She was frowning at the void again. He thought about saying something but decided against it. Why ask for trouble?

"C'mon. Let's go find a phone," he said. "I gotta call in and let them know what's going on."

"What about Michael?"

Gibbons shrugged. "If we had the van, maybe we could've found them."

"Bells is going to kill him. He took them to that place, the Belfry."

The look on her face was so sad, Gibbons didn't know what to do: lie to her to make her feel better or tell her the truth. The way he saw it, Bells was too damn unpredictable to say what he'd

171

do with Tozzi. But Gibbons didn't want to lie to her and tell her everything would be okay, because he wasn't so sure himself. He remembered how shook up Freshy had been when Stanley told him to go to the Belfry. He could just imagine what kind of place that was.

Gibbons pointed up the block. "Let's find a phone. Who knows? Maybe our guys have already located them."

"You don't really think so, do you?" She was either very depressed or very sarcastic, he couldn't tell for sure. He must've done something wrong. She was definitely in a mood.

He shaded his eyes and peered down the deserted street. Cinder-block factory walls lined the sidewalks on both sides. They were covered with spray-painted graffiti, and not particularly good graffiti at that. Down at the end of the street, two blocks away, a small cluster of very old red brick buildings sat by themselves like an island in the middle of muddy overgrown lots surrounded by Cyclone fencing. A sign hung out over the sidewalk on the closest building, but Gibbons couldn't make out what it said. What he did see was the glow of an orange neon sign in the front window, probably a Bud sign. There was a green and white neon sign in the same window. Probably Rolling Rock.

"There's a bar up there," he said. "C'mon. I can call in from there. I could use a good stiff drink anyway."

"Me too," Lorraine said.

Gibbons looked at her sideways. There was *definitely* something wrong. Lorraine wanting a drink in a sleazy bar before sundown? That wasn't her at all.

"Let's go," she said, and started walking toward the bar. She cast a long, lonely shadow that reached from the middle of the street all the way over to the graffiti-covered walls. Olive Oyl walking into the sunset. Olive Oyl in mourning. Olive Oyl royally pissed off.

Gibbons pressed his fingers into his sore jaw. He couldn't figure her out for shit.

SEVENTEEN

5:15 P.M.

"Wake up, my little kumquats."

The doors swung open, and the back of the truck was flooded with light. Tozzi had to squint against the sudden brightness. He felt a tug on his handcuffed wrist as Gina tried to shield her eyes with her forearm.

Bells was standing outside on a loading dock, gun in hand, beaming at them. "C'mon. Get up. We're home."

"Whose home?" Tozzi hauled himself to his feet with a groan. His joints were stiff from the cold damp interior of the truck.

He tried to help Gina up, but she shrugged him off. Tozzi's coat was hanging inside out from their handcuffed wrists, like a muff. They'd both refused to wear it.

"What'sa matter? You two kids can't get along?" Bells laughed as he motioned with his gun for them to get out of the truck.

As Tozzi stepped into the sunlight, he gathered up the ends of his coat so Gina wouldn't trip. Then he wondered why the hell he was worrying about her. She was so goddamn nasty—let her trip.

Bells started doing that little voodoo dance of his, moving on the balls of his feet. "C'mon, Gina. Let's move it. I thought you were dying to see my place here."

"Go scratch, will ya, Bells?" If looks could kill . . .

There wasn't much to see from the cracked cement loading dock, just a big dirt lot with abandoned cars and dumped stoves and refrigerators poking out of the overgrown weeds. Tozzi squinted at the horizon, looking for big buildings. Maybe he could figure out where they were if he could identify something, but between the overhanging tin roof on the loading dock and the truck in the way, he couldn't see very much.

A freight elevator was already open, waiting for them. With its wooden gate up, it looked like a big mouth ready to swallow them.

Gina was rubbing her arms, inching out into the sun, but the muzzle of Bells's gun corralled her back into the shade. "This way, Gina."

"Don't talk to me, okay?"

"Why so mean, Gina? What'd you do to her, Mikey? You didn't try to take advantage of her back there, did you? Shame on you." Bells was getting a big kick out of himself, but there was an edge to his good humor that made Tozzi nervous. "Shall we?" Bells cocked his head and escorted them into the elevator.

When they were inside, Bells dropped the gate and yanked on the rope that started it. It must've been a very old building, Tozzi thought. You didn't see many of these rope-start elevators anymore. Bars of light and shadow passed over their faces as the rickety elevator moaned and groaned its way up. No one spoke, but Bells whistled softly to himself. It took Tozzi a second to recognize the tune. "Would You Like to Swing on a Star?" The elevator was so slow, Bells had time to go through two verses and then some.

It stopped with a jolt, and Bells threw the gate up with one hand. Jiggling the gun barrel, he indicated that they should get out. "Go on in. Go on. Don't be shy." He grinned at Tozzi. " 'Or would you rather be a pig?' "

Tozzi scanned the large loft space. It was nothing special. The walls were crumbling, open-faced brick, and the hardwood floors were grimy and scarred. A room had been made out of a corner of the space, but the wallboard walls had never been painted. A dingy kitchen had been set up in the opposite corner from the room: cheap metal cabinets, Formica counter in an imitation wood-grain pattern, a square table with five mismatched chairs. The stove was old, but the big refrigerator looked fairly new. Two imitation-leather sofas—one black, the other green—and two burgundy imitation-leather lounge chairs were grouped near the kitchen. Newspapers, magazines, and full ashtrays were scattered all around. The place had the feel of a men's clubhouse where guys hung out, drank beer, ate pizza, played cards, made coffee, and shot the shit.

Rows of single-paned, arch-topped windows lit the space with natural light. There was a good view of the Hudson and the Manhattan skyline through the east wall windows. Using the Empire State Building as his gauge, Tozzi figured they were either in Hoboken or Weehawken, not too far from the Lincoln Tunnel. Tozzi shook his head in disbelief. He lived in Hoboken, probably less than a half-mile from here. If all of this hadn't happened, he'd be over at his apartment right now, resting up for the black-belt test he wasn't going to be taking tonight. Shit.

Bells went to the kitchen area and started looking through the drawers. "Sit down. Make yourselves comfortable." He pointed to the sofas with his gun.

Tozzi started to move toward the black sofa, but Gina stayed put. She gave Tozzi a dirty look, but he ignored her and kept walking, pulling her along with him. He was sick of her shit.

He sat on the end of the sofa, and she sat as far away from him as she could with Tozzi's bunched-up coat between them as a barrier. They both kept their wrists bent against the cuffs, determined not to even touch each other.

Gina glowered at Bells, who was crouched down looking through the bottom drawers under the counter. "What're you gonna do with us now, Bells?"

Bells kept rummaging through the drawer. "Kill you. What'd you think?"

"You're not funny."

"I'm not trying to be." He continued his search for whatever he was looking for.

Tozzi cleared his throat. "Hey, Bells, what's the story here? I mean, let's stop fucking around."

Bells stopped his search and stared at him. "I'm not fucking around, Mikey-boy. *You're* the one who was fucking around. Both of you, together. And that's why I'm gonna do what I gotta do."

"You mean kill us."

"That's right."

Gina looked at Tozzi, her face drawn. "Is he really serious?"

"You know everything. You tell me."

Bells laughed to himself as he stood up and dropped a length of heavy steel chain onto the countertop. "You two are getting to be like a comedy routine." He lifted the chain with the hand that wasn't holding the gun and dangled it from one end. It was short. Maybe two, two and a half feet long. "Too bad you gotta go. You're very funny."

Gina went to cross her arms, but the cuffs stopped her. "Oh, go to hell."

"You want some coffee or something? I think I've got some soda here." He opened the refrigerator and checked. "Pepsi, ginger ale, beer, and fizzy water. Have something. This is gonna take me a while. What can I get you, Mikey? A beer?"

"Nothing." Tozzi was looking at the green phone with the long cord that was sitting on the counter. *"Gina, it's me. Gimme a call."* He was wondering if Bells had called her from here.

"Whatta'ya want, Gina? A ginger ale?"

"No. I'll just have to pee."

Bells jingled the chain and grinned. "Not if I'm fast." If the devil had a face, this was it.

Tozzi leaned forward and let out a sigh. It was time to show his cards. "Look, Bells, you're making a big mistake here. There's an army of federal agents out looking for you. Don't make it any worse for yourself."

Bells dropped the heavy chain on the counter, and the sudden noise made Gina jump. His eyes glowed as he stared at Tozzi. "Why would they be looking for me, Mikey?"

"Because you killed two agents from the Federal Bureau of Investigation today. What the hell do you think?" Tozzi could feel the blood rushing to his face.

Bells shook his head. "My, my, my. For a rat, you think you know a lot. But you don't know nothing. For one thing, I only shot one guy, the old guy with the swollen face in Macy's. That other guy on TV, the one up on the Turnpike—what's his name, Paterson? I don't know nothing about him. That's a frame."

Bells was too calm, too rational. He was fearless, and Tozzi didn't like that. Unless Bells wanted something or feared something, there'd be no negotiating with him.

"You telling me you didn't shoot Petersen, the one on the Turnpike?"

Bells shook his head. "Wasn't me."

"But they think you did it, and they're looking for you."

Bells shrugged as he rummaged through another drawer.

178

"It's not just the cops looking for you. Your own people are looking for you, too. You know that, don't you?"

"Why's that, Mikey? 'Cause they think I shot a fed? You been watching too many movies, my friend."

Fury ballooned inside Tozzi's head. "You *did* shoot a fed. And you shot my fucking partner, jerkoff. The cops, the FBI, everybody's gonna bust balls until they have your ass nailed to the wall. And don't act like you don't know that because you do."

Bells just looked at him, calm as could be. There was almost pity in his face for Tozzi.

Tozzi's head was throbbing, he was so pissed. He was losing his cool, lashing out, while Bells was the one keeping his center, letting it all come to him. Tozzi had been practicing aikido for almost six years now, and what had he learned? Nothing. Aikido principles are supposed to apply to all situations, not just when someone's throwing punches at you. He shouldn't be losing it like this. But apparently Tozzi just hadn't gotten it yet. But Bells, he was like some kind of Zen master; he had it all together. He was making Tozzi the aggressor even though Bells was the one who had kidnapped him. Jesus!

Tozzi threw himself back against the couch in frustration and yanked on the handcuffs.

"Hey! Watch it," Gina complained.

"Shut up!"

"You shut up!"

Tozzi bit his bottom lip and looked up at the cracked plaster ceiling. He couldn't believe he was letting everything get to him like this. He'd been in bad situations before. It wasn't like this was a first for him. Then he thought about Gibbons and sighed. It was his first bad situation without Gibbons. Maybe that was the problem. Gibbons never got flustered, and he never let himself get stuck. Gotta keep moving, he'd always say. Life was like

179

driving a car in deep snow. If you can't go forward, go backward. Do anything you have to to get something moving because the most important thing is to keep things moving. That was Gibbons's philosophy.

Tozzi dropped his chin and watched Bells going through that drawer. He took long, measured breaths, in through the nose, out through the mouth—aikido breathing exercise—until he felt a little calmer. Gotta keep things moving, he kept repeating to himself, trying to get centered. You can't just sit there. Gotta keep things moving. Even going backward is movement.

"Bells, look." Tozzi opened his sport jacket and pointed to the beeper clipped to his belt. He'd totally forgotten about it until just now. Stupid. That's what happens when you're not centered.

As Tozzi went to unclip the beeper, Bells thrust out his gun hand. "Whatta'ya doing?"

"Relax, Bells. I just wanna show you something. No tricks. Shoot me if I try something funny."

"Don't get wise, Mikey."

Tozzi unclipped the beeper and held it out to Bells. "See this?"

"Yeah?"

Tozzi wrapped his fist around the transmitter so they wouldn't be overheard. "It's not really a beeper."

Bells narrowed his eyes.

"It's a transmitter, Bells. It broadcasts everything we say to a surveillance van."

Gina smirked. "What is this, *Star Trek*?"

Tozzi ignored her.

Bells's suspicious expression didn't change. Neither did his gun hand extended at Tozzi's head.

"Here's the deal, Bells. You wanna escape, I'll help you. You take off, go wherever you wanna go, and we'll keep talking as if you're still here. Better yet, if you don't trust me, just put the thing somewhere where it'll pick up some conversation. Someplace like a diner or a store. It'll throw them off the track."

Bells looked skeptical. "Lemme see that thing."

Reluctantly Tozzi uncurled his fingers and tossed the transmitter to Bells, who caught it in his left hand. He examined it at arm's length. Tozzi feared that Bells would smash the transmitter to bits with the butt of his gun, and then they'd really be up shit's creek because it was the only bargaining chip he had. But he kept thinking about Gibbons's philosophy. Gotta keep moving. Gotta keep gambling if you wanna stay in the game.

Bells held the beeper like a microphone and started to scatsing into it to the tune of "Swinging on a Star." He started to laugh then and tossed it back to Tozzi: It landed in the folds of the coat. "Nice try, Mikey-boy, but no cigar."

Tozzi picked up the transmitter and wrapped it in his fist again. "I'm telling you the truth, Bells. I'm an FBI agent."

"Is that so?" Bells nodded. "Interesting."

"I'm telling you. I can help you out here if you listen to me."

Gina rolled her eyes. "Give it up, will ya?"

Tozzi glared at her sideways. He wished she'd shut the hell up.

"You're throwing away a good chance to save yourself, Bells. Your only chance. Believe me."

Bells's face turned hard. "Believe *you*? Why the fuck should I believe a professional liar like you?"

"Don't be stupid, Bells—"

"I'm *not* stupid. That's why I would *never* listen to you, my friend. You are the lowest kind of rat there is. Any fucking cop who goes undercover and gains a man's trust just so he can send the guy to jail is less than shit on my shoe."

Gina nodded. "He's got a point."

"And you're no better, my dear Gina." The gun shifted its attention to her. "What can you say about a woman who turns her back on a man's sincerest offer? Huh? I tried to be nice to you, Gina, but you turned your back on me. You said to yourself, 'Fuck him. Who needs him?' Right? You probably even heard her say it, huh, Mikey?"

"I don't know what you're talking about, Bells." In fact, Tozzi didn't. He had no idea what this "sincerest offer" business was all about. But once again Bells's voice on Gina's answering machine came echoing back to him. He glanced at Gina and the wedding ring hanging around her neck. What the hell was going on between these two?

Bells was wearing the devil's face again. "What can I say, Gina? You turned out to be a real class-A bitch. Worse than that, you betrayed me."

Gina spat. "You're crazy. You don't know what the hell you're talking about."

Tozzi was stumped. "What *are* you talking about?"

"It's none of your business," Gina snapped, then turned back to Bells. "When are you gonna let us go, Bells? I'm getting sick of the both of you."

Bells started to shake his head, back and forth. He kept shaking his head.

"What's that supposed to mean?" she demanded.

Bells tilted his head sideways like a curious dog. "It means I'm not gonna let you go. I'm gonna kill you. I thought I told you that."

"Oh, cut the shit, will ya?"

Tozzi felt like there was a baseball lodged in his throat. He couldn't understand why she didn't believe him. She saw him kill Gibbons that morning. The man was crazy. He'd do it again in a minute.

Bells shook his head in pity. "You don't get it, Gina, do you? Do you know what this place is?"

"I don't know, and I don't care."

Bells looked at Tozzi. "Do *you* know?"

Tozzi shook his head.

"You never heard of the Belfry? That's not what *I* call this place, but I know a lotta guys do."

"You got *bats* in the belfry," Gina said.

"And that's not all." Bells grinned.

"So what is this place?" Tozzi asked.

"This is where I make people disappear." He said it as if he were admitting that he collected stamps.

"Mikey-boy, don't look so shocked. This is what I do. You mean to tell me the FBI didn't even have a clue? I'm flattered, really. I'm better than I thought."

Gina threw her hand out. "Go ahead. Pat yourself on the back. You're good at that, Bells."

"That's not all I'm good at. See, I'm so good at making people disappear, that's my main gig now. I'm, like, the official executioner for the family."

Now Tozzi looked skeptical.

"It's true, Mikey. I am the capo of retribution. You like that? Capo of retribution. Nice, huh? See, whenever somebody does something wrong, and they decide the guy has to be whacked, we lure him up here, and I do the deed. I must've done at least thirty guys up here. No shit. I got it down to a science. First I either shoot 'em or strangle 'em, whatever seems right at the time, then real quick I stab 'em through the heart a couple of times to stop the blood from pumping all over the place. Blood spurts if you shoot a guy, makes a big mess. Then I let 'em sit for

183

a while until the blood congeals, ya know? When they stop dripping, I drag 'em in the bathroom." He nodded toward the boxed-off room in the corner. "I cut 'em up, wrap the pieces nice and tight with plastic garbage bags and duct tape, then I get rid of the packages. Never all in the same place, just in case. Dumpsters, landfills, sewers, out in the Meadowlands, in the river—I know all kinds of places. My record is perfect. As far as I know, none of them have ever been found. Not a hand, not a foot, not even a finger. I'm very good at this."

Bells was bragging, but Tozzi had a bad feeling that he wasn't stretching the truth. He'd given Tozzi the creeps the first time they'd met, but Tozzi never thought he was this bad. He was a friggin' vampire, this guy.

Gina glared at Bells. "You're sick, you know that?"

"I know." Bells grinned. His eye was on the chain swinging in his hand, but the gun in his other hand was still leveled at them. "You know, Gina, I forgot to tell you. Everybody I ever brought up here I did basically the same way, cutting them up and making packages and all. All except one."

"Save your breath. I'm not interested."

"Maybe you should be." Bells looked up and grinned at her. "It was the only woman I ever did."

Gina was suddenly restless. Her chest was heaving, and her face started going through contortions trying to settle on an emotion.

Bells pointed with his gun to the windows that faced the skyline. "Go look. Out in the backyard."

Gina couldn't help herself. She stood up and started for the windows, though her eyes never left Bells. Tozzi got up to follow her before he got his arm yanked again. It was already sore.

Bells came up behind them, swinging the chain, as they stood at the window and looked down at the junky back lot.

"See that compacted car way back by the fence. That rusty thing. See it? About the size of a refrigerator."

Tozzi spotted it right away, even though it was mostly covered by tall weeds.

"You see it, Gina?"

"I see it."

"Margie," he said.

Gina bit her knuckle. She tried to hold back her tears, but it was a losing battle.

"I put her in the trunk of an old Chevy and had her compacted."

Tozzi felt queasy. "You kill her first?"

"Nope."

Bells sounded proud of himself. Tozzi could just imagine the poor woman's screams as the compactor ground its gears, crushing the fenders and the roof before it got to the rear end. But who was this Margie? And why did he kill her?"

"I really didn't want to do it," Bells said. "Swear to God. But you forced me, Gina. The two of you forced me. I kept warning her to stop playing games with me, but she didn't listen. And you egged her on."

Silent tears rolled down Gina's cheeks. Despite her nasty attitude all day, Tozzi felt bad for her. He wanted to do something for her, but he was afraid she wouldn't want any comforting from him.

Bells stopped twirling the chain. He moved to Gina's side and wiped her cheek with the gun barrel. "I gave you plenty of chances, Gina. You can't say I didn't. But you kept on playing games with me, even after Margie was gone. All I wanted was a simple answer. That's all. But you kept telling me to go fuck myself. Well, now it's my turn to tell you to where to go. And make you go there."

185

Tozzi was puzzled. "What's this all about? I don't—"

The gun barrel moved like a viper and slipped into Gina's mouth. She reared back, but the gun followed her retreat. Bells bore down on her until she was on her knees, the gun making her gag.

"Easy! Easy!" Tozzi yelled. He was tempted to take a poke at Bells, who was well within reach now, but he didn't dare, not with the gun in Gina's mouth. "Can't we talk about this, for chrissake?"

Bells's eyes were on fire. "Nothing *to* talk about, Mikey-boy. I've been fucked over by both of you. What's done is done. Now you die. Period."

"C'mon, Bells. Be reasonable."

"Reasonable is for jerkoffs. I have rules. I stick to those rules, and I expect other people to do the same."

Tozzi glanced down at Gina, his heart pounding. She was choking on the gun, writhing, trying to get away from it, but it stayed right with her. "Bells, Bells, listen to me. I don't understand what your complaint is. Not with Gina. Who's this Margie? What's she got to do with anything?"

Bells suddenly whipped the chain around Tozzi's handcuffed wrist. He dug a padlock out of his jacket pocket and dangled it in front of Tozzi's face. "Put the chain around the radiator—that one right there—and lock yourselves to it."

"But, Bells—"

"Put the chain on the radiator!" Bells yelled as he jammed the gun farther down Gina's throat.

Tozzi fumbled with the ends of the chain, getting down on his knees and doing as he was told before Bells killed her. He looped it around the steam pipe and gathered the end links around his handcuffed wrist as fast as he could, then clicked the ends together with the padlock. Tozzi yanked on the chain with the handcuffs to show Bells that it was secure. He and Gina were locked to the radiator.

Bells pulled the gun out of Gina's mouth, and she slumped to the floor, rolling over on her stomach. Tozzi touched her shoulder, but she pulled it away. She was sobbing with her face against the filthy wooden floor.

Bells went back to the kitchen. He pulled out something from under the sink and took it to the center of the loft. Sticking the gun in his waistband, he unfolded a large, aqua-blue plastic tarp. Tozzi didn't have to ask what that was for. To catch the blood.

"So who was Margie?" Tozzi was determined to at least satisfy his curiosity before he died.

Bells stepped on the stiff plastic to make it lie flat. "My wife," he said without looking up.

Tozzi looked at Gina, who was still turned away, resting her head on the outstretched arm chained to the radiator. He was down on the floor on his side, his arm extended the same way. His wife? he thought. In cahoots with Gina? But the message on her answering machine . . .

"You look confused, Mikey-boy."

"I am." Tozzi strained his neck to look at Bells.

"Well, ask Gina. She'll tell you all about it."

Tozzi tended to doubt that. He pulled out the beeper again and held it up in his fist. "It's not too late, Bells. Take the transmitter and go. It's your only chance."

"Put that fucking thing away, will ya? Transmitter, my ass. You insult my intelligence."

"You're being stupid, Bells. So you say you didn't shoot Petersen. Okay, fine, maybe you didn't. But what about Gibbons?"

"Who?"

"My partner. The agent you shot in Macy's. They'll get you for that one." *If I don't get you first, you son of a bitch.*

"How they gonna get me on that one, Mikey? Who saw it happen? Who's gonna testify? It was too crazy in there. No one will be able to point the finger at me. Except you and Gina."

"And Stanley and Freshy."

"Stanley, I don't worry about. And Freshy? He's stupid, but he's not that stupid."

"And what about us? You really gonna kill us? They know you're the one who kidnapped us. They'll know it was you."

Bells grinned. "I don't think you'll be in any shape to take the stand against me. Either of you."

Tozzi sucked in his breath and wished his heart would cool it with the drum solo.

"Listen, you two, I gotta go and get some tape and plastic bags. I don't think I have enough, and I don't like running out in the middle of the job, ya know what I mean? Besides, this'll give you guys a chance to collect your thoughts, say a rosary, whatever you want. I'll be back in a little while." Bells headed for the freight elevator.

"But, Bells, wait a minute."

Bells had his hand on the wooden elevator gate. "*Wait.* I hate that word. *Wait.* I never wait for anything. *Do.* That's the word I like. Just do it. Do what you gotta do. Do the right thing." Bells stepped into the elevator, and the gate rushed down, banging against the floor like a guillotine.

Bells yanked on the rope, and the rickety elevator started to descend.

"Have Gina tell you the story about her and Margie. You'll enjoy it."

Tozzi looked at him through the wood slats of the gate. The floor was even with Bells's waist. "You can yell for help if it'll make you feel useful, but no one will hear you. Trust me on that. Others have tried. See you later."

188

Bells's head sank into the pit. The vampire had made his exit.

Tozzi stared at the back of Gina's head. Her hair wasn't so blond or silky in this light. She was still on her side, facing away from him, but he could see the rise and fall of her back as she breathed. He gripped the chain and yanked on it, making it rattle against the steam pipe. He knew it was useless to try pulling on the chain, but he had to try anyway.

Tired squeaks and bumps rose from the elevator shaft. Maybe it would break down, and Bells would be stuck. But then he'd just turn into a bat and fly back up, Tozzi thought. After all, it was his belfry.

EIGHTEEN

5:41 P.M.

The freight elevator finally stopped at the bottom with a thud. Gina listened, staring at the brick wall, thinking. Her glasses were on top of her head, and the arm under her face was wet with tears, but she wasn't crying now. She just didn't have any more tears, not for Margie. She'd cried enough for that girl. They'd used to cry together. When Margie was alive, that's all they seemed to do, the two of them, cry. They cried when they were happy, and they cried when they weren't. They were so stupid. You can't make happiness. Gina knew that, but it was hard to disappoint Margie when she got an idea in her head. Gina knew that Bells was no damn good, and she'd warned Margie that it was nuts to try to do anything behind her husband's back. But Margie had been her friend since fifth grade. St. Elizabeth's in Bayonne. Gina never could say no to Margie, not when she started crying like that. The only thing Margie ever wanted in life was a baby; she'd even talked about it way back when they were in school. So many tears they cried over that. Enough tears to rust out a car.

Gina stared at the furniture on the other side of the loft. The armchairs cast long shadows across the turquoise plastic tarp spread out on the floor. Outside, the sun was setting, throwing a warm wavy orange light through the windows. It was going to be dark soon. Bells would come back, and . . . that would be the end of that. Gina didn't want to cry anymore, and she didn't want to panic, not in front of Mike, but as she thought about it, her breath became short and her chest got tight. She couldn't stop thinking about Margie out there in the trunk of that compacted car. She wondered whether Bells would decide to put her in a car, too, and dump the block of metal in the backyard next to Margie. Or would he just cut her up and wrap up the pieces like a side of beef the way he'd said? She closed her eyes against the nausea.

Her arm was falling asleep under her head, so she wiggled her fingers and squeezed her fist a few times to get the blood circulating. She didn't want to move too much, though, because that was the arm that was handcuffed. She didn't want to have to deal with him right now, and she knew that if she moved too much, it would give him an opportunity to say something and try to be nice again. Why do men always try so hard to be nice? Because they're trying to get something out of you, of course. But why were they always trying to be nice to *her*? she wondered. She was a bitch, for chrissake.

She could feel the heat of his body lying behind her. They were almost in the spoon position, except he was keeping his distance. Because he'd finally caught on that she was a bitch, no doubt.

Of course, that didn't stop him that day after the christening up at her place.

Well, maybe she wasn't so much of a bitch that day. She did kind of like him then. Kind of. Well, more than just kind of. She did like him. A lot. And she kind of thought he was interested in her, too. And not just to get laid. Although that was on her mind, too. It had been an awful long time.

But afterward, when they'd gotten off the couch and started

wandering around the living room, picking up their clothes, it was awkward. It was like, now what? Then the phone rang, and he heard Bells on the answering machine, and she could feel him getting weird on her. At the time, she'd thought he was jealous, but then later on after she found out from Freshy that he and Mike were in business together and they were trying to get a loan from Bells, she figured the bastard wasn't there because he really liked her. He was there because of Freshy. It was almost like networking. Cementing the relationship. Getting tight with the family.

Now come to find out, what he was really doing was spying. A cop worming his way into people's lives so he could pick up information on them. She meant nothing to him. He was just using her.

Except at the time, he was pretty nice. And he seemed genuine. He was tender. He was fun. Cops don't take acting lessons, do they?

She turned her head just enough so that she could see him out of the corner of her eye. The sunlight was blinding, and she had to shade her eyes.

The jerk was staring at her. "You okay, Gina?"

She turned over and sighed. What the hell did he want from her now?

"Are you all right?" he repeated.

"Don't talk." She knew she sounded bitchy, but she couldn't help it. She always sounded bitchy.

He blew out a sigh, and she felt his breath on her neck. He yanked the chain again as if this time it might come loose. What, by magic? He was only doing it for her benefit. To show that he cared, that he was worried about her, that he wanted to rescue her. She wished to hell he'd just give it up because she wasn't impressed. Besides, every time he did it, the handcuff just pulled on her wrist and irritated it even more than it already was.

The radiator hissed. Gina reached up and touched the pipe. It was hot. Well, at least they wouldn't die cold, she thought. Then she worried about getting burned.

"Don't touch the pipe," he said. "You'll get burned."

She clenched her jaw and touched it again, out of spite.

He sighed again, exasperated with her. Why didn't he just tell her she was a bitch? That was what he was thinking.

She felt him fidgeting. He was straining his neck, looking all over the place. "You see anything like a piece of two-by-four or a length of pipe, anything like that?"

She just looked at him. "Why? You gonna build an addition?"

He made a face. "Maybe I can break the pipe and get us out of here."

She closed her eyes and shook her head. That's the other thing men always do. Fix things. Men need their tools. She wondered what kind of "tools" Bells had up here. Butcher knives, or Black and Decker kind of stuff?

"Is there anything lying around over on your side?"

"Please. Do you really think you're gonna break an iron pipe with a piece of wood?"

"It's an old building. These pipes must be a hundred years old—"

"What're you, a building inspector now?"

"Would it kill you to cooperate a little? I'm trying to get us out of this." He was testy, but he still wouldn't tell her she was a bitch. Too much of a gentleman maybe. Yeah, right.

She turned over and faced him. "Can I ask you something?"

"Oh, now we're gonna be formal?"

"I just wanna know one thing before I die. That day we went back to my apartment. Did you go to bed with me because it was

193

part of your undercover assignment or because you really wanted to?"

"What?"

"Don't say 'what.' Just answer me."

His face turned very serious. "I don't make love for the government. I was genuinely attracted to you. I still am."

She burst out laughing. She couldn't help it. She shut her eyes because she couldn't look at him he was so earnest, so . . . typical. Where do men learn this crap?

"I'm glad you think this is funny." He was hurt now.

She couldn't stop laughing.

He raised his voice to be heard. "I tried with you. I really did. But you shut me down every step of the way."

"Stop." She was clutching her belly. "Stop." She was gonna split a gut laughing.

"I really felt something for you, Gina. And I was stupid enough to think you might've felt something for me. But I was stupid. I didn't realize you had something going with Bells."

She stopped laughing and glared at him, glared at the suggestion that she and Bells might mean anything to each other. "You're so full of shit—"

"I'm *not* full of shit. You treated *me* like the one-night stand. How many times did I call you and ask you out? I tried with you, Gina, but you didn't want any part of me."

She didn't believe a word of it. He'd just wanted to go to bed with her. He thought she was a bitch. He had to; she acted like one.

He shrugged, resigned. "You just didn't give a shit about me." He was trying to get the last word in.

She pushed the hair out of her face with a quick swipe and put her glasses back on. "You expect me to believe this?"

"Yes."

194

"You really . . . felt something for me?"

"Yes."

"Not just that Sunday. I mean, afterward."

"Yes!"

"You were thinking in terms of a relationship? Something that could lead to something sort of permanent?"

"*Yes!*"

"Really?"

"*Yes!*"

"Then prove it. If I'm gonna die tonight, I want to make love one more time, and for once in my life I want to know for sure that it's for real." She was trembling deep in her chest.

"You're not gonna die tonight, Gina. Get that out of your head."

"Don't try to comfort me. You're not my father, goddamn it. Just put up or shut up. Unless everything you just said is a load."

"It's not a load. I meant everything I said." His face was red. His deep-set eyes were smoking.

"Then kiss me. Make love to me. I want to know that I was really loved at least once in my life." She was staring into his eyes, her hand clenched around his belt. She was serious.

"But—"

No fucking buts, she thought as she put her face in his and kissed him, hard, like a bite. His free hand found its way to her back, then to the back of her neck. She pulled at his belt, grinding her lips into his face, afraid that she'd hear the elevator coming back, and that would be the end of everything.

He turned his head to the side to escape her kiss. "Slow down," he said. "Take it easy."

"I can't. Not enough time." Her throat was constricted. She felt teary, but she wasn't going to cry, not now. She tilted her head back, reaching out for his lips with hers.

195

He pulled her closer, his hand on her back again. He started nuzzling her neck. But he was being too tender. She didn't want tender. She wanted fire. She squirmed to get to his lips again.

"Don't you at least wanna take off your glasses?" he asked.

"No. I wanna see what I'm doing this time."

"Oh."

She found his lips and grabbed the back of his head, gripping the hair in her fingers. She wasn't going to let him go. She didn't want him to see the tears.

It was dark when Tozzi opened his eyes. The streetlights outside threw a cold greenish glow into the loft. Gina was staring at him, her glasses shining in the shadows. He must've dozed off.

"Sorry," he said, clearing his throat.

"For what?"

"Falling asleep."

She didn't answer, but he thought she might have shrugged. It was hard to tell with her arm stretched out above her head.

Her blouse was buttoned, and her pants were on. He started working on his own zipper, putting himself back together, which wasn't easy with one hand. She reached over and helped him with the button on his pants. She didn't seem to be mad or anything, which he'd half-expected. But there was no reason for her to be mad. Not if she'd felt the same thing he had. Maybe it was the handcuffs or the thought that this could be the last time he'd ever have sex again, or possibly it was the excitement of doing it when Bells could come back at any moment, but making love to Gina DeFresco was beyond belief. He'd gone to heaven before with a woman, but this time he saw God.

Too bad she didn't really like him. That would've made it even better.

After his shirttails were tucked in, he reached over and

touched her cheek, hooking the loose strands of hair behind her ear so he could see her face better.

"Will you do me one favor?" she said. Her voice was low and husky.

"Sure."

"Don't say you love me."

"Why?"

"Just don't say it."

"Why?"

"Because I don't want to hear it."

"What if I really mean it?"

"You only think you mean it. That's why I don't want to hear it."

Tozzi felt her hair in his fingers. "You're something else, you know that?"

"Stop. You're warming up to say it, and I don't want to hear it."

"Why not?"

"Because it doesn't mean anything. Men are always in love after they get laid. They're like dogs. Dogs are so good when you feed them. The rest of the time they just pee on the rug."

Tozzi let go of her hair.

"Nothing against you in particular, Mike. You are what you are. You can't help it."

His jaw tightened. She was ruining what had just been the most incredible sexual experience of his entire life. She was doing it on purpose. She couldn't just enjoy it for what it was. No, she had to put her spin on it. She couldn't just shut up and at least let *him* believe that in the last hours of his life he'd finally found love. Or the beginning of what could have been love. Or—

Shit. She was making him as loony as she was.

She lifted her head and shifted her position so that she was up on her elbow. "What do you think happened to Bells?" She wasn't talking softly now, which pissed Tozzi off. She was finished with the sex part obviously.

Tozzi tilted his wristwatch toward the light. "He's been gone, what? About two hours?"

"How long does it take to buy tape?" She sounded like she was anxious to get this show on the road. They'd done the sex— let's get going with the violence.

Tozzi thought about Bells turning into a bat. "Maybe he has to wait for the moon to come up."

"Bells doesn't wait for anything. You heard him." She was sullen and resentful, almost talking to herself. "The selfish bastard does whatever he wants, whenever he wants. Always."

Tozzi wondered if this was first-hand knowledge. He was dying to know what the hell her relationship with Bells was, but he knew he wasn't going to get a good answer if he asked. And right now, he wasn't sure he really wanted to know. The gold wedding band around her neck glimmered dully in the greenish light. Tozzi had a feeling he might not like the truth about them. He balled his fist and yanked on the chain in frustration.

"Will you stop doing that? You're gonna pull my arm out of the socket. It doesn't do any good."

Tozzi stared up at the chain. It was shinier than the wedding band. He wondered how much slack there was. Twenty inches? Thirty inches? It was hard to tell. His eyes slid down to Gina's waist.

"Let's try something." He started to pull the coat through the loop. "See if you can squeeze through the chain."

"What?"

"Like this." He pulled the coat all the way through so that it

198

was all on his side. "Try to get through the loop. So we can get outta here."

"I don't know what you're talking about." She knew. She was just giving him grief.

Tozzi spoke to her as if she were a five-year-old. "See this chain right here, the big chain on the radiator? It's just a loop around the pipe and the handcuff chain. Try to thread your whole body through the loop."

"Why don't you thread *your* body through the loop?"

Tozzi was getting impatient with her. She was just being obstinate. "I'm too big. I won't fit. You might fit, though. What've you got, a twenty-eight-inch waist?"

"Twenty-six." She was insulted.

"Great. It should be a piece of cake."

"And what about my hips. They're . . . bigger."

"They're not that big. You've got nice hips."

"Listen, I've got a huge can and I know it, so don't lie to me. Just forget about it. I won't fit."

Tozzi rolled his eyes. Now he had to be her goddamn psychiatrist. "Gina, there's nothing wrong with your hips. They're in perfect proportion to the rest of you. Just give it a try. You'll fit through. Try it."

"You're just saying that."

"I am not just saying that. You have a beautiful body."

"No, I don't. My tits are too small, and I have a rear end like an elephant."

Tozzi squeezed his eyes shut and counted to ten. "Gina, do you *want* to die?"

"Of course not."

"Then do something to save yourself. Try to wiggle through the chain. You can do it."

"You didn't say wiggle before. See, you do think I have a big can. Liar."

"I'm getting mad now, Gina. Just give it a try."

She frowned up at the chain above her head. "The radiator's hot. I'll get burned."

"It's not that hot."

"What if Bells comes back? He'll go nuts if he catches us trying to escape."

"Gina, he's gonna kill us anyway. What else can he do to us?"

She frowned at the chain again. She was out of excuses. "I'm too big," she muttered. "It won't work."

"Just try."

"The chain's not big enough."

"Take off your pants."

"What?"

"Pull down your pants. You're wearing those silk satin panties. If it gets a little tight, the panties will help you slide through."

"They're not silk. They're polyester."

"Whatever. They're slippery." Tozzi was losing his patience.

She looked up at the chain again. "All right. But you'll see. I won't fit."

"Try," he whispered.

She clasped her hands together and started to wiggle and squirm, snaking her way through the chain. Tozzi held the back of her thigh, guiding her through.

"Don't push," she said.

She worked her shoulders through the loop and shimmied until the chain was around her waist. That part went much faster than Tozzi had expected. She must've been right about her tits. She kept shimmying, but she didn't make much progress.

"See? I told you I wouldn't fit."

Tozzi reached for the button on her pants, but she slapped his hand away.

"I'll do it." She was gonna be modest now.

She unbuttoned her slacks and pulled down the zipper. Tozzi pulled them down around her knees.

"This pipe is hot," she complained.

Tozzi touched it. It was hot, but not that bad. "Hurry up and you won't get burned."

"Yeah, like you really care a lot."

"You wanna die like Margie?"

She glowered at him. "Don't talk about Margie." She got her hands to her waist and started to push down on the chain as if she were trying to work her way out of a tight girdle.

"That's it," Tozzi encouraged her. "If you got your shoulders through, you'll get your hips through."

"Says who?"

"That's what they say about babies when they're born."

"Shut up about babies!"

Tozzi was stung by her sudden anger. What'd he do wrong now? He wasn't about to ask her, though. Not now. She was almost through.

"You're almost there," he whispered. "Keep going, keep going."

She was straining and grunting, and it looked like she'd cleared one hip.

"I'm stuck," she said. "I'm stuck! It hurts!"

"Don't panic. Just keep going. You're almost there."

"But the chain's digging into me."

"Keep going."

"But—"

Thunk!

They both heard it, and they both froze. The elevator.

"It's him!" she hissed.
"Keep going. Hurry up."
Thunk!
"Oh, shit!" Her face was as tight as a knot.
So was Tozzi's stomach.

NINETEEN

Gibbons was trying not to stare at Lorraine, but it was hard not to. It was just too weird. He winced against the mounting pain in his tooth as he took another sip of his scotch. He looked down at Lorraine's drink sitting on the bar. She was having a scotch, too, which was not like her at all. But that wasn't the weird part. The weird part was that he was sitting here in this dive, drinking scotch with his wife, a Princeton University history professor who usually only drank white wine and never very much at that, and she was talking to a stripper, that young kid behind the bar in the stacked heels and bikini bottom and nothing else. And what was even weirder was what they were talking about: some guy named Boethius, a philosopher from the Middle Ages.

Gibbons stared blankly at the rows of bottles behind the bar. Maybe the bulletproof vest hadn't saved him that morning. Maybe he really was dead. Maybe this was the lounge act for hell. It was just too weird.

The stripper was leaning on her elbows, flipping through a yellow paperback edition of something called *The Consolation of Philosophy* by this guy Boethius. She had a cute jet-black Dutch-boy haircut that fell forward over her cheeks as she looked down at the book. Her boobs were dangling down over the bar. They

203

were cute, too. He wondered whether Lorraine had noticed that the kid wasn't wearing anything. She had a way of being oblivious to certain things. When she'd spotted the book on a chair behind the bar, Lorraine couldn't help asking who was reading it. The Middle Ages was her period, after all, and when the stripper told her she was reading it for a lit class she had to take, Lorraine's teacher mode kicked right in, and she started unloading everything she knew about this Boethius guy. The kid was eating it up. She knew she was getting a hand-feeding, and Gibbons was willing to bet that Lorraine's words were gonna find their way onto this kid's final.

Gibbons checked the place out. Two old geezers were down at the other end of the bar, clutching drafts and ignoring each other. There must've been some customers in the back room because the bartender had brought a tray of drinks back there a little while ago, but Gibbons hadn't actually seen anyone. It was a good thing the patrons were more interested in drinking than seeing the show. Lorraine's lecture had stopped the action. Philosophy and T&A don't exactly mix.

"So Boethius was really that important," the kid was saying. "I couldn't figure out why our professor had us reading him. He's a little on the boring side."

Lorraine took a quick sip of her scotch. "Boethius is *very* important. He was the main disseminator of Platonic thought in Western Europe."

The kid's eyes widened between the wings of her haircut. "Our professor never told us that." She had one of those sweet, ingenuous voices that reminded Gibbons of girls who wore bulky turtlenecks and corduroy skirts out in the sun. Not g-strings by the cool blue light of a jukebox.

"The works of Plato were unknown to Europe in the Middle Ages. The Arab world knew Plato, and it was through Arab interpreters of Plato that Boethius formulated his philosophy. If it weren't for him, the importance of Plato and his followers might never have influenced Western thought. And can you imagine what would've happened then?"

Gibbons's eyes slid toward his wife over the rim of his glass. A world without Plato. Perish the thought.

He gritted his teeth in a grin of pain as a flurry of throbs shot through his jaw. He flipped his wrist over to look at his watch, then glanced at the front door. He'd called in to the field office for the fourth time a half-hour ago, and they gave him the same old shit: Stay put, men are on the way. It had been almost three hours since Buddha Stanzione threw him and Lorraine out of the surveillance van and left them on the street. You'd think Ivers would've sent some guys right out, *pronto*, considering the situation. Well, they could take their goddamn time now. The trail was stone cold. Bells might've been in the area three hours ago, but he was long gone by now. They could count on that. Gibbons drained his glass and motioned to the scurvy-looking barkeep to do him again.

Lorraine pointed at her empty glass, too, but she didn't miss a beat with the kid. She just kept on yapping. "I'm sure your lit professor told you about the Wheel of Fortune. Fate personified as a woman? Lady Luck, she's sometimes called. She's often portrayed wearing a huge wheel on her body with tiny mortals caught in the spokes. The ones at the top of the wheel are joyous, while the ones at the bottom are in misery. Chaucer spoke of the Wheel of Fortune in several of his poems, if I remember correctly. Well, this popularization of human fate being cyclical and out of the individual's control comes directly from Boethius."

The stripper nodded, raven hair bouncing like the beautiful Breck girl. She was taking down notes on cocktail napkins. A

205

small stack was piling up on the bar. Gibbons still couldn't believe this—Lorraine oblivious to the whole scene here, acting like this kid with the nice gazongas was one of her students and this was her office down at Princeton. Maybe this was how she was dealing with the whole trauma thing. First she sees him getting shot, then she sees Tozzi getting kidnapped, then she gets kidnapped herself—maybe this was like denial for her. Still, it was very weird. Never in a million years would he have thought he'd ever see his wife in a place called Joey's Starlight Lounge. Never.

Gibbons glanced at his watch again. What the hell was taking them so long? Apprehending Bells was supposed to be top priority. Two agents—no, three if you counted him—had been assaulted by this guy in less than twenty-four hours, and this is the kind of response you get? Frigging Bells had shot him and left him for dead. Same with Petersen, and for all Gibbons knew, Petersen might have croaked in the hospital sometime today. And Tozzi? Well . . .

He looked down at the bar in front of him, and as if by magic, a fresh drink was sitting there, waiting for him. He picked it up, took a long sip, and basted his bad tooth in liquor for a while before he swallowed. He'd been trying not to think about Tozzi because he didn't like what common sense was telling him was most likely true. If Bells had had no compunction about taking nearly point-blank shots at FBI agents twice today, what was he gonna do with the one who was actually wearing a wire on him, the one he had handcuffed like a prisoner on a chain gang? It was time to face reality. Tozzi could be dead.

Gibbons stared down into the amber liquid in his glass, and the bar and the jukebox and the kid with the tits and even Lorraine flew out into the stratosphere, leaving him alone in an empty black hole, just him and the bartop and what was left of his scotch. Tozzi dead. He felt like pulling into himself and grabbing onto whatever he could. Tozzi dead. Things wouldn't be the same. He wouldn't be able to work anymore. Couldn't deal with a new partner and wouldn't last ten minutes on a desk job. Tozzi dead. Lorraine would be different. She'd blame him, blame the Bureau, which would amount to the same thing. Tozzi dead. It could never be the same. None of it. Nothing. Tozzi dead. Just pull back and hang on to what's left.

He reached for his glass, but he couldn't lift it to his lips. What was the point? Tozzi was dead.

Gibbons let out a sigh so deep and sad, it felt like his ghost had slipped out his nose and left him there. He really didn't care, though. Everyone in this place was alone and separated. Lorraine and the stripper kid weren't talking; they weren't communicating. Lorraine was spouting, and the kid was sopping it up, thinking about how she was gonna ace this lit course with all this stuff she was getting down on the cocktail napkins. The two old drunks sitting together down the end of the bar didn't even acknowledge each other, let alone anyone else. The bartender was busy counting out the cash in the till. Gibbons was tempted to strike up a conversation—something he never did unless he was looking for information about a suspect. Bartenders were supposed to be good at listening to other people's troubles. They probably don't care any more than the next guy, but they know how to make believe. That was okay. Gibbons would take the make-believe understanding. He just needed to talk to someone, anyone. Because Tozzi was dead.

"Say," Gibbons started, but the bartender's gaze sailed past him to the front door. His sickly face was drawn. All of a sudden he was tight-mouthed and owl-eyed. He kept counting the money in his hand, but he wasn't looking at it.

Gibbons looked at the reflection in the mirror to see what had spooked him.

Holy shit! It was Bells.

The mobster breezed past the blue glow of the jukebox, ignoring the bartender, who obviously knew who he was. He was holding a big plastic Ace Hardware bag, something heavy inside. He was heading for the back room. Gibbons instinctively reached inside his jacket for Excalibur as he got up off his stool. He heard the words in his head before he started to say them: *Freeze! FB—*

His fingers fell into the empty holster. He forgot. He didn't have Excalibur.

But Tozzi was dead.

Gibbons moved fast, as if he were weightless. He swept an empty longneck Bud bottle off the bar in front of the closest drunk, and before the drunk realized it was gone, Gibbons had it jammed in Bells's back, his other arm wrapped around the bastard's neck, pulling him backward.

"Freeze, motherfucker! FBI!" Gibbons's breath was hot, ignited by his wailing tooth. He was breathing fire.

Lorraine spun around in her seat. "Gibbons!"

"Jesus!" The stripper stood up and covered her nipples with Boethius.

Bells was relaxed, almost limp.

The bartender's eyes bulged. He looked toward the back room. "Stanley!" His voice was a sharp rasp, like an old dog's bark.

The name didn't register with Gibbons until eight figures emerged from the gloom of the back room: Bells's right-hand man Stanley, Buddha Stanzione, that little shit Freshy, and Buddha's pack of gorillas.

Gibbons cursed under his breath behind Bells's head. The gang was all here. Wonderful.

"Hey, Bells." Stanley's greeting was tentative.

Buddha's eyes were cold. "We been waiting for you, Bells."

Freshy was nervous, shifting his weight from one foot to the other. He avoided looking at anyone for too long.

The gorillas, like their boss, only had eyes for Bells. It was as if Gibbons weren't even there.

Gibbons glanced into the mirror over the bar. The women were frozen, the drunks confused. He looked at the bartender's face, wondering whether the guy realized that he was holding a beer bottle to Bells's back and not a gun. It was hard to tell. The bartender's slack-jaw expression was hard to read.

"Let him go," Buddha muttered.

Stanley chimed in. "Let us deal with him." He sounded a little uncomfortable siding with Buddha against his man Bells. Of course, with all these gorillas hanging around, he didn't have much choice.

Gibbons glanced at the mirror again. Bells was looking right at him, flashing this shitty little grin, like he had something up his sleeve. He was still holding the bag from the hardware store, which got Gibbons to wondering about what he had in there. But it was the smug, lizard-eyed look on the bastard's face that he couldn't figure out. You'd think the guy would be a little shook up under the circumstances, but instead he was very cool. He actually seemed to be enjoying himself.

Bells raised his eyebrows at Gibbons in the mirror. "Vest?"

Gibbons didn't answer, but he was surprised the bastard recognized him.

"You were wearing a bulletproof, right? Son of a gun." He shook his head and chuckled, like a multimillionaire who'd just lost ten grand at the roulette table, like it didn't matter, it was only money.

"C'mon, Gibbons. Let him go," Stanley repeated.

Bells smiled at the little capo. "I didn't see any cars outside, Buddha. You must've parked on the side behind the hedges and come in the back way, right? I should've thought to check. How stupid." He rolled his eyes to the side and looked at Gibbons in the mirror. "I guess you didn't know they were here either, huh?" He was still smiling like none of this mattered to him.

Buddha was getting that constipated look, like he wanted things to get moving. The gorillas moved closer, crowding in around the capo's back.

"Forget it," Gibbons said to the whole bunch of them. "He's under arrest, and I'm taking him in."

Buddha shook his head.

Gibbons ignored him. "He'll stand trial for what he did. The right way. Not your way."

Bells started laughing, softly and to himself. Gibbons frowned. What was he doing, building his case for an insanity plea? Gibbons dug the beer bottle into his back out of spite.

"He's ours," Buddha mumbled. "We'll take care of him our way."

"Forget it." Gibbons listened for the door behind him to open. If it was true that timing was everything, now would be a great time for those guys from the field office to show up. Gibbons waited, but he didn't hear anything. So much for timing.

Stanley stepped forward. He had a curious look on his face.

"Stay where you are." Gibbons jammed the bottle into Bells's back and jerked him back.

"Easy, my friend, easy, easy." Bells was smooth.

Stanley took another step closer and craned his neck to see

behind Bells's back. Gibbons felt his stomach sink. He knew right there and then that he was screwed.

Stanley turned to the pack. "Freshy, you still got his piece?"

"Yeah." Freshy pulled Excalibur out of his pocket and held it up for everyone to see.

"That's what I thought." Stanley moved closer and stared down at the beer bottle. His big jaw broke into a big grin as he shook his head. "Nice try, Gibbons." He took the bottle out of Gibbons's hand and waved it at Buddha and his bruisers.

On Buddha's nod, the gorillas moved in and grabbed Bells. He didn't say a word, and he didn't look particularly upset either. One of them looked in the plastic bag and pulled out a box of heavy-duty lawn-and-leaf plastic bags and a couple of rolls of duct tape. The gorilla reached in again and came up with an electric knife sharpener.

Lorraine covered her mouth. "Oh, my God . . ."

"Upstairs," Buddha grumbled. "Everybody."

"I'll make coffee," Bells quipped as the gorillas shoved him through the back room.

Stanley had his gun out. "Mrs. Gibbons?" he said to Lorraine. He was being polite about it, extending his arm to show her the way.

She looked at Gibbons, her brows slanted back in distress. "Do we have to . . . ?"

Gibbons shrugged. "Looks that way, doesn't it?"

She went to his side and squeezed his arm. It was the first sign of connection he'd gotten from her all day. He looked into her face and finally saw that she was there—not Professor Lorraine, *his* Lorraine. He wanted to hug her and give her a kiss that lasted until their breath ran out and then some, but Stanley's gun was prodding his back, and Buddha was giving them dirty looks. Gibbons took Lorraine's hand and locked fingers with her.

They followed the crowd into the back room, where Buddha and company had been waiting to ambush Bells. Gibbons couldn't believe that he'd been that out of it that he didn't hear them come in. He couldn't imagine these baboons being quiet. They passed through a back door to a dim hallway with a cold cement floor that led to a loading dock at the back of the building. The stink from the Dumpster would have been worse than it already was if it hadn't been so chilly out. Freshy opened the gate of the freight elevator, and the gorillas hustled Bells inside, his arms pinned back behind him. They weren't gentle with him, but from the relaxed look on his face, nothing seemed to bother him. Stanley prodded Gibbons again, and he and Lorraine stepped inside, standing against the wall away from Bells. Stanley and Buddha took the middle position as Freshy dropped the wooden gate.

Stanley tugged on the rope that started the elevator. "We figured you'd come back here, Bells." It sounded like an apology.

Bells just smiled and nodded.

"Yeah. I went up to look for you before, but the place was all dark."

Bells's face hardened, then just as quickly it relaxed again.

Gibbons caught Stanley's eye. "This is the Belfry?"

Stanley nodded.

Gibbons shook his head. "Son of a bitch."

"What did you do with my cousin Michael?"

All heads turned to Lorraine. Her clear demanding voice was startling among all these grumbling wiseguys.

Bells let his gaze bore through her like a slow drill press, but

Lorraine wasn't cowed. "What did you do with them?" she repeated. "Did you kill them?"

Freshy shuffled his feet, looking from Bells to Stanley to Buddha to Bells. He was worried sick about his sister.

Gibbons studied Stanley's face, looking for a clue. Had Bells killed them already? Were they up there dead on the floor? He remembered the duct tape and the garbage bags Bells had bought. His heart was pounding in syncopation with his throbbing tooth.

Buddha was looking into Bells's face for a clue of his own, but Bells revealed nothing. They just had to wait for the tired old elevator to get there. It seemed to take forever. When it finally stopped with a clunk, Lorraine had Gibbons's hand in a vise-grip. He'd forgotten about his tooth, but his heart was pounding down a brick wall in his chest.

The room beyond the gate was dark. Freshy raised the gate so fast, it banged at the top and dropped back down halfway. "Gina!"

Stanley stepped out and groped for the light switch. Fluorescent bulbs flickered on the ceiling, and suddenly the place was revealed: the kitchen, the couches, the plastic tarp bunched up on the floor. But where were Tozzi and Gina? Gibbons honed in on Bells's eyes, ready to follow his gaze. But Bells was watching Buddha.

The gorillas wrenched Bells's arms and shoved him out of the elevator. Stanley pointed his gun up and motioned for Gibbons and Lorraine to get out, too. Buddha was the last one out, the little emperor.

Gibbons felt Lorraine putting the squeeze on his hand again, digging her nails into the flesh over his knuckles. She was frantic, ready to explode, staring at something against the wall. Gibbons followed her gaze to a paint-peeled radiator under a closed window. Then he noticed the two shiny items on the floor next to the radiator—a short chain padlocked around the steam pipe, and a black patent-leather shoe with a velvet bow on the front, a woman's shoe.

"Oh, Jesus." Freshy's face crumpled as he lunged at Bells. "You son of a bitch!"

One of the goons stepped in his way, and Freshy literally bounced off him. Before Freshy even thought about making another attempt, the gorilla moved in on him and changed his mind.

"Whad'ja do with my sister?" Freshy yelled over the gorilla's head.

"And my cousin," Lorraine added.

Bells made a big show out of looking at the radiator, then looking around the loft. He shrugged. "Beats me." He was trying to be cool and unconcerned, but Gibbons could see the shadow of a blue vein surfacing on one temple.

Buddha walked up to Bells and got in his face. "So what's the story, Bells?"

Bells pulled down the lizard lids again. He was pissed, and he was trying not to show it.

"Talk," Buddha grunted. "Tell me things."

"Like what?" Bells was arrogant.

"Tell me about that funny money you tried to pass off on me this morning." Buddha was like a spike—hard, short, and sharp.

Bells just looked at him for a second, then looked at Gibbons and pointed with his head. "Not in front of him." He nodded toward the boxed-off room in the far corner. "In the bathroom."

The little emperor didn't seem to like the idea. "Dom," he said to one of the gorillas. He nodded toward the bathroom. "Go check it out."

Ice water ran through Gibbons's heart. What if Gina and Tozzi weren't dead? What if they'd gotten loose and were hiding in the bathroom? Even if Tozzi had a gun, there were too many of them. But Tozzi was stupid enough to take them all on. Shit.

Big Dom reached around to the small of his back and pulled out a big black-matte automatic. A 9-millimeter, Gibbons assumed, with a big clip, fourteen, fifteen bullets. Big Dom moved toward the bathroom, leading with the gun like a point man on jungle patrol. When he got to the door, he waited and listened.

Gibbons balled his fists. Lorraine clutched his arm.

Suddenly Big Dom threw the door back and crashed into the bathroom, sweeping the small space with his weapon. He went all the way in, closed the door behind him, and came right back out, nodding to his boss. "It's okay, Mr. Stanzione."

Gibbons started breathing again. Lorraine loosened her grip.

But Gibbons's relief didn't last. If Tozzi and Gina weren't in there, where were they? He glanced at the bunched-up plastic tarp between the green couch and the cabinets under the kitchen counter.

On Buddha's order, the gorillas let go of Bells, and Dom escorted him at gunpoint into the bathroom, followed by the little emperor, who walked with a swagger, hands in his pants pockets, the train of his camel hair overcoat swishing behind him.

After the bathroom door closed, Lorraine suddenly went into overdrive. "Stanley, where are they? What did he do with them? Tell me. Please, Stanley."

Stanley shrugged, his eyes slanted back in sympathy. "I don't know, Mrs. Gibbons. I wish I could tell you something."

"But, Stanley, you've worked with him. You must know—"

Stanley just shook his head and shrugged. "Sorry, Mrs. Gibbons."

Freshy piped up. "Hey, Stanley, what about—?"

"*Hey!*" A shout came from the bathroom, then a clunk and a crash. Then the lights went out, and the room went black.

"Nobody move!" Stanley shouted.

"What the fuck?"

"What happened to the lights?"

"Mr. Stanzione? You all right? You all right?"

The gorillas panicked. Gibbons could hear them scrambling in the dark.

"I said don't move! Nobody!" Stanley yelled.

Two shots rang out, muzzle strobes lighting the room, but they came from the elevator. Gibbons grabbed Lorraine and pulled her to the floor, covering her with his body. Jesus!

"Do what the man said. Don't move." It was Bells's voice, and it was coming from the elevator. The gate banged closed, and the elevator motor groaned to life.

Two more shots lit the darkness, making Gibbons's ears pop. He pressed his chest to Lorraine's back, making her go down flatter.

"Don't do anything stupid now," Bells warned in singsong. " 'Or would you rather be a pig?' "

The elevator ground its way down, and Bells fired again, keeping everyone at bay. The elevator was so slow, it was hard to say whether he still had a good shot at any of them or not, but Gibbons wasn't taking any chances, not with Lorraine there.

Twenty seconds passed, and the gorillas came out of the bushes, stumbling over the plastic tarp and cursing, groping for the bathroom.

"Mr. Stanzione? Mr. Stanzione? You all right?"

Gibbons heard one of them banging on the bathroom door, then there were more curses.

"What happened?" Stanley shouted from somewhere behind Gibbons.

"Jesus Christ!" Freshy breathed. "Jesus!"

"Gibbons?" Lorraine was shaky.

"Stay down." Gibbons got to his feet, but stayed in a crouch, his hand on Lorraine's hip.

The lights flickered back on then, and Gibbons squinted against the sudden brightness.

"What happened?" Stanley shouted as he ran to the bathroom.

Gibbons followed him.

"Holy shit!" Stanley's big jaw dropped as he looked in from the doorway.

Gibbons looked over his shoulder. The gorillas were crowded around the little monkey emperor who was doubled over, writhing, clutching his head. Two halves of a broken porcelain toilet tank cover were on the floor. Big Dom was sitting motionless with his legs stretched out, heels together, his head slumped forward like a Raggedy Ann doll. A switch blade was sticking out of the back of his neck. Severed spinal cord, Gibbons thought, surgical precision. On the wall above Big Dom was an open junction box.

It wasn't hard to piece it all together. Bells had taken them both on. He must've grabbed Big Dom's gun and hit the circuit breakers. His efficiency in the dark with the rest of it was chilling.

Suddenly fearing for Lorraine, Gibbons wheeled around to go to her, but he froze when he saw her standing where he'd left her, looking at Freshy, who was on the verge of tears. It was a still shot of grief becoming a reality, the victims' relatives frozen in gut-gnawing pain, finally believing what they'd been trying so hard to deny. Gibbons felt a heaviness in his chest that threatened to bring him to his knees with sadness for Lorraine. And for Tozzi.

The turtle-slow elevator stopped groaning then. The echo of the wooden gate banging open sounded up the empty shaft. It was a message from hell. The devil was on the run.

TWENTY

Tozzi couldn't believe he was so stupid.

"This way," Gina said. The alley was dark, and she was hobbling because she'd lost her shoe and the ground was cold and uneven. It couldn't have been easy running on the cobblestones with one bare foot, but she wasn't complaining. She hadn't even complained when they got halfway to his apartment on the other side of Hoboken and he realized that he didn't have his keys. He never carried anything that could give away his real identity when he was undercover. The keys were stashed in the trunk of his car back at Freshy's house in Bayonne. He couldn't believe he hadn't remembered that. Stupid.

They were heading back uptown to the Macy's warehouse where they made the floats for the parade. It was Gina's idea. She said they could hide out there. But Tozzi didn't like the idea of going back uptown toward the Belfry. "C'mon. Let's go straight to the police station," he suggested.

"That's farther than your apartment," she gasped, pulling him along by the handcuffs. "The warehouse is closer. We'll call the cops from there." As she ran up the alley, she made these scared little *eeep* noises.

Five minutes later, they emerged from the alley onto Fourteenth Street, where several cars were waiting at the traffic light.

219

Tozzi held her back as he scanned the faces in the front seats, looking for Bells, but Gina bolted across the intersection, terrified to be out in the open. There was an all-night gas station across the street on the corner, one of those modern ones with no garages, just an attendant's booth. The whole corner was lit up like daytime with fluorescent lights.

Tozzi pointed to the rear of the station. There was a lone pay phone over by the air pumps. "Look. We can call from over there."

"No! Where're we gonna wait? Out here in the open? Bells will find us for sure. C'mon, the warehouse is just up this way."

She had a point. Bells must've known by now that they'd escaped, and he knew they'd be on foot. Standing out under all these lights would be crazy. Tozzi gripped her hand and followed her back into the shadows of the side street. She started making the *eeep* noises again.

Back at the Belfry she'd really panicked when she'd heard the elevator coming up. She started to hyperventilate, and then she started *eeep*-ing, struggling to get some air into her lungs. He tried to calm her down, but she was frantic, terrified that Bells was going to get them. And after all that complaining that she wouldn't fit through the chain loop, she suddenly managed to get out of it somehow. Must've ripped a piece of her butt off doing it. They rushed over to the kitchen and tried the door to the stairwell, but it was locked, and it was a three-story drop out the window. The elevator was almost there, so he grabbed Gina and made her get down behind one of the leather couches, pulling the plastic tarp over them. He figured he just might be able to take Bells by surprise that way. But he practically had to lie on top of Gina to keep her still, and even with his hand over her mouth, she was still *eeep*-ing too loud. The elevator stopped with a *thunk*. They lay there frozen, eyes wide, listening for Bells,

Tozzi wondering what the hell he was going to do handcuffed to Gina. But he didn't hear any footsteps getting off the elevator.

"Bells? You here? Bells?"

It was only Stanley, and he didn't even get off the elevator, just called out and left when he didn't get an answer.

After Stanley left, Tozzi and Gina went down the elevator, cut through the empty lot, squeezed through a broken fence, and found a pay phone on the street. He quickly called in to the field office and explained the situation to the night clerk. He said he'd take Gina to his apartment on the other side of Hoboken, and they'd wait there for someone to come for them. But he'd forgotten about the keys. Stupid.

"This way." Gina pulled him off the side street down another alley. Up ahead there was a open bay on the right, light from inside pouring out onto the cobblestones. When they got to the bay, Tozzi had to shade his eyes against the unexpected onslaught of glitter and color. It was . . . incredible.

The warehouse was as big as an airplane hangar, and it was full of floats decorated with crepe paper and fabric, ribbons and paint in every color imaginable, floats with giant papier-mâché squirrels and life-size bears, parrots and giraffes, whales and skin divers, seals and penguins, dinosaurs and cavemen, pirates, crystal-blue elves and silver fairies, knights on armored chargers, cowboys and Indians, clowns and acrobats, robots, rabbits, walruses, extraterrestrials, silly dogs and cats, hula girls in front of a looming volcano, flowers as big as trees. It was more than the eye could take in.

"Can I help you?"

Tozzi blinked as an old geezer got off a stool just inside the bay and walked toward them very slowly. He was frowning at them, and he tried to sound threatening, but he must've been pushing ninety.

"I said, can I help you?"

Gina dug into her pants pocket and came up with a laminated Macy's employee ID card. She held it out to the old man, who took it from her and tipped his head back so he could read it through the bottom half of his bifocals. She glanced at Tozzi. They were thinking the same thing: Hurry up!

"Okay," the old man finally said, handing back the ID. He headed back to his stool without another word.

"C'mon," Gina said. She led him through the rows of parked floats, all waiting to be towed off to Manhattan for the parade tomorrow. At another open bay way over on the other side of the warehouse, workmen were already hitching up floats to idling tractor trucks.

As they squeezed through the narrow aisles between the floats, Tozzi kept an eye out for Bells. He was half-convinced the guy really was supernatural. The bastard could show up anywhere.

"Up here," Gina said when they emerged from the floats. She led him up a steel grid staircase against the wall to a posh lounge that overlooked the floor of the warehouse. Gina pulled him inside, locked the door behind them, and closed the maroon venetian blinds that covered the plate-glass windows, blocking out the colorful view. She pulled Tozzi over to the other side of the room, where a beige telephone was sitting on a cherry sideboard. She picked up the receiver, got an outside line, and handed it to him. "Here. Call."

Tozzi reached over and punched out 911. It only rang once.

"Police," the bored voice on the other end said.

"This is Special Agent Mike Tozzi, FBI. I want to talk to the commanding officer on duty. This is an emergency."

"Hang on, sir."

Tozzi looked at the closed venetian blinds as he waited. He didn't like not being able to see out.

"This is Lieutenant Frankel. How can I help you, sir?"

"My name is Tozzi, FBI. I'm inside the Macy's warehouse uptown. I'm unarmed and handcuffed to a civilian. We're being pursued by an armed individual—"

The lieutenant interrupted. "Do you know this individual's identity?"

"Yes. His name is Tony Bellavita, aka Tony Bells. White male, about five foot ten—"

"Oh, yes, I'm familiar with Mr. Bellavita. I'll send some men up right away. Where in the warehouse are you?"

"A room that's up a flight of metal stairs, dark red blinds over the picture windows. It overlooks the whole warehouse. I think there's only one room like this." He looked at Gina, and she nodded. "Yes, it's the only one up high like that."

"Is anyone hurt?"

"No."

"Okay, sir. They're on their way."

"Thank you."

The lieutenant hung up, and Tozzi reached over and replaced the receiver. "They're sending a cruiser," he said.

"Good." Gina looked exhausted. She started for the couch that was next to a buffet table set up with a platter of fancy cookies wrapped in yellow cellophane, a dozen plastic liter bottles of soda, paper cups, and an ice bucket. But before she made it to the couch, Tozzi pulled her over to the window.

He didn't like being cooped up in here. He parted the blinds and peered out as she dragged up a straight-back chair and collapsed into it next to him. He scanned the warehouse floor below, following the aisles between the floats. Then he looked all the way back to the open bay where the old geezer was posted, and his heart stopped. "Oh, shit!"

"What?" Gina got up and parted the blinds for herself. Right away she saw what Tozzi saw. "Oh, my God!"

Bells was standing in the open bay, scanning the rows of floats. The old man was off his stool, waving at Bells to stop, but Bells ignored him and walked right in.

Gina gripped his arm. "What're we gonna do? He's here!"

Tozzi stared out the window. He couldn't believe this. How in the hell—?

But then he glanced at the cookies and soda on the table and remembered Gina's secretary, the black girl back at Macy's in Manhattan that morning. Bells had been looking for Gina, and the secretary told him that Gina would be taking all those kids over here to the warehouse in Hoboken. Bells must've figured that he and Gina might come here since it wasn't far from the Belfry and Gina knew this place. Or else the son of a bitch really could read minds. Shit!

"C'mon." Tozzi pulled Gina to the door. He shut the lights and parted the venetian blinds again. "We gotta get outta here."

"Why? Why can't we stay here? He doesn't know we're here."

"Wanna bet?"

"How could he know?"

"I'll tell you later."

Tozzi tracked Bells as he strolled through the floats, looking underneath each one as he passed by. He waited until Bells disappeared from view behind the big volcano on the Hawaiian float. "C'mon, fast. Let's go." He opened the door and practically flew down the steps. Gina resisted, but a sharp yank on the handcuffs got her moving. There was no time for discussion.

They dashed from the staircase to the Wild West float, hunkering down behind the rear tires for cover. Tozzi's heart was thumping. Gina's eyes were wide behind her glasses. Her free hand was clamped over her mouth. She was *eeep*-ing again.

He whispered in her ear. "C'mon. Let's go."

Out under the stars, Tozzi turned over on his hip, rustling the noisy bed of shredded tan-colored crepe paper that was supposed to be sand. His back was getting stiff lying out here in the cold, surrounded by a bunch of goofy-looking candy-colored dinosaurs wearing bikinis and jams, getting glitter and dried glue in his eyes and up his nose, freezing his ass off. Tozzi glared up at a seven-foot orange papier-mâché Tyrannosaurus rex in a purple tank top and Ray Bans, standing on a surfboard. He glanced over at Gina next to him and knew they were both thinking the same thing: Did the cops get Bells yet? The police lieutenant Tozzi had talked to said he knew who Bells was, but they weren't taking any chances. That's why they were here lying low. Bells could still be out there, looking for them.

Their float was in line with all the other floats waiting for clearance to go through the tunnel. Every year on the night before Thanksgiving, one tube of the Lincoln Tunnel is closed off at midnight to bring the floats through. Tozzi lifted his head and saw that the line stretched from the toll plaza all the way back into Hoboken. Sight-seers lined the route just as if it were a regular daytime parade, and that made Tozzi uneasy. The crowd would be a good cover for Bells—if he was still out there. He looked at Gina sideways and thought about going up to the cab of the truck that was pulling this float and asking the driver for help, but she'd go nuts again if he did.

After they'd gotten out of the warehouse, she had a real panic attack. He'd thought she was gonna have a heart attack the way she was carrying on, crying and *eeep*-ing and flailing all over the place. She kept ranting that everybody was in cahoots with Bells, and they couldn't trust anyone now. All she wanted to do was hide, hide from Bells. Tozzi had other ideas, but it's hard to act independently with a struggling, kicking, hundred-and-what-ever-pound nutcase handcuffed to your wrist. But the way he figured, as long as they were safe and she was quiet now, he'd wait until they got into Manhattan, then they'd go for help.

Gina was curled up on her side, her eyes glistening with the tears she wouldn't let go of, just about in the fetal position, frowning at her bare foot. It must've been frozen. But the rest of her couldn't have been. She was wearing the coat. He was pissed at her for being so goddamn difficult, but he couldn't stay pissed because he felt bad for her, too.

Tozzi frowned up at the surfing dinosaur looming over his head. "We shouldn't be just sitting here, you know. This is stupid."

"No, it's not," she mumbled.

"Yes, it is. We should've gone back to my apartment. Even if we couldn't have gotten in, we should've just waited there."

"How do you know Bells doesn't know where you live?"

"I was undercover. I told him I lived down the shore."

She turned over and looked at him. "You don't know Bells. He doesn't miss a trick. He could've followed you home one night. He'd follow you for a whole month if he wasn't sure about you. You don't know how bad he can be."

Tozzi hesitated before he asked. "And how do you know so much about him?"

She was quiet for a moment. "We used to go out."

Now he was quiet.

"Oh, don't give me the attitude, will ya? It was way back in high school."

"Oh . . ." Tozzi wanted his coat back. Let her freeze. But

226

instead of asking for it, he squeezed the surfing dinosaur's black toenail and broke the papier-mâché crust. Way back in high school, huh?

"Hey, stop that." She pulled his hand away from the dinosaur's foot. "Don't break him."

Tozzi glared at her. He was dying to know, but he didn't want to ask. He watched his breath on the cold air for a minute, mulling it over. Shit. He *had* to know. "You sleep with him?"

"Who? Bells?"

"Yes, Bells."

"What do you care?"

"I'm curious."

"It's none of your goddamn business if I did or I didn't."

Tozzi stared up at the half moon. "You're absolutely right. It is none of my business." But he still wanted to know.

She got up on her elbow. "What do you think, I was a virgin before you? Is that it? You're disappointed?"

"Don't be ridiculous."

"Then why do you want to know?"

"Forget about it. I don't want to know." Tozzi glared at the moon. He did want to know. And he was all set to be disappointed in her.

"You do want to know, or else you wouldn't have asked. All right, I'll tell you. I don't care. It's no big deal. Yes, I did go to bed with Bells. There."

Tozzi shrugged. He wasn't gonna ask. He *wasn't* gonna ask.

"A long time ago," she added. "When we were in high school."

Tozzi was fuming inside. He wanted to know if it ended in high school. When was the last time? *"Gina, it's me. Gimme a call."*

227

"It wasn't love or anything," she went on. "It just sort of happened."

Bullshit.

He coughed into his fist. "Why are you telling me all this? I don't want to know about you and him."

"I'm telling you because you *do* want to know. But this isn't what you wanted to hear. You think I'm a slut now because I slept with him."

"Did I say that?"

"No. But you're thinking it."

"How do you know what I'm thinking?"

"C'mon. Do you think you're deep, or what?"

Tozzi wanted to rip the dinosaur's foot off.

"He wasn't a killer when we were in high school," she said. "At least, I didn't think he was. I mean, I didn't even know he was a made man until this past summer. Don't get me wrong. I knew he was no angel, but I thought he was just small time, like my brother."

Tozzi didn't answer her.

She kept talking. "Of course, when your whole family is basically mob associated, who else are you gonna meet when you're a kid? In my family, we were taught that Italians were the only people you could trust, and preferably Sicilians. My father wouldn't even hire a plumber unless his last name ended in a vowel. You should've heard the screaming when I asked if I could go to the movies with Brian O'Boyle in seventh grade. It was like I'd told them I wanted to shave my head and become a Hare Krishna or something. I always tried to get away from all that bullshit, but it's hard when you've got one of those clingy Italian families. When you don't do what's expected, they scream and cry and pout and tell you you're gonna go to hell unless you straighten up and fly right."

228

Tozzi could relate. He had the same kind of family. When he got married to the Episcopalian chandelier heiress from Rhode Island, his family acted like it was a funeral. His mother pouted the whole day, and his father kept complaining that there was no macaroni. What kind of wedding reception doesn't have a little baked ziti, at least?

The jealousy that gripped Tozzi's gut started to relax, and he turned to face her. Then he noticed the dull shine of the gold wedding band hanging around her neck, and his stomach tightened up again. "Can I ask you something?" He tried to keep the judgmental tone out of his voice.

"What?"

"That ring. Is that a wedding band or what?"

She got quiet. Behind her glasses, her eyes were liquid under the streetlights. Tozzi wasn't sure if she was crying.

"Never mind," he said. "It's none of my business. I'm sorry. Forget about it."

She let out a deep sigh. "It's Margie's."

"Margie?"

"Yeah, Margie. Bells's wife."

Tozzi remembered the compacted car in the lot behind the Belfry. "How'd you end up with her ring?"

She was quiet for a while. "Margie and I were best friends. Ever since fifth grade." She fingered the ring, her eyes lowered.

She hadn't really answered the question, but Tozzi wasn't going to press her. He could see that this was a sensitive subject. If she wanted to talk about it, she would. "I take it you just found out that Margie died the way she did."

She nodded. "Yeah . . . sort of. When she first disappeared at the end of the summer, I knew right away Bells had done something to her. I mean, I didn't *know* know, but I knew in my heart."

"How?"

The truck's engine suddenly rumbled to life, and every other tractor truck in line followed suit. They were about to get rolling. Tozzi watched her face, eager for her to continue. Bells was a suspect in several murders, but they didn't have enough evidence on any one of them to justify charging him. The FBI didn't know anything about his wife.

Gina shrugged, rubbing the ring between her fingers. "Margie and Bells had been having problems."

Tozzi waited to see if she'd explain, but she didn't. "Serious problems?"

"Yeah. Serious to them. Margie couldn't get pregnant."

Tozzi nodded. "It happens."

Gina shook her head. "You don't understand. It happens to other people, not to Bells. He wanted kids. Badly."

"They couldn't adopt?"

"Bells? Never. They had to be *his* kids, *his* flesh and blood."

"I figured." Tozzi sort of felt the same way about adoption.

The truck started to roll. The caravan was heading for New York. Tozzi turned his watch toward the streetlights. It was just after midnight.

Gina had gotten quiet again. "So what happened with Bells and Margie?"

"Well, Bells's solution to their problem was more sex. Just increase the odds. But Margie told me it was horrible. Every morning and every night, like a chore. She said she felt like a hooker—wham, bam, thank you, ma'am. She wanted to go see a doctor, find out why she couldn't get pregnant, but Bells didn't want to hear about it. See, she'd already made the big mistake of suggesting that maybe it was his sperm that was defective, not her equipment. After that, he started coming home with all kinds of teas and vitamins, all this New Age crap. Half of it made her sick to her stomach. She told me she felt like Mia Farrow in *Rosemary's Baby*. She said she expected him to walk in the door some night with a witch doctor. Crazy."

Tozzi just listened, but this reminded him of some of the people in his aikido class. A few of them were big believers in alternative medicines. He looked back toward Hoboken. Testing was over by now. He'd missed his black-belt test again. He'd forgotten all about that for a while. Damn.

Gina continued the story. "Margie was a real mess. She called me every day at work, crying and complaining. Finally I told her. I said we're going to a doctor. To hell with Bells. She said no, she couldn't, Bells would kill her, but I went ahead and found this guy up in Hackensack anyway, a fertility specialist. He checked her out and said yeah, it was her who had the problem. Something about her eggs not coming down the right way, I don't know. When we came out of his office, I thought Margie was gonna walk out into traffic. She was bawling her eyes out like a little kid. She said she was gonna kill herself. I didn't realize how much *she* really wanted to have a kid, too. I thought it was just Bells, but it wasn't just him. She was all nuts about it, too."

"So what happened?"

Gina shrugged and looked him in the eye. "I did something real stupid."

"What?"

"I promised her she'd have a baby, no matter what. I told her I'd help her."

Tozzi's pulse picked up. "You mean, you—? Artificial insemination? Bells went for that?"

She shook her head no. "Not me. I found Margie a surrogate. A nice Sicilian girl in her twenties, an illegal alien. The girl said she'd do it for twenty grand. But Bells wouldn't go for it. He said it wasn't natural. Margie didn't care, though. She made a deal with the girl on her own. I don't know where she got the money. They were crazy, the two of them. Bells kept insisting that he could get Margie pregnant the normal way, so after he'd fall asleep after they had sex, she'd go into the bathroom and suck out his sperm, then save it in the refrigerator. A couple of times she had the girl waiting outside so she'd get it fresh. Threw it out the window in sandwich Baggies. Can you imagine? Crazy."

Tozzi was only half-listening. This girl from Sicily sounded like a story. Maybe *Gina* was the girl from Sicily. Maybe the real story was that Gina had offered to be her best friend's surrogate. But could Gina really be pregnant with Bells's child? Maybe that was why he'd called her at home, to see how she was doing. Why else would he be so obsessed with her? Tozzi felt sick. "So did it work?"

Gina frowned and shrugged. "I don't think so. Anyway, you can't get pregnant that way. I read all kinds of pregnancy books for Margie. Except she never listened."

But Tozzi was thinking about turkey basters now. Gina would never do something like that, would she? The thought of her putting Bells's sperm up her, even if Bells's dick wasn't attached, made him nauseous.

The truck shuddered as it crawled forward in its lowest gear. The beach-blanket dinos shook like trees. Tozzi lifted his head and saw the caravan of garish floats waiting in line behind them, fifty engines rumbling in unison.

Gina shook her head. "The weird thing about him is that he wants girls. Don't men always want sons? Not Bells. He wants girls. At least three. Isn't that sick?"

Tozzi shrugged. He'd heard that girls were easier to raise and that they gravitated more toward their fathers than their mothers. As in Daddy's girl, he guessed. But what the hell did he know about kids?

The truck slowed down and started to buck as it passed through the toll booths. The prehistoric party animals started to do the Jerk.

"Where do they park these things for the night?" he asked. "Do you know?"

"Somewhere on the Upper West Side. That's where the parade begins."

"Okay. When we get there, we'll flag down a police car and have them take us to the closest precinct so we can get the cuffs off. Okay?"

"Why don't we go to your office?"

"The police'll have the right kind of tools for getting us out of these." He lifted their handcuffed wrists. "We don't have stuff like that down at our office."

"Oh. Okay." Her eyes were moist, her face soft. He tried to remember if she'd looked this nice the afternoon they'd made love at her place. Or was it just a wham, bam, thank you . . .

As they rolled down toward the mouth of the tunnel, he spoke fast, as if they were about to go underwater. "When we get inside the tunnel, breathe through the sleeve of the coat. You know, carbon monoxide."

She shrugged. "Okay. But I thought they pumped air into the tunnels."

"Not enough for me."

The vaulted tile ceiling of the tunnel swallowed them. He breathed into his sport jacket sleeve and watched to make sure that she did the same. Her eyes glimmered behind her glasses, the satiny blue sleeve of his inside-out coat covering the lower half of her face.

Tozzi lay back and looked up at the surfing Tyrannosaurus.

233

The artificial lights inside the tunnel cast evil shadows across the toothy face. With those sunglasses, he looked like Jack Nicholson now. Tozzi frowned and looked at something else. He was trying to stop thinking about turkey basters.

"You take it easy, Mr. Bellavita."

"Yeah, you too, Rick."

The cop saluted with two fingers as he rolled up his window and drove off.

Bells smiled and saluted back. He watched the police cruiser disappear down the street before he turned and started walking up the steep incline of the sidewalk along the viaduct that led out of Hoboken. Officer Rick had been sent out to find "some FBI guy" who'd called in complaining that Bells was after him. Bells had lent Officer Rick's father the money for his sister's wedding last spring, which he was still paying off. When the good officer found Bells at the Macy's warehouse but couldn't find the FBI agent, he decided to give Bells a "Pasadena" and gave him a lift to the edge of town, advising him to make himself scarce for a while. Bells grinned to himself. It always helped to have friends on the force.

When he got to the crest of the viaduct, Bells stopped and stared out at the line of floats waiting to go through the tunnel. Gina and Mikey-boy were on one of these things. He'd seen them trying to sneak out of the warehouse, jumping on the float with the cool dinosaurs. He could've caught up with them, but there were too many people around by then—workers, truck drivers, people out in the street. He couldn't have done anything. But that's okay, he thought. This'll be better.

The last float in line was waiting at the bottom of the hill. There was a guy standing guard down there. Bells stared at him. The guy wasn't big and he wasn't small. Bells kept his arms folded, fingers under his armpits, his breath forming clouds on the cold night, like the headless horseman's horse. He wasn't wearing a coat, but he wished he were. Big Dom's big automatic didn't fit in the pocket of his suit coat, and he didn't like the feel of that big hunk of metal in his belt at the center of his back. He looked down at the guy standing guard and thought about throwing the goddamn thing away. Too friggin' noisy. But then he thought about Buddha and his entourage and decided he'd better hang on to it.

Up ahead, closer to the tunnel entrance, the line of floats was crawling like a fiesta-colored caterpillar, real big but real slow. The last dozen floats hadn't even started to move yet. When the caterpillar got where it was going on the New York side, the head would be asleep before the tail even got started. That's what his old man used to say when they used to come up here to see the floats off when he was a kid. It was a ritual with his father. He never saw a whole lot of his old man back then, basically because his father was a nighttime kind of a guy. But coming to see the floats on the night before Thanksgiving was perfect for him. It was a family thing he could do with his son late at night. Bells always used to look forward to it.

Every year his father would say the same thing about the floats looking like a big friggin' caterpillar. After the first few years, it got to be like a game, Bells waiting for when he'd say it. Bells always figured when he'd have kids, he'd take them here the night before Turkey Day and tell them the same thing. The big friggin' caterpillar with the head asleep and the tail awake. Yup, that's what he'd tell them. His three girls. That's what he wanted. He hadn't given up hope yet. He'd never give up hope.

Three girls. He'd always seen it that way, him with his girls. Like that old Jackie Gleason movie where he's got this daughter, and he spoils her rotten, but the kid's real sharp, doesn't miss a trick. That's why he wanted girls. Girls had it all over boys. Especially if you brought 'em up right.

Bells started walking down the hump of the viaduct toward the last float, Santa's float. A sleigh and eight tiny reindeer. Except these babies weren't tiny. He never cared much for the Santa Claus float when he was a kid. It was always pretty much the same thing every year. But his daughters? He knew they would get a big kick out of Santa because Bells would make sure Santa brought them everything they could ever want. Even ponies, if that's what they wanted.

He could never figure out why men got so nuts about having to have sons. Sure, there's the carrying-on-the-name thing, but if you look at it objectively, boys are real pains in the ass. They're rough, they break things, they have more problems growing up, they're prone to more diseases and defects. Then they just grow up stupid. Like dogs. You show a guy a piece of meat, he goes right for it. No subtlety. By and large, men don't think beyond what's in front of them. That's why he never wanted a crew. Dealing with Stanley was enough. Ten Stanleys would drive him nuts.

The difference between boys and girls was so obvious, he couldn't believe everyone didn't think the way he did. For example, you watch your average guy play pool. He'll never even think about using bank shots or combination shots unless there's absolutely nothing left he can do. With most guys, everything's gotta be direct. Now, girls aren't like that. They're subtle. They're cool. They can learn how to *play* the game. See, winning a game is different from mastering a game, and guys just play to win. Girls don't do that. They want to do things the right way. You bring a girl up right, she can really be something. That's why he wanted girls.

His wife Margie hadn't been brought up right. She was

brought up on the moon. She couldn't have babies, she was useless. Just as well, though. She would've brought 'em up all wrong. They would've tried to do things behind his back. Just like she did.

Now, Gina DeFresco was sharp, but she hadn't been brought up right either. Not really. She was stubborn, like a guy. Hard-headed. She also lived in a dreamland. She wanted people to think she was tough, but she wasn't. Back when they were in school together, she was always reading stuff about the past, drawing these fantasyland pictures of castles and unicorns and shit in her notebooks, wanting to live somewhere else, in some other time, looking for something better, looking for magic. She wasn't brought up right. You make your own magic happen, now, in the present. That's what he was going to teach his girls. He wasn't gonna let them get polluted with all that stupid some-day-my-prince-will-come crap.

Gina was like most girls, though. Always wishing and a-hoping for Prince Charming to come down the pike. Just brought up wrong, that's all there was to it. She was probably in fantasyland right now, thinking she was safe. Just jump on a float and fly away, escape from reality. Dumb, Gina. Very dumb. But that's the way she is. She's looking all over the place for magic when she should've learned how to make her own magic. She's very unrealistic. Still, she isn't totally worthless.

As he walked closer to Santa's float, the guy standing guard finally noticed him and froze where he stood. Bells exhaled a laugh through his nose. See? So obvious. The guy's tense, stiff, instantly belligerent. Typical male. He reminded Bells of Mikey-boy.

Mikey-boy the FBI agent. Mr. Gallant. Prince Charming. In his mind, maybe. Hopelessly predictable. And teamed up with Gina, even worse. She was gonna tell him they could escape on this magic carpet in her mind, the big fuzzy caterpillar, and he was gonna listen to her, the jerk. That was the other problem with guys: they listen to women. Any guy who listens to a broad doesn't see the bank shots, the combinations, the angles. He's too direct. The lady complains—*bang*—he tries to please her. Action, reaction. Call and response. Ninety-nine point nine percent of the people in this world just weren't brought up right. They don't think; they just react. They're no better than snails.

Bells strolled over to Santa's float and checked out the reindeer. The guy standing guard had that high-testosterone look, the bug-eyed frown—it's mine, and you can't have it. The guy followed Bells around the side of the float as Bells gazed up at the sleigh-tower where Santa would be riding tomorrow.

When Bells moved closer and touched the shredded white paper that was supposed to be snow, the guy barked: "Hey! Whatta'ya doin' over there?"

Bells grinned. "I'm dreaming of a white Christmas."

"Well, go dream someplace else."

Bells left his hand on the paper snow for a moment, then put it in his pocket. He didn't move away from the float, though. Just looked at the guy as the guy glared at him.

"Is there something you want, pal?"

Bells shrugged and shook his head.

"Then move away from the float . . . please."

Bells smiled. The *please* told him a lot. He had the guy thinking twice about him. Good.

The truck's engine rumbled, and the paper snow shivered. Bells waited.

The guy took a step closer. "Hey, mister, I don't want any trouble here."

That meant he did, but he didn't. He wanted trouble only if he knew for certain that he could kick the intruder's ass. Bells stroked the paper snow and looked at him, waiting for him to make up his mind.

"Hey, pal, I'm not playing games here. You understand what I'm saying?" He moved in a little closer, testing the distance to see if Bells would react. A typical predator, a coward with big teeth. Won't attack until he's sure there won't be any retaliation.

Bells just looked at him, dragging his fingers across the paper shreds.

"Get your hand off that. You're gonna damage the float."

Bells smiled when he heard the guy say "damage." Official language. High-test males love jargon. It sets them apart, makes them special. Just like cops.

"I'm telling you for the last time, pal. Get away from the float."

Bells did nothing. The truck engine revved, and the float started to move. Bells closed his fist on a handful of paper snow and let the movement of the float uproot it. He looked at it in his hand, then let it go. White shreds floated to his feet, a few strands sticking to his pants.

The guy charged like a bull. Bells had caused "damage," so now the man had a reason to act, reasonable cause. Guys always need defensible reasons. He rushed up to Bells and reached for his lapel. "Hey! I told you—"

Bells brushed the guy's hand aside and in one fluid motion spun the poor bastard around and pulled the guy's back to his chest.

"Hey! Whatta'ya doin'?"

Bells had his wrists crossed on the guy's chest, gripping both of *his* lapels. Bells pulled, using the guy's jacket collar to cut off the blood supply passing through the large arteries along the sides of his neck. Bells could never remember the right name for those arteries. A Green Beret he knew a long time ago told him, but he forgot. The Green Beret showed him this move, told him that you could make a person black out in ten seconds doing this, but that you had to be careful because one person in a hundred will die when you do this to them. He even let Bells try it on him, telling Bells not to worry, he wasn't one of those people because he'd had it done to him plenty of times before. Bells never found out if that was true or not because he shot the jerk through the eye before he came to. He owed Buddha money, and there was no way he could ever pay up. He might have been a Green Beret in the army, but he was a bum out on the street. He should've stayed in the army.

Bells held on tight, waiting for the guard to stop struggling. It wasn't long before the guy slumped to the pavement, out cold. As the big tires of the flatbed rolled past his motionless body, Bells wondered if he was dead, if he was one of those one-in-a-hundred people. Bells looked down at his blunt bulb-nosed face and decided that this dweeb couldn't be one in a hundred in anything.

He turned and walked toward the float as it tried to crawl away from him. When he caught up with it, he put his palms on the paper snow and vaulted on board, then went to the steps of the sleigh-tower and climbed up. Sitting in Ole Saint Nick's seat, he looked out at the big friggin' caterpillar as it slithered into the tunnel. Gina DeFresco was somewhere on board with Prince Mikey-boy and the cool-ass dinosaurs. As soon as they got to Manhattan, they'd probably flag down a cab or something, and Bells would do the same, follow them wherever they went. It would all work out fine. New York was full of dark little nooks and crannies where you could off someone quick and just walk away from it, no problem.

Except this wasn't gonna be a single hit. It was gonna be a combination shot.

TWENTY-ONE

11:54 P.M.

Gibbons held his chest and took shallow breaths. He was having chest pains—not bad ones, but bad enough. They weren't the same pains he'd been feeling all day. These were new pains. He tried not to think about them. He had enough to worry about.

He was sitting on the black-leather couch in Bells's grubby loft, opposite the green-leather couch where Buddha was sitting with a big plastic bag full of ice on his head. The corners of the bag drooped over his ears, and now the little shit looked even more like Napoleon. Everybody was standing around waiting for His Highness to make a declaration, but the little bastard was still smarting from the bop over the head Bells had given him with the toilet-tank cover, and he hadn't said a word since it happened.

Gibbons looked over at Lorraine on the other end of the couch. He was getting edgy. It was a bad situation. The longer Buddha and his gorillas kept them there, the more likely they'd end up killing them. True, Gibbons was the law, but he and Lorraine had heard too much. At the very least, these guys were facing a kidnapping charge that could send them away for a good long stretch. Gibbons knew they weren't gonna let that

241

happen if they could help it, and Buddha Stanzione wasn't known for his charitable nature.

The loft was as solemn as a church as they all waited for the little emperor to show some signs of life, and that just aggravated Gibbons more than he already was. He wanted to know what the hell happened to the backups he'd called for hours ago. He wanted to know what the hell happened to Tozzi. He wanted these bastards to at least let Lorraine go. But he wasn't getting what he wanted, and he was ready to strangle someone. Except that his chest hurt so bad, he didn't think he had the strength.

Then something occurred to him that drained the blood from his face. What if the chest pains weren't from the bullet shots he'd taken? What if he was having a heart attack? Jesus. He couldn't have a heart attack now. He couldn't leave Lorraine alone with these animals. No, it couldn't be. It wasn't a heart attack, he kept telling himself. If he croaked, they'd kill her for sure.

Gibbons started sweating. He couldn't wait around for the emperor anymore. He might not have the time. "Hey, Buddha," he said, breaking the silence, "wake up over there. You looking for sympathy or what?"

Stanley and the four double-knit gorillas glared at him, but Gibbons didn't give a shit. He was sick of waiting around.

"Wake up, Stanzione, will ya? We supposed to sit around here all night? Big Dom's gonna start stinking up the bathroom pretty soon. You guys smell bad enough. I don't wanna have to smell him, too."

Buddha opened his eyes and rolled them toward the bathroom. He'd forgotten about the dead gorilla in the can.

Gibbons laughed despite the pain. "Yeah, let's hang around for a while. Maybe the cops'll come by, and you can tell them how Big Dom got that way."

Buddha looked at Stanley. "Shut him up." The little emperor shut his eyes again.

"You heard him, Gibbons." Stanley was as solemn as an altar boy.

"Tell him to go fuck himself."

Stanley's eyes bulged. "I'm warning you, Gib."

"Go tell your old lady."

Lorraine took his hand and squeezed it. She was warning him to behave. She was being as solemn as the rest of them.

Gibbons rubbed his chest and felt his pounding heart. His shirt was soaked through with sweat under his jacket. He kept telling himself it wasn't a heart attack. It could be a combination of things: no lunch and no dinner; lack of sleep; the effects of the booze and the pain-killers had finally worn off; maybe the two didn't mix and he was reacting to that. It could be anything. But it wasn't a heart attack. It couldn't be. Still he was anxious to get things going, to do something to save Lorraine before he . . . couldn't.

He turned to Freshy, who was pacing the floor around the bunched-up plastic tarp. "What'sa matter, Freshy? Nothing to say? You used to have a big mouth. Why don't you say something?"

Freshy just glared at him from under his brows and continued his pacing.

"C'mon, Fresh. Speak up. What're you, a wuss now?"

Another quick glare.

Buddha raised his voice. "I said, shut him up."

Stanley stepped toward Gibbons, pulling his gun out of his belt. He held it in his palm and raised it over his head, about to bash Gibbons over the head with it.

Gibbons was ready to duck the blow—or at least try to—when Lorraine suddenly jumped up and got between them.

243

"Stop!" she screamed.

"Sit down!" Stanley shoved her out of his way.

"No!" She got in his face again.

Gibbons started to get up off the couch, but the pain in his chest wouldn't let him move. He felt like his chest was a lemon being squeezed. He wanted to rip Stanley's head off, but he couldn't move. One of the gorillas came around the couch and grabbed his shoulder to keep him down. Gibbons cursed and threw an elbow into the couch. It just made the pain worse, and he had to hold his breath to keep himself together.

Stanley raised the gun again, but Lorraine hung on to his arm.

The sweat was pouring off Gibbons, and the gorilla had him by the shoulders. He had to do something. For Lorraine. To save her.

"Wait!" He tried to breathe evenly, but he sounded like a balloon with a slow leak. "Whatta'ya bothering with me for?" He pointed at Freshy. "*He's* the one you should be pissed off at. He's been working for us, ratting on you guys. How do you think Tozzi got introduced to you people?"

All heads turned toward Freshy, who started blinking out of control. "Wha-wha-whatta'ya talkin' about? He's crazy, Mr. Stanzione. That ain't true. No how, no way. He's crazy."

The icebag rattled on Buddha's head. "Stanley," he said, "how did Bells meet this FBI guy Tozzi?"

Stanley was staring holes into Freshy. "Through him. Freshy told Bells not to worry, the guy was okay."

"No, no, no. You don't understand, Mr. Stanzione."

Stanley had his finger on the trigger, muzzle leveled on Freshy. The four gorillas had their pieces out, too. Buddha only had to give the word. Freshy's mouth was moving, but nothing was coming out. He seemed to be backstepping in place, like a mime with the shakes.

Buddha's icebag rattled again and broke the tension. The little emperor was not happy. "So?" he said.

"You don't understand, Mr. Stanzione. You don't understand. Lemme explain, lemme explain."

"So explain." The ice cubes shifted and rattled very softly, like termites about to bring a house down.

Freshy gulped and blinked a few more times before he started. "All right, here's the deal. No bullshit, okay? Yes, it's true. I was working with these guys . . . the, the FBI guys."

Stanley and the gorillas got restless real fast. They wanted the go-ahead from Buddha to blow his brains out.

"But, listen, listen." Freshy was holding up his index fingers, head cocked to the side. "I wasn't doing it to help them. No fucking way, I swear to God. I was stringing them along, telling Bells everything I found out from them. Everything. I swear to Christ on my mother's eyes. I'm not lying, I swear."

Gibbons exploded. "Bullshit! You were working for us."

Stanley's gaze bounced back and forth from Freshy to Gibbons and back to Freshy. His face looked like a fist. "If you're lyin' to us, you little bastard—"

Freshy backed away from him. "No, Stanley, no. I'm telling you the truth. I told Bells everything I knew. I was loyal to him, man. Absolutely. The FBI didn't know what I was really doin'. They thought I was playing straight with them. That's what Bells told me to do. I swear."

Gibbons watched Freshy doing his little tap dance, but it didn't seem to be working. Stanley and the gorillas weren't buying his story, and for the moment Buddha was ominously noncommittal. Gibbons was glad. The heat was on Freshy now and off them. He had no problem giving up Freshy for the slaughter.

The little shit had turned on Gibbons and helped Stanley take him and Lorraine hostage. And if he was telling the truth and really had double-crossed the Bureau, he deserved to be thrown to the lions.

Freshy still had his index fingers up. He was blinking like a strobe light. "You think you're smart, Gib. I know what you're trying to do here. Well, I got some news for you. For all of youse."

Gibbons winced and bared his teeth. "Spare us the bullshit, Freshy. Nobody wants to hear it."

"Oh, no? Well, lemme tell you something. That agent that got shot up on the Turnpike this morning? Paterson?"

"Petersen."

"Petersen, Petersen, right. Bells did do it. I know it for a fact."

Stanley barked. "Bull-*shit.*"

"No, Stanley, no, not bullshit. Before the meeting he had last night with Mr. Stanzione downstairs in the bar, were you with Bells? Were you?"

Stanley didn't answer right away. He looked at Buddha. "I was home."

Buddha's ice cubes rattled.

Stanley glared at Freshy. "But so what? What does that prove?"

"C'mon, Stanley, get real. Bells had an appointment with that guy Petersen. The guy was bringing money he wanted Bells to shy for him. And what did Bells always say? You want free money, find some jerkoff shy who'll give you a loan and then whack him. Free money. I heard him say it a hundred times. You guys never heard him say that?" Freshy looked to the gorillas for corroboration.

Buddha held on to his icebag and looked up at the gorillas. "Did you?"

The polyester primates nodded in unison.

"See what I'm saying here? I thought I was doing the right thing, telling Bells everything I found out from the FBI so we could keep a step ahead of them. How the fuck was I supposed to know he was gonna turn around and whack a fed? I didn't know that. I swear to—"

BA-BOOM!

The locked stairwell door flew open and crashed against the brick wall behind.

"Freeze! FBI! You're under arrest! Drop your weapons!" Four agents rushed in, guns drawn, high-stepping over their battering ram on the threshold. Gibbons recognized two of them, young guys from the Newark office whose names he couldn't remember. The first one in had wavy red hair and reminded Gibbons of cub reporter Jimmy Olson from the *Superman* comics. He nodded at Gibbons in recognition but kept his eyes on the bad guys. Gibbons clutched his chest and smiled with his teeth, wanting to cheer, even though the bastards should've been here hours ago.

Then suddenly he heard Lorraine's squeal behind him. "Gibbons!"

Freshy had his arm crooked around Lorraine's neck, bending her backward. Excalibur was in his other hand, the barrel buried in Lorraine's scalp.

Once again Gibbons reached for the gun he didn't have, even though he was looking right at it. Son of a—

Pain seared through his chest. He held his breath, hoping it would pass, but it didn't. He kept telling himself it wasn't a heart attack, it wasn't a heart attack, but the words kept bouncing back at him like a racquetball: It *was* a heart attack, it *was* a heart attack. He remembered hearing guys who'd had cardiacs say that the pain was like a truck parked on your chest. Gibbons wasn't sure if his pain felt exactly like that, but he had nothing to compare it to. But the more he thought about it, the more it did feel like a heavy weight, and the more he tried to deny it. It wasn't like it was an eighteen-wheeler parked on his chest. More like a pickup truck, he thought, a little pickup, that's all.

He blinked and squinted up at Lorraine with Excalibur to her head. He sniffed in a sharp breath. "Let her go, Freshy. Let her go *now*." He wanted to yell it, but he could barely get it out.

Jimmy Olson heard Gibbons, and he repeated the order. "Let the woman go."

Freshy ignored them both.

Stanley and the gorillas were ignoring the agents, too. The greaseballs had pulled their guns as soon as the agents broke down the door, and now they were holding them on the squeaky-clean street agents from Newark. Freshy had Lorraine, and Gibbons and Buddha were sitting on opposite couches, just staring at each other. It was a friggin' Mexican standoff. Gibbons couldn't believe it. This never happened in real life. Not like this. But if he dropped dead, the wiseguys would have the clear advantage. That's why he couldn't croak now. Not until he knew Lorraine was safe. He sniffed in another short breath and kept his eye on that little shitass Freshy.

"Drop your weapons. Now!" Jimmy Olson was very stern.

"Drop your own fucking weapons," Stanley growled.

Young Olson looked grim, and so did his buddies. The FBI philosophy is to always have overwhelming manpower and firepower when you go into a situation like this. So much for philosophy.

The room fell silent all of a sudden. You could almost feel everyone thinking hard, trying to figure out what he could do to break the stalemate. Gibbons's hand was still on his chest, palm over his heart. He was counting the beats, hoping they were regular beats, though he wasn't sure he knew what regular was. He watched Lorraine breathing fast under Freshy's arm around her neck. The minute stretched. Nobody from either side was coming up with any brilliant moves, and the pickup truck was still parked on his chest.

The icebag rattled.

"So?" Buddha said.

That's all he said.

Gibbons stared at him, fighting to hide his discomfort. "Yeah? So what?"

That was all he could say without giving himself away.

They just stared at each other.

After another long minute, Jimmy Olson coughed. "Ah, Agent Gibbons?"

Gibbons rolled his eyes toward him.

"You're the senior agent here. Perhaps you should handle the negotiations."

Gibbons frowned. Thanks a lot. No wonder Perry White was always so pissed off at Jimmy Olson. Gibbons closed his eyes and forced himself to breathe through his nose until he thought the pain let up a little.

He opened his eyes and looked at Buddha. "Let's make this simple, okay? You let my wife go, we'll leave. Okay?"

The four freshman from Newark bristled, but they kept their mouths shut. Gibbons knew these young guys were mentally tallying up the charges they could make against these mooks. And they didn't even know about the stiff in the john yet. But Gibbons didn't give a shit about making cases against these zeroes. All he wanted was his wife back, unharmed. Before he died.

He stared hard at Buddha. "So? Say something."

The little emperor took the icebag off his head and felt the goose egg. He looked at Gibbons. "Sounds okay to me." He looked up at Stanley then and nodded with his head toward Freshy.

Stanley interpreted the gesture. "Let her go, Fresh."

"No, no, wait." Freshy shuffled his feet, and his burst of jitters joggled Lorraine like a marionette. "Listen, listen."

Stanley shook his head. "No, *you* listen. Mr. Stanzione says to let her go. That means let her go." The Tazmanian Devil was working his jaws.

So was Gibbons. Gun or no gun, chest pains or no chest pains, he was ready to pounce on the little shit.

Freshy backed up, hauling Lorraine back with him. "Just listen to me, listen to me. Okay? You still think I'm a rat, that's what you're thinking. But you're wrong. I'm not. I did the right thing. At least, I thought I was doing the right thing. I swear. Why don't you gimme a break here?"

"Let her go." Buddha spoke to him directly now, and Freshy reacted as if it were a ghost talking to him.

"No. No. Listen to me, Mr. Stanzione. Please." Freshy was shitting bricks. "Bells fucked you over, right? He gave you counterfeit money, right? Okay, so let me take care of him for you."

"You?" Stanley couldn't believe this twerp would even suggest that he could take on Bells.

Gibbons couldn't believe it either, but this made him nervous. If Freshy seriously thought he could go *mano a mano* with Bells, he'd lost it, which wouldn't have bothered him at all, except for the fact that he was holding Excalibur to Lorraine's head. The pickup truck was still on his chest. Tears came to his eyes, but it wasn't because of the pain. The thought of him sitting here helpless when Lorraine could die at any moment from a slug fired from his faithful revolver totally overwhelmed him. . . .

But only for a few seconds. He opened his eyes, set his jaw, and sniffed in as deep a breath as he could stand. Personal emotions never help in situations like this.

"How do you think you're gonna get Bells?" Gibbons wasn't mocking Freshy, just putting it to him hard, trying to make him think straight and be rational.

Freshy appealed to Buddha. "I know how I can do it. I really do. If Bells is with Tozzi, I can find him."

"How?" Buddha's face turned sour.

"The transmitter thing Tozzi's wearing. I can track 'em in the FBI van, find out where they are, sneak up on Bells, and—"

"No one sneaks up on Bells." Stanley was absolutely certain about that.

"Oh, no, no, no, I will, I will. Don't worry about that, Stanley. I'll get up right behind him, real quiet, and I'll stick this gun right in the back of his head, and I won't wait. No way. I'll do it fast. *Ba-da-boom.* I'll blow him away. Clean. One shot. Right through the brain. Before he can do anything."

Gibbons's chest felt squeezed again. All of a sudden the pickup truck had a cow in the back.

Lorraine's eyes were wild. Did she suddenly notice that Gibbons was in distress? Oh, Jesus, he hoped not. He didn't want her to worry.

Freshy was smiling like a maniac, sweat pouring off his face. "I wanna make my bones, Mr. Stanzione. I wanna get made some day. Let me make my bones now. I'll do this for you, Mr. Stanzione. I will. I'll get Bells for you. Then someday when—I mean *if* the time comes, I'll be all set because I already killed for you."

A sour Edward G. Robinson expression was frozen on Buddha's face. He looked up at Stanley. "What the hell's he talking about?"

Stanley raised his eyebrows and shrugged. "He's a wackarino, Mr. Stanzione. What can I tell you?"

"Drop your weapons," Jimmy Olson said again, but nobody paid any attention. It was only to convince himself that he was doing something useful.

"Gibbons?" Lorraine knew something was wrong with him, but Freshy yanked her back and shut her up.

"Just give me this one chance, Mr. Stanzione. That's all I want. Just let me try. I know I can find him with that equipment that's in the van. Just let me try."

Buddha put the icebag back on his head and closed his eyes. "You're giving me a headache."

"Please, Mr. Stanzione, please. I can get outta here. If I take her with me, I can do it. These guys won't shoot as long as I got Mrs. Gibbons. You see what I'm saying? I got a hostage. I'm the only one who can get out. Just let me *try*."

Buddha looked around the room, the ice cubes rattling gently on his head. Freshy was right. It was an even standoff; everybody was covered. Except he had the hostage.

Gibbons swallowed on a dry throat.

Buddha shrugged. "Go 'head, do what you want." He didn't seem to care. He looked at Gibbons and the young agents. "I can't stop you."

The capo was clever. He wasn't gonna incriminate himself in front of five FBI agents. Freshy might get lucky and actually pull it off.

Freshy's face was underbelly white. "You serious, Mr. Stanzione? Really? I can do it?"

"I said you can do what you want, kid. Nothing I can do to stop you."

Freshy grinned. "Okay, okay. Right. I understand. I got it."

He started backing toward the elevator, dragging Lorraine with him.

Lorraine reached out. "Gibbons?"

Gibbons was fuming. He was ready to take off his shoe and hurl it at the little jerk, do anything to keep him from leaving with his wife. He was just about to tell Jimmy Olson to shoot the bastard when Freshy suddenly stopped.

"Hey, Gib," Freshy said.

"Hey, what?"

"C'mon, get up."

"What?"

"C'mon. You're driving."

"What're you, funny?"

"No. I said you're driving. Now get up." He jammed Excalibur into Lorraine's head to make his point. All of a sudden the little shit had balls.

The ice cubes rattled. Buddha was snickering.

Gibbons gritted his teeth, held his breath, and bore down on the pain in his chest. Another cow just got in the back of the pickup.

TWENTY-TWO

12:39 A.M.

Tozzi and Gina separated to get by a garbage can left in the middle of the sidewalk. "Bread and butter," Tozzi said as they kept walking.

Gina peered at him over the turned-up collar of the inside-out coat, which she held closed under her glasses, covering her face.

Tozzi immediately felt stupid for having said that. He was just trying to get her to talk to him.

"So where is it?" she said. "I thought you said it was up here."

Tozzi pressed his lips together and slowed down. He and Gina were on foot on Seventy-eighth Street on the Upper West Side, in the middle of the block between Amsterdam Avenue and Columbus Avenue. When their float had stopped on Eleventh Avenue over by the river, they'd hailed a cab, and Tozzi told the cabbie to take them to this block because he was sure the Twentieth Precinct was here. But the cabbie wouldn't take them down the block because Columbus on the other end was jammed with people out to see the balloons being blown up for the parade, he said, and he didn't want to get caught in traffic. Gina started to argue with the guy, told him he could back up on the one-way street after he dropped them off, but the cabbie refused. Tozzi didn't want to waste any more time arguing, so they just got out and walked. But now he just couldn't figure it out. He was almost positive the Two-Oh was on this block. They must've moved it.

He frowned up at all the brownstones along the street. "I could've sworn it was here. Damn. C'mon, we'll find a cop car."

He started toward Columbus, and she followed without any argument, though he kept sneaking looks at her, wondering why she wasn't giving him any shit about his mistake. He couldn't figure her out. She'd given him shit about everything else today. What was she, tired?

Up ahead at the end of the block, Tozzi could see the crowds of midnight strollers milling around the Museum of Natural History—parents with little kids, trendy young couples, packs of teenagers—all here to see the inflating of the giant balloons. He could make out Woody Woodpecker and Underdog beginning to take shape. The half-inflated balloons were like nightmare behemoths springing up from the ground. The whole scene was like Mardi Gras—but New York style.

They picked up their pace, both of them eager to find some policemen. Though they hadn't said much since their float had taken them through the tunnel, they were both thinking about Bells, worried that the cops in Hoboken hadn't stopped him, that he might show up again like the boogie man. Tozzi stared at the shadowy figures walking briskly on the other side of the street, imagining that one of them could be Bells. He tried to be rational about it, though, telling himself that the chances of Bells finding them here in the middle of Manhattan were pretty slim. But then again, Bells wasn't your average bad guy. He was more than just weird.

He glanced sideways at Gina. She looked like an Arab woman with her face buried in that coat. He just couldn't figure her out.

You would've thought that making love would've made her a little chummier with him, but instead she'd sunken into herself, become quiet and distant, lost in her own thoughts. What was the phrase they used these days? Emotionally unavailable? He wondered what she was thinking about. He wondered about this alleged "Sicilian girl." Could Gina really be pregnant? But who'd the hell want to have Bells's kid? Except maybe she wanted to have a baby. Maybe she wanted Bells's. *"Gina, it's me. Gimme a call."* Tozzi tried not to think about it. Getting to a police station and getting the handcuffs off—that's what he should be focusing on.

But it was hard to focus when all he could think about was that message on her answering machine, and what would've happened if they hadn't escaped from the Belfry, and the fact that he was freezing his ass off. His handcuffed hand was pink and chapped. Gina kept hers tucked up the long sleeve of the coat, but his fist was hanging out like a frozen Cornish hen. He wished she'd at least hold his hand—just for a little warmth. But even that kind of connection was more than he could hope for with her.

The dark brownstone stoops along Seventy-eighth made Tozzi nervous, and it annoyed him that his heartbeat was keeping up with their marching footsteps. It was stupid to worry about Bells now. He was probably long gone, heading for the hills to escape the manhunt. But still, Tozzi was edgy. So much for maintaining aikido principles. Maybe it was good that he had missed his black-belt test tonight. He wasn't ready. You're supposed to be able to keep calm and centered, at least to some extent, when you're a black belt. Tozzi sure as hell didn't feel centered now.

Logically he knew that Bells wasn't going to pop out from behind the garbage cans, but of course Bells wasn't the only dangerous nutcase in the New York metropolitan area. Any old mugger, rapist, crack addict, chain snatcher, demented street person, or plain ole asshole with a chip on his shoulder could show up to give them a hard time, and he still felt vulnerable handcuffed to Gina. If he ended up in a situation where he had to confront an attacker, there wasn't a whole lot he could do to defend himself that wouldn't put Gina in danger. Of course the way he was feeling right now, he wasn't so sure he wanted to defend her. He felt that she was excluding him. After all they'd been through today, why wasn't she leveling with him about her relationship with Bells? Why did he feel that she was holding something back from him?

Margie's wedding ring was something else that bothered him. How did Gina get it, and why did she wear it around her neck? Was it supposed to be like wearing a cross to ward off the vampire? Apparently it didn't work with Bells. It was pretty ghoulish if you asked Tozzi. What the hell was it supposed to mean? Maybe Gina was into headgames even more than Bells was. Maybe she was playing with Bells's head. Maybe Gina wasn't so innocent. Maybe Bells got fed up with her messing with his head, messing with his *wife's* head. Maybe Gina was the one Bells really had it in for, not him. Maybe he was just a side dish for Bells. Maybe it was Gina who was the meat.

He watched her glasses glinting under the streetlights as they walked. *"Gina, it's me. Gimme a call."*

Tozzi had made love to her twice, and for a while today he'd thought he understood where she was coming from. But he didn't understand shit. If anything, he understood less than he did before.

He wondered if Bells felt the same way about her, if he was just as confused and aggravated by her. He wondered if Bells understood her any better than he did.

He wondered how many times Bells had been to bed with her.

Then his face got hot as he became angry with himself for even thinking this. He was a born paranoid, a conspiracy theorist before they even had a name for people like him. He was always looking for the shady side, for the ulterior motives. It was probably what made him a good organized-crime agent, but it was also what kept him from ever having had a single decent long-standing relationship with a woman in his entire life. He didn't know how to trust people. Gibbons was the only one he could really trust. And now Gibbons was gone. Who was he gonna trust now?

Tozzi sighed on the cold air, and his despair flew off into the night, like a bird heading south. Couldn't worry about all that now, he thought. There were more immediate problems to take care of. He curled his wrist around the cold steel handcuff. Unfortunately his life couldn't be fixed with a hacksaw.

As they approached the end of the block, Tozzi breathed a little easier. Columbus Avenue was brighter and full of people. They'd be able to find a cop there. He looked at her again, searching her face for a clue, but the streetlights glanced off her glasses, and he couldn't see her eyes. It didn't matter. He couldn't read her even when he could see her. He scanned the area around the back end of the museum, looking for a cop car in the roving mass of people.

They were almost at the corner of Seventy-eighth and Columbus when suddenly she stopped walking, and his arm was jerked again. She nodded at something down on the ground, her face still covered. A homeless person wrapped in plastic bags and newspapers was asleep in the shadows of a stoop, the legs sticking out in the streetlight. Tozzi's heart started to pound. What? Did she think it was Bells? Immediately he was annoyed with himself for being so paranoid. It was a homeless person. It wasn't Bells. How the hell could it be Bells?

"How's it going, Mikey-boy?"

Tozzi jumped when he heard the voice right behind him. He turned his head to see Bells standing there, grinning in his face. He was holding a gun down low, aimed at Tozzi's back. Tozzi's heart was in his throat.

Gina's eyeglasses flashed. She didn't say a word.

"Shouldn't leave without saying good-bye to the host, Mikey-boy. It's not polite."

Tozzi turned around all the way to face him, tugging on the cuffs and forcing Gina to do the same. Bells backed up a half-step, keeping the gun leveled on Tozzi's midsection. Tozzi forced himself to stare at the son of a bitch's laughing eyes.

Tozzi could not believe this. "How?"

Bells shrugged. "Must be magic."

Tozzi was speechless.

But Bells was enjoying himself. "So whatta'ya say we all go back to my place and carve up some turkeys? How's that sound, Gina?"

She snarled from behind the collar of the coat. "Why don't you do it right here? With all these people around."

Bells rolled his eyes toward the edge of the crowd out on Columbus twenty feet away, then he grinned at her. "They're not that close. We have enough privacy here. I could do it here if that's what you want, Gina. Whatta'ya think, Mikey? Think I could get away with it?"

Tozzi didn't answer. He was unarmed, handcuffed to Gina, dead tired, on a shadowy side street—of course Bells could get away with it.

"I'll bet you fi' dollars I can shoot the both of you and be halfway back to Jersey before anyone even notices."

Tozzi started to nod to himself, thinking Bells was absolutely right. He could do it. Then all of a sudden Tozzi was very calm. He knew Bells could kill him if he wanted to, and under the circumstances there was nothing Tozzi could do about it. And so he really didn't give a shit. He wasn't afraid anymore.

"C'mon, Mikey. Bet me. It's only fi' dollars." Bells inched forward, the gun still leveled on Tozzi.

Gina let go of the collar. "For God's sake—"

Bells glared at her. "I'm not talking to you. I'm talking to Mikey-boy." The grin wrapped around his face like a boa constrictor. "So what's it gonna be, Mikey-boy? You gonna take me up on it?"

"You know, Bells, I really don't care what you do. It's all in your hands now. I can't stop you. There's not a thing I could do." Tozzi was centered. His pulse was even.

Bells frowned. "Whatta'ya mean, it's all up to me?"

"It is. You do whatever you gotta do, Bells. It's outta my hands."

The shadows etched deep lines around Bells's mouth as the wiseass grin gave way to a scowl. Tozzi had taken the joy out of it for him. There was no fun in killing if the victim wasn't scared. Tozzi had turned the situation around and thrown it back in Bells's face. It was pure aikido.

Bells's face transformed again, the snake grin slithering back. "What is this, Mikey, some kind of reverse-psychology thing? Do you really think you can psyche *me* out? Think again, my friend."

Tozzi just shrugged. He looked bored.

The grin on Bells's face drooped. So did the gun in his hand.

Tozzi didn't hesitate. He swatted Bells's hand, and the gun clattered to the sidewalk. Tozzi kicked it into the shadows under the stoop where the homeless person was sleeping. A metallic clank rang out as the gun hit a garbage can.

Bells turned toward the noise, and in that second Tozzi went to knee him in the groin. But Gina beat him to it, kicking him in the nuts with her foot. Tozzi's knee caught him in the face as he doubled over with pain from Gina's blow.

"Bread and butter," Gina yelled, and Tozzi knew exactly what she was thinking.

They stepped forward, one on either side of Bells, and hooked their handcuffed wrists under his chin, yanking him up and over, slamming him down on his back on the concrete sidewalk. Bells groaned, curling up on his side and clutching the back of his head.

Tozzi smirked at her. "Why couldn't you cooperate like that before?"

"Why couldn't you?"

"Never mind. Let's find the gun."

They started for the shadows, but Bells suddenly shouted "Stop!" and Tozzi felt something slash his calf. He high-stepped out of the way and saw Bells on the ground with his pantleg rolled up, a shimmering blade in his hand. "Back off," he ordered, and slashed a wide circle around himself, forcing them to get away from him. He scooted on his butt into the shadows under the stoop, feeling with his free hand for the gun.

Gina tugged on Tozzi's arm, ready to bolt. Tozzi felt his leg. There was no pain, but his pants were sliced, and he could feel the wetness of blood.

"C'mon!" Gina urged. "Before he gets the gun."

Bells was reaching into the shadows around the sleeping legs when suddenly a zombie face sprang out of the dark. "It's mine!" she declared in a sandpaper shriek. The woman was a fire-eyed, wool-capped, Thorazine-deprived demento used to defending her space.

Bells brandished the knife in her face. "Move, bitch."

She pointed the gun in his face. "You move!"

Bells backed off on all fours like a retreating spider. He looked up at Tozzi and Gina, then glanced at the woman. He stared Tozzi in the eye and grinned, holding the knife pointed up. It glinted like a candle. "So who needs a gun?" Slowly he started to haul himself to his feet, wincing with pain.

"Come on!" Gina yanked on the handcuffs.

But Tozzi was unmovable. His first instinct was take Bells on, confident that he could handle a knife attack—then he remembered that he and Gina were Siamese twins. He'd never done aikido for two, and it was no time to experiment.

Reluctantly he started to backstep toward the crowd on Columbus, led by Gina's tugging, but he didn't like this. Bells was crazy, and he was out for blood. There were people all over the place. No telling what Bells would do. They couldn't just run away. Bells liked to take hostages, and there were plenty to choose from in this crowd. All Tozzi could imagine was Bells snatching some little kid, a toddler, a baby from its stroller, and holding the knife to the kid's throat. He and Gina couldn't just run away to save themselves. He was going to have to keep Bells on the string and lead his mind, keep him following them until they could find a cop, a couple of cops, a *lot* of cops with a *shitload* of guns so that they could take this sick fuck down.

"Where ya goin'?" Bells said. He was on his feet, a little unsteady, still holding the back of his head. He tottered forward.

Tozzi looked over his shoulder. Gina was frantic, pulling him to move faster. Tozzi could hear the voices in the crowd—kids oohing and ahing, parents telling them to look at this, look at that. On the other side of the avenue, Woody Woodpecker, Spi-

der-Man, and Bart Simpson were becoming giants as the balloons filled out. Farther up the block, Garfield, Pink Panther,
Bugs Bunny, Betty Boop sitting on a quarter moon, and Goofy
in a Santa suit were bobbing and weaving as they puffed out
their chests and came to life. He looked down at the zombie
with the gun and Bells doing the Transylvania shuffle as he
lurched toward them. This was too fucking bizarre.

"Where ya goin'?" Bells repeated, a malicious growl stuck in
his throat.

"Where you wanna go?" Tozzi answered.

Gina was yanking his arm out of the socket. He grabbed her
wrist to keep her still. It was like trying to hold back a wild
horse. They waded into the crowd, Tozzi stepping backward,
Bells lumbering, Gina pulling.

Tozzi locked eyes with Bells, intent on maintaining that contact with him and ignoring the voices all around him, the voices
of kids. He didn't want to look at them, and he didn't want Bells
to look at them. Tozzi didn't want to be distracted by them, and
he didn't want them to give Bells any ideas.

"C'mon! Let's go!" Gina kept yanking on his arm, but he
ignored her, walking backward at an even pace, letting Bells
keep up.

Bells held the knife down by his side, and in the carnival
confusion no one noticed. No one except for one little boy, a
toddler with long dark eyelashes who was bundled up in a pow-
der blue snowsuit, wearing a red harness attached to a leash that
was tied to a stroller where another, younger child was fast
asleep. The mother had her hands on the stroller's handle, but
she and her husband weren't paying attention. They were looking up at the giant Bart Simpson balloon while their little son
was reaching out for the bright shiny object in a killer's hand.
Tozzi's heart leaped as he imagined what would happen next.

The kid would grab Bells's leg, and Bells would seize the opportunity, slashing the leash with the knife and snatching the kid away. Knifepoint to the snowsuit. A new hostage. Jesus Christ, no . . .

"Bells!" Tozzi glanced at the kid, praying that he wouldn't touch Bells and that Bells wouldn't notice him. But Bells followed Tozzi's eyes and saw the toddler down by his leg.

The kid reached up to touch the shiny metal. Bells pressed the flat of the blade against the sleeve of the blue snowsuit. He looked up at Tozzi and grinned.

"Bells," Tozzi repeated. "Bells—"

Then Tozzi saw that goofy moon face looming over Bells's shoulder. He couldn't believe this. It was Freshy.

"Hey, Bells! Bells! Over here!" Freshy's face was drenched with sweat.

"Michael!"

"Tozzi!"

Tozzi frowned and peered over the surface of the crowd. Gibbons and Lorraine were swimming through the crush, fighting to get to them. Gibbons? Tozzi zeroed in on his partner's face. He looked terrible, but he wasn't dead. He wasn't dead.

Gibbons cupped his hands around his mouth and yelled, "He's got Excalibur." He pointed at Freshy.

Tozzi wrinkled his brow. What the hell was Freshy doing with Excalibur? He glanced down at the toddler. Bells had the blade under the red webbing of the leash, sawing through it. The parents were oblivious to all of this because they were going gaga over the big Bart Simpson. Freshy was no more than an arm's length behind Bells, shaking like a leaf. Tozzi couldn't see where he had Gibbons's gun, but it wasn't going to be worth much in Freshy's hands. Freshy didn't have the balls to pull the trigger, not on Bells. Of course, under the circumstances Tozzi wasn't so sure he wanted Freshy to try. In this crowd he was bound to hit somebody besides Bells. Like the little kid. Shit.

But as he watched the red webbing start to fray under the knife's edge, Tozzi changed his mind. Shoot the fuck. Kill him. Go 'head, Freshy. Do it before he grabs the kid.

Gina had stopped pulling on Tozzi's arm. She was staring at her little brother. "Freshy! What're you doing?"

Freshy raised the gun and stuck the muzzle into the back of Bells's neck.

Tozzi's stomach sank. Freshy should've kept some distance between himself and Bells. Now Bells could do something because he knew where the gun was, and he knew where Freshy was. Also, Freshy shouldn't have waited. He should've shot the bastard right away when he had the chance. Bells continued slicing through the kid's leash. The gun to his head didn't seem to bother him at all.

Gibbons moved around to Freshy's side, pushing people out of the way to make room. "Easy, kid. Take it easy."

Freshy's hand was shaking like crazy. He looked like he was going to cry. He kept looking back to Lorraine, but she was totally confused. "What is it?" she said. "Say it."

Freshy's mouth bent into a clown frown. "I, I . . . I dunno."

People in the crowd were starting to notice the nervous guy with the gun, and a circle of panic quickly opened up around them. The toddler's mother yelped and pulled on the red leash, but Bells had his fingers around the harness, and he wasn't letting go.

"Josh! Josh!" The woman was screaming, staring at the knife, about to blow a gasket, and the husband had that shaky look like he knew he should do something heroic, but he didn't have a clue where to start, so instead he yelled at the kid along with his wife, "Josh! Come here right now! Josh!"

Tozzi moved in front of the parents, dragging Gina with him. He took the leash in the middle, ready to yank the kid out of harm's way, praying that the frayed leash wouldn't break.

Before he did anything, he looked over his shoulder. Where the hell were the cops when you needed them? But then he realized how dense the crowd was. It was as bad as Times Square on New Year's Eve. Even a mounted cop would have a hard time getting through this mob, which meant there weren't going to be any nick-of-time rescues from the cavalry.

He stared at the knife. The blade was flat against the kid's chest, the fingers of the same hand clutching the harness. A flip of the wrist, and Bells could pierce the snowsuit easy.

Bells grinned at Tozzi, daring him to try his luck.

Tozzi let out a slow breath and caught Gibbons's eye. "Anybody know any good jokes?" he called out.

Bells's grin stretched, but he didn't say a word.

Gibbons nodded toward Freshy. "You hear the one about the guy who wanted to get made?"

"No." Tozzi kept his eye on Bells.

Gibbons kept his back to the crowd and his eye on Freshy. "Well, there was this guy who wanted to make his bones in the worst way, so he told this capo he'd whack this wiseguy who'd pissed the capo off by paying off a loan with funny money."

Bells perked up and laughed. He looked at Gibbons. "I heard that one, but that's not how it goes." He glanced at Excalibur and acted as if Freshy were holding a Popsicle to his head instead of a pistol.

Gibbons looked at Bells. "So how does your version go?"

"The little fuckhead who wanted to make his bones? *He* was the guy who gave the wiseguy the funny money."

Freshy barely squeaked, ". . . not true . . ."

Bells turned all the way around to face Freshy. "Yeah, the

little fuckhead gave the other guy, who was supposed to be his friend, thirty-two grand in counterfeit bills, and that guy turned around and gave it to the capo, not knowing it was phony baloney. Now I wonder where the little fuckhead got it? What do you think? You think maybe he shot some undercover agent up on the Jersey Turnpike for it? You think it goes something like that?"

Freshy had Excalibur in Bells's face, but he was shaking and sweating as if it were the other way around. "No, no, no . . . that ain't the way it goes. No—"

"No, huh? So tell us, Fresh. Where were you last night when that undercover guy got shot? Huh?"

Tozzi suddenly remembered that Freshy had disappeared last night. The first time he had seen Freshy was after three at Joey's Starlight Lounge, while Bells and Buddha were having their meeting in the back room. Tozzi wasn't sure what time Petersen had been shot, but he could account for Bells's time a lot better than he could Freshy's.

Freshy's eyes were blinking out of control. "Y-y-you're fucked up, Bells. You are."

"C'mon, Freshy, tell us where you were last night. What's your alibi?"

Freshy's lips trembled. He couldn't get the words out.

"You wanna hear *my* alibi, Fresh? Here, I'll tell you. I was with Buddha from two till around four"—Bells glanced at Tozzi and grinned—"before that I was with your sister, Fresh. I left her place around one thirty. Go 'head, ask her."

Tozzi's stomach bottomed out. His face was burning. He felt betrayed. Unconsciously his fingers tightened around the red leash as he pulled on it. Bells pulled back.

"Mommy!" the kid suddenly wailed.

"Josh!"

Tozzi stared at Gina. "Is that true?"

Her eyes roved from one face to another, but she didn't answer the question.

"Mom-meee!"

"Joshua! Josh—"

Tires screeched at the top of Seventy-eighth Street. Tozzi looked back toward the edge of the crowd, where a smoke-gray Lincoln was stopped in the middle of the street next to the blue surveillance van. The car doors flew open, and Buddha and his gorillas jumped out. "There they are," one of the gorillas shouted, and they rushed into the crowd.

"I told you they were following us," Lorraine said to Gibbons.

"Get 'im," Buddha shouted to his apes from the back of the crowd.

Bells turned toward the yelling wiseguys, and Tozzi suddenly yanked on the leash, whipping the kid out of the bastard's grasp. He hoisted the little boy up like a fish on the line and swung him back to his mother.

Buddha roared, "Get 'im, goddammit."

Freshy turned white. His knees started to buckle. Excalibur fell from his fingers, clattering to the pavement. He looked down at the ground, but Gibbons was already there, trying to recover his weapon.

Bells grinned into Freshy's face. The knifepoint was suddenly under Freshy's chattering chin. "What now, my love?"

Tozzi quickly snatched Bells's wrist and, dragging Gina along, used his other hand to bend the hand back over the wrist in a *kote gaeshi* pin that pointed the knife back at Bells's own chest.

Freshy didn't waste time. He bolted, heading for the balloons, going over the crowd rather than through it, like a running back diving over the defensive line to make that last half-yard for the touchdown. Bells slithered out of Tozzi's grasp and went after him, muscling his way through the crowd.

Gibbons yelled. "Stop! You're under arrest. Both of you!" Excalibur in his hand was pointed at the sky.

But neither Bells nor Freshy could hear him, not with all these screaming citizens running for their lives. Gibbons started pushing his way through the panicked sea of people, Lorraine right behind him. But Buddha was making better progress with his phalanx of gorillas cutting through like an icebreaker.

Tozzi glared at Gina, his jaw so tight he could've shattered a molar. "C'mon," he growled, and didn't wait for her to object. He yanked her arm and plowed through the crowd. He didn't give a damn if he pulled her goddamn arm right off.

Bells had been with her until one thirty. And she never said a word.

Bitch!

TWENTY-THREE

Gibbons felt like someone had pounded a spike into his jaw. The chest pains were gone, but the tooth hurt so bad now, he was having a hard time keeping his eyes open as he shoved people out of his way, trying to get to Bells and that little shit DeFresco. With Excalibur back in his possession, Gibbons was itching to use the .38 as payback for all the bullshit he'd had to put up with that day. After all, fair was fair. Bells had shot him; he should get to shoot Bells. At least one shot. And Freshy, that conniving little bastard, he'd been fucking around with everybody, the mob and the Bureau. But worst of all, he was the one who'd gunned down Petersen. Why the hell else would he be running away now? For that, the little shit deserved the rest of Excalibur's load.

"Stop! FBI!" he shouted over the heads of the screaming crowd. "Stop, goddammit!"

Freshy continued to flee with Bells right on his tail. They moved through the commotion like salmon leaping upstream. Either they didn't hear Gibbons's order or they were ignoring him because Gibbons was no more than ten feet behind Bells, and neither one of them looked back.

Gibbons kept shoving and pushing through the flailing arms when suddenly someone threw an elbow back at him and caught him in the face, right on top of the tooth. A gong went off in his brain, no, an explosion with a mushroom cloud rising out of the top of his head as the pain quadrupled and his body went stiff. His fingers squeezed Excalibur's butt so tight it was a miracle the gun didn't discharge.

Seconds later, when Gibbons was able to open his eyes again, he saw red. His whole field of vision was like an infrared scanner homing in on those two lying, murderous, scum-of-the-earth assholes. He was gonna take those two down if it was the last fuckin' thing he ever did. Gibbons shoved harder, unconcerned with the citizens he was bruising in his wake. He had his sights set on Bells and Freshy. Dead or alive, they were his, goddammit.

"Gibbons!" Tozzi shouted.

"Gibbons!" Lorraine screamed.

"Freshy!" Gina yelled.

Tozzi was trying to get to Gibbons, but it was slow going with Gina on one arm and Lorraine hanging off the other. He noticed that Buddha's gorillas were making much better progress, and that worried him. He had no doubt that they were all armed, and from the shade of scarlet on Buddha's face, Tozzi knew they were out for blood and weren't going to worry about pinpointing their targets. Once they started shooting, innocent people were going to get hit. And then there was Gibbons, who was acting like a maniac now, manhandling bodies like a college-club bouncer, desperate to get to Bells and Freshy. Tozzi hoped to God his partner still had his bulletproof vest on.

Lorraine dragged on his sleeve. "Michael, we have to do something. Gibbons is out of his mind. He's going to get himself killed."

Gina jerked the handcuffs. "Do something. Bells is gonna kill my brother. Can't you do something, for chrissake?"

Tozzi scowled at her. "Why should I? He shot an FBI agent. Gary Petersen may be dead, for all I know. Why should I help a friggin' cop killer?"

"That's bullshit," Gina snapped. "I don't believe it. Freshy's a jerk, but he's no killer. Believe me."

"Believe *you*? Why the hell should I believe you? You've been jerking my chain right along. Why didn't you tell me you were with Bells last night?"

Her eyes flashed hot. "I wasn't *with* him last night. He just showed up at my place at midnight."

"Why? Who goes visiting people at midnight? Tell me that."

Gina started screaming. "You think I slept with him? Is that it? You think I'm his girlfriend?"

"You're on the right track."

Bells's voice on the answering machine sliced through the madness all around them and rang in Tozzi's ears: "*Gina, it's me. Gimme a call.*"

"You're a jerk, you know that? I knew it right from the start, right after I took you back to my place. I saw you snooping around, checking out my things, looking for clues, looking for signs of another man. And you were sneaky about it, too. You were jealous before you even had anything to be jealous about. Jealous and clingy. Just like him."

"Him who?"

"Bells. Who the hell're we talking about?"

"You're crazy."

"No, *you're* crazy. You and Bells are two of a kind. That's why he came to my house last night. That's why he comes buzzing around me all the time, bugging me at home, at work, everywhere. He thinks he owns me. Are you thick or what? Don't you get it?"

Tozzi's face was burning. "No! I don't get it."

She pulled out the chain around her neck. Margie's gold wedding band dangled under her chin. "He came by last night to give me this. He wants me to marry him."

Tozzi was stung, but he wasn't really surprised. "Congratulations," he shouted.

"You don't understand," she shouted back. "Margie had told him about the Sicilian girl I found to have their baby. He told me this last night. But he thinks *I'm* the Sicilian girl. He's sick in the head. He thinks Margie's cuckoo plan worked, and I'm pregnant with his kid. That's why he won't leave me alone."

Tozzi's face was burning. He'd thought that she was the "Sicilian girl," too. "You really expect me to believe this?"

"I don't give a shit what you believe. It's true."

"So, are you?"

"What? Pregnant?"

"Tozzi! Tozzi! Behind you."

Tozzi looked over his shoulder to see who was shouting to him. About three arm-lengths away, a young redheaded guy in a suit was waving to him. There were three other young guys in suits with him. It took Tozzi a second to realize who they were. The redhead's name was Connell, from the FBI's Newark office. They all had their weapons drawn, pointed at the sky, as they fought their way through the crowd. Connell was carrying a shotgun over his head.

"We followed Buddha and his goons here," Connell shouted. "They were following Gibbons in the surveillance van. But we lost them in the crowd. Have you seen them?"

Tozzi nodded toward the advancing gorillas on his other flank. "They're over—"

Lorraine shook his shoulder and screamed. "Michael! Look!" She was pointing ahead toward the museum.

Tozzi squinted, trying to see what the hell she was getting hysterical about. Then he spotted them, and his jaw dropped. He couldn't fucking believe it. Freshy, Bells, and Gibbons were climbing up the partially inflated Bart Simpson balloon. Freshy was frantically clawing his way up. Bells was right on his heels with his knife in his hand. And Gibbons was bringing up the rear, cursing and screaming and waving his gun at Bells's backside. They were on Bart's striped shirt, climbing up his gigantic body like three ants in a row.

Tozzi glanced back at Buddha's gorillas, who'd spotted them, too. They were all pointing at Bart with their guns, and they all had automatics. The agents from Newark only had revolvers. Tozzi had nothing. Except for Gina on his wrist. He glared at Bells, the second ant in line, and wished to Christ he had a rifle with a scope so he could blow that mother's ass to kingdom come. *Shit!*

"Michael! Do something!"

"My brother! They're gonna shoot my brother! Do something!"

Tozzi squinted at Bells. Goddamn you . . .

"Stop, you sons of bitches. You're under arrest." Gibbons crossed another blue stripe in the big balloon kid's shirt. He was starting to lose his footing now, sliding back into the depressions created by his own weight. He was falling behind, but he wasn't about to let these two dirtbags get away, not after what they'd done to him, to Lorraine, to Petersen, to the Bureau, and worst of all, to his weapon. He shoved Excalibur back into his shoulder holster and grabbed two fistfuls of balloon canvas, hauling himself up.

Bells slashed a wide arc at Gibbons. "Back off, old man."

"Stick it up your ass." Gibbons kept climbing.

"I said, back *off.*" Bells slashed again, forcing Gibbons to stop and lean back.

"You're under arrest, Bells." Gibbons pulled out his gun again. "Drop the knife on the count of three, or I'll plug you one. I mean it. One . . ."

"Whatta'ya after me for? I didn't shoot that guy up on the Turnpike. He did." Bells pointed with the knife at Freshy.

Freshy's legs were dangling off Bart's drooping bottom lip like a cigarette as he struggled for shelter in the big open mouth. "I heard that, Bells," the legs shouted. When Freshy made it into the mouth, he poked his head over the side. "I didn't do it, Gib. He did."

Gibbons cocked the hammer and pointed Excalibur up at Freshy. "Who did it?" he barked.

"Not me. It was h—"

Crack!

Freshy ducked back into Bart's mouth as Gibbons fired and hit the big bottom lip.

The crowd down below screamed en masse.

"Whatta'you, crazy?" Freshy screamed.

Bells nodded down to Gibbons. "That's right. He was the one who did it."

Gibbons snarled. "You shut up. Freshy," he shouted. "Who did it, Freshy? Tell me the truth right now, or I'll hit you next time."

Freshy's voice came out of Bart's mouth. "Gib, I swear to God. I didn't—"

Crack!

Helium rushed out of a second hole in Bart's lip. Freshy peeked over the side, and his hair was blown to one side by the escaping gas. "All right! All right!" Breathing in the helium, Freshy sounded like Donald Duck. "Don't shoot, don't shoot. It was me, it was me. I did it. But I had a reason, Gib, a *good* reason."

Gibbons exploded. "I don't wanna hear it." He was itching to empty his load and do to Freshy what *he'd* done to Gary Petersen.

"No, listen, Gib, really. You gotta listen to me. I had a reason. I had to frame this prick over here before he killed my sister." He pointed down at Bells.

"What!" Bells glared up at him. "Kill your sister? I wanna fucking marry her."

"Yeah, then kill her like you killed Margie if she can't get pregnant. You're a sick fuck, Bells. I wasn't gonna let you do that to my sister. No way. You don't know how to take no for an answer, Bells. You were bothering her all the time, she told me. I figured the only way to get you off her case was to get you in jail, man. On death row. It's the only way to get rid of a sicko like you. I swear to Christ, Gib, that's why I did it. I didn't wanna kill that guy Petersen, I just wanted to wing him. *Attempted* murder, you know? All I wanted was for Bells to take the fall for it. I swear to God."

Bells's eyes were glowing. He stabbed the balloon with the knife and pulled himself up by the handle, reaching out for Bart's lip. Helium rushed into his face, making him squint like a mad Chinaman. He yelled like the bad Donald Duck, "You're dead, you little fuck! You're dead!"

"Stop!" Gibbons was peering down Excalibur's barrel, drawing a bead on the back of Bells's thigh, intent on stopping him, when suddenly he heard the hiccuping crack of automatic gunfire coming from down below. Three bullet holes appeared in Bart's shirt right next to Gibbons's arm. He lost his footing and spun completely around, dangling by a handful of canvas. A gush of helium rushed into his face.

"Shit!" he yelled in Donald Duck's voice. He gritted his aching tooth. Shit!

"Get 'im," Buddha yelled to his gorillas. "Get Bells."

Muscle-bound arms, each one holding an automatic, rose above the crowd, firing up at the balloon.

"Michael," Lorraine screamed, "do something."

Gina chimed in from his other side. "Yeah, do something."

"Stop hanging on me, the two of you," Tozzi shouted as he shrugged them off. It was worse than a freestyle aikido attack where everybody gets a piece of your *gi* jacket and tries to drag you down. Christ, testing would've been a piece of cake compared to this. He glanced up at Bart Simpson, Freshy in his mouth, Bells on his chin, Gibbons dangling from his shirt. Gina was clutching his hand with both of hers. He couldn't stop staring at Bells. His gut was churning, his face on fire, thinking about him and Gina.

"Gina, it's me. Gimme a call."

"Connell," Tozzi yelled over his shoulder, "gimme the shotgun."

"Right." The redheaded agent passed the shotgun to Tozzi over the crowd, extending it by the barrel. Tozzi reached out for the butt with his fingertips and finally pulled it in.

"What're you going to do?" Lorraine screamed. Her eyes were wild, hair all over her face. She clutched his arm again, but he shrugged her off before she could latch on.

Tozzi pumped the slide. "What the hell're you doing?" Gina was hanging on his arm again, but he out-muscled her this time. "What're you doing? You're gonna kill somebody with that thing. You're crazy!"

He raised the shotgun to his shoulder and squinted down the sights.

The tape played in his head, over and over. *"Gina, it's me. Gimme a call. . . . Gina, it's me. Gimme a call. . . ."*

"You're crazy!" Gina screamed. "You're not gonna hit Bells. Bells is like the devil, he can't die. You're gonna hit my brother. You're gonna hit Freshy!"

Lorraine shrieked in his ear. "That's a shotgun, Michael. You'll hit everybody. You'll hit Gibbons!"

Tozzi shrugged Lorraine off with his left elbow and fought Gina for the use of his right arm.

"Don't do it," Gina screamed, her face contorted as she strained to pull his hand away from the trigger.

But Tozzi was determined. He was motivated.

"Gina, it's me. Gimme a call. . . . Gina, it's me. Gimme a call—"

Gimme a call, my ass, he thought.

Ka-BOOM!

The crowd was rocked by the explosion, screaming and scattering in fast forward.

Tozzi pumped the shotgun again.

Gina strained. "No! Stop!"

Tozzi took aim. Call this, asshole.

Ka-BOOM!

"Noooooo!" Gina was doing pull-ups on his arm, but there was no stopping him.

"Oh, my God!" Lorraine pointed up at the balloon.

Bart Simpson had a ragged four-foot hole in his side and a matching one in the middle of his forehead. Helium whooshed out of the huge holes like a hurricane, and Bart started to collapse. In less than ten seconds, Gibbons, Freshy, and Bells were covered in folds of canvas, hidden from view.

"The balloon," Tozzi shouted to the young agents. "Get the guys on the balloon. Arrest them. Go!"

Tozzi whipped around, shotgun pointed up but at the ready. He scanned the scene, looking for Buddha and the gorillas in the dwindling crowd, but all he could see were the soles of people's shoes as they ran for dear life. The wiseguys were gone. He looked back toward Seventy-eighth Street just as the headlights of Buddha's gray Lincoln flashed on and the car went into reverse, braking and blowing its horn at fearful pedestrians as it backed up the block toward Amsterdam Avenue.

The corners of Tozzi's jaws were pulsating. He could feel Gina next to him, but he couldn't look at her. He was too angry, too hurt, too angry at himself for being hurt.

"You could've killed them," she squawked, but her bitchy heart wasn't in it. "God!"

Tozzi still wouldn't look at her. Even if he could've thought of something to say, he couldn't have gotten the words out. He just wanted her off his wrist and gone.

The street cleared out fast, and NYPD squad cars zoomed in, bubble lights flashing, sirens blaring. Uniforms came running, but the show was over. In the distance, Tozzi watched Gibbons pulling himself out from the heavy folds of canvas, refusing help from the cops. Connell and the boys from Newark had Freshy and Bells in handcuffs. Bells stood erect, as smug as Dracula. Freshy bent over and hid his face like the punk that he was. Looming over them all, Bart Simpson's giant head lolled over on its side, slowly melting into the puddle of balloon that had been his body.

A kid on a skateboard rolled up next to Tozzi. He must've been about ten or eleven, scrawny, with long dirty blond hair under a backward baseball cap. He gazed up at the sad billowing balloon head, mesmerized by the sight.

Gibbons stomped across the street toward Tozzi, his eyes locked onto his partner's. His face was swollen, and he looked mad as hell. Worse than the Grinch who stole Christmas.

The kid on the skateboard looked up at Tozzi. "Hey, man, you killed Bart. Cool."

Gibbons walked up to Tozzi and snatched the shotgun out of his hand. "Yeah, *real* cool . . . dickhead."

TWENTY-FOUR

THANKSGIVING DAY

Tozzi sat slumped down on the couch in Gibbons's living room, staring blankly at the TV set. The Macy's Thanksgiving Day Parade was on, and a bunch of leggy cheerleaders from Oklahoma were doing high kicks down Broadway in the cold drizzle. Lorraine was in the kitchen working on the turkey. Gibbons was in there with her, getting in the way.

Tozzi was having a hard time paying attention to the parade. The hallway off the living room that led to the bedroom kept calling to him. He knew there was a phone in there, on the end table next to the bed. He couldn't stop thinking about that phone and the fact that he could just go in there and use it. It was like knowing there was a ticking bomb in the next room, and he still had time to do something about it . . . if he knew what to do.

The problem was: Would he end up disarming it or setting it off? He wasn't sure. The possible detonator was in his wallet in his back pocket. A scrap of paper with Gina's phone number on it. He'd copied it from the phone book before he'd left his apartment that morning, but he wasn't exactly sure why.

Well, actually he did know why. Unfinished business, that's why. Unanswered questions that were keeping him from making up his mind about her. She baffled him. He liked her, but he despised her, too. She could be a total bitch, but he admired her for not taking any shit from anyone. She was a street-smart, smart-mouthed, second-generation Italian, as hardheaded as any greenhorn right off the boat. She had balls, chutzpah, spirit, something. She was a lot like him.

Last night, after "the Bart Simpson Incident," he didn't say a word to her. He was too pissed off about her not telling him that she'd been with Bells the night before. As soon as they got to the local police precinct, and that NYPD sergeant had unlocked the handcuffs with a master key, and he and Gina were free of one another, he'd just walked away, afraid of what he might say to her if he got started. He assumed she'd gone off to tend to her brother's legal needs, which were going to be considerable despite the fact that Gary Petersen had pulled through and was going to be all right. Naturally, Freshy was a fuck-up as a killer, too. He'd shot Petersen three times at point-blank range, but missed all the vital organs. The worst injury Petersen sustained was a partially collapsed lung.

Tozzi stared down the hallway that led to the bedroom. The smell of roasting turkey was all over the house, but he wasn't very hungry. He couldn't stop thinking about that ring, Margie's wedding band. He could see why Bells had given it to Gina. As sick as it was, it was just the kind of thing he'd do. But why was Gina wearing it around her neck on a chain? That seemed even sicker. Tozzi had been up most of the night thinking about all this, and it was driving him nuts. It was also driving him nuts that he was letting Gina drive him nuts like this.

A commercial came on the TV then, and of course, the volume doubled, demanding Tozzi's attention. The Keebler elves were making cookies in their tree house again. This was the second time they'd run this damn commercial. Tozzi stared at the ceiling and tried to ignore the obnoxious little elf voices.

This was stupid, he thought. He stood up and self-consciously arched his back. The damn couch was so squishy, it was giving him a backache. Of course, he'd been sitting on it for more than an hour, brooding, just getting more and more pissed off.

This really was stupid. He glanced down the hallway, then glanced at the kitchen doorway. He thought about it for a second and almost changed his mind again, then called out to his cousin before he did. "Lorraine, I have to make a phone call."

Her voice sailed out of the kitchen. "Go ahead. You don't have to ask."

"It better not be long distance." Gibbons's growl stopped him in his tracks.

Tozzi didn't want them to know who he was calling. "I'll charge it to my phone." He hoped he didn't sound too suspicious.

"Don't worry about it," Lorraine said, canceling out Gibbons's warning. "Use the one in the bedroom."

"Okay." Tozzi was already heading for their bedroom, pulling out his wallet to get the phone number.

But when he got to the bedroom, he stood on the threshold and stared at Gibbons's and Lorraine's bed. He'd never thought of them sleeping together. Not making love, just sleeping, every night, together. It sort of shifted his perspective on them all of a sudden. They'd been a couple a long time, but Tozzi had never thought of them as *together*. But they were. Gibbons came on like a tough guy, all alone on the mean streets, but he wasn't. He had Lorraine. And she had him. And this was where they had each other. Suddenly Tozzi felt like he shouldn't be here.

He looked at the slip of paper in his hand and read the number. Maybe this wasn't such a good idea. What was he gonna say to Gina? How was he gonna start the conversation? He didn't know what he wanted to say. What he really wanted was for her to do the talking. He wanted answers. He wanted her to have one of those automated telephone systems. Press one if you want to know why I'm wearing Margie's ring. Press two if you want to know more about the Sicilian girl. Press three if you want to know who I really care about. . . .

Stupid.

Tozzi grabbed the receiver and started to punch out the numbers. He was an FBI street agent, for chrissake. He'd just been involved in a major arrest. And a kidnapping. He was calling her to follow up on the case, see if she was all right, what her condition was, if she needed anything. A courtesy call, that's all. It was the professional thing to do. Don't make a big deal about it. He'd do all the talking. If she had anything she wanted to say to him, she'd say it. He wasn't gonna pull teeth to get it out of her.

He punched out the last digit and sat down on the edge of the bed, listening to the first ring, ignoring the Keebler elves running around in his nervous stomach. He was just calling to see if she was all right. Just keep it professional, he told himself.

It rang twice.

Keep it professional.

Three times.

Don't even try to drag it out of her. If she wants to talk, she will.

Four times.

Forget it. She isn't home. It's Thanksgiving, and her brother's in jail, and—

"You have reached 555-7846. I can't come to the phone right now, but if you leave a message, I'll get back to you. And don't forget to wait for the beep. Bye."

Tozzi frowned. The answering machine. She sounded friendlier on the machine than she was in person. At least toward him.

His heart was slamming as he listened for the beep. He was about to hang up—

Beeeeep.

"Gina, it's me—" he started, then suddenly remembered Bells's voice on her machine. *"Gina, it's me. Gimme a call."*

He started again. "This is Mike Tozzi. I was just calling to see how you were doing . . . I mean, how you are . . . your condition, that is, after the . . . the incident yesterday. Ah, please feel free to call me if you have any questions."

He hung up the phone fast. His face was red. He sounded like an ass. What kind of questions was she gonna have? He was the one who had the questions. She was gonna have a real good laugh when she heard this.

Then he realized that he hadn't left his phone number on the message. Shit.

The FBI's number is in the book. If she really wanted to talk to him, she'd find it.

But does she know that he's with the Manhattan field office, not the Newark office?

Newark will just tell her to call New York, right? Sure. Probably. He couldn't call her machine again to leave the number. That would sound even more stupid. And desperate. He didn't want her to think he was desperate because he wasn't. He was just being professional.

He stood up, looked down at the phone, and sighed.

Of course, the professional thing to do would be to call back and leave his number, right?

He sat down and punched out her number again before he lost his nerve. He listened to her message, then waited for the beep.

Beeeeep.

"Gina, it's Tozzi again. I forgot to leave my—"

285

"What do you want?" She picked up. She was there. She sounded really bitchy.

He cleared his throat. "I just wanted to—" He stopped himself short. He was tired of the bullshit, tired of playing games. "I just have one question, Gina. The wedding ring. Why are you wearing it?"

"What? You're sick. I'm hanging up."

"Just tell me that. That's all I want to know. I won't bother you anymore if you just tell me."

"You're nuts."

"Yeah, I know. We've established that. Now just give me a straight answer about the ring. What is it, like an engagement thing, wearing a wedding band like that?"

She sighed into the phone. "I told you. Bells gave it to me. It was Margie's."

"Yeah, but why were you wearing it?"

"Margie was my best friend, you stupid dickhead. I loved her. And I miss her. What was I supposed to do with it? Stick it in a drawer and forget about it?"

"Oh. . . ."

"You happy now?"

"I was just curious. Sorry to bother you."

"Oh, now you're gonna apologize? Spare me."

"All I said was that I was sorry to bother you. It is a holiday. I'm not apolo—"

"Just shut up. I'm not in the mood. I'll call you." She hung up the phone.

Tozzi stared at the receiver. "I'll call you"? What did she mean by that?

He hung up the phone and furrowed his brow. Nah. She's not gonna call. She didn't mean it that way.

He went back into the living room and returned to his place on the couch.

That's not what she meant. She won't call.

The Goofy balloon was drifting down Broadway on TV.

So what *did* she mean?

Gibbons leaned back from the kitchen table and glared at the TV through the doorway. The camera switched from Goofy to that perky little brunette from the *Today* show. She was holding a microphone, and you could see her breath as she spoke.

"And for those of you just joining us here in Herald Square, New York City, for the Macy's Thanksgiving Day Parade, we regret to tell you that one of our big balloons met with tragedy last night. The Bart Simpson balloon was the apparent victim of a mob rubout. Sources tell us that Bart sustained extensive punctures from heavy gunfire while he was being inflated for the parade, and we're told that the damage may be irreparable. A sad loss for fans of the hit cartoon program—"

"Will you turn that off, for chrissake?" Gibbons yelled at the back of Tozzi's head. "At least put on some football if you're gonna watch that thing."

Tozzi turned around and stared at his partner through the doorway. "I don't like football."

"What're you, a friggin' communist? Everybody likes football."

"I don't."

"Well, you're screwed up anyway."

"Guess so." Tozzi turned back to the parade.

Asshole.

Gibbons was still steamed up about Tozzi using the shotgun to deflate the balloon.

Lorraine was over at the counter, pulverizing potatoes in the food processor. She never made mashed potatoes because she

287

didn't like them herself, but she was making them today. For him.

She dropped a glob of margarine into the hopper. "How's the tooth?"

"What tooth?"

"You know what I mean."

Gibbons stuck his tongue in the space where his molar had been. "It's better than it was, I guess." He'd been in so much pain this morning, he begged his dentist to open up the office and yank it. It was still very sensitive now, even with the pain-killers, and the sutures smarted whenever he touched them. That's why Lorraine was making mashed potatoes. Mashed potatoes and gravy, and cream of carrot soup—that was going to be his Thanksgiving dinner. That and the inside of the pumpkin pie. He figured he'd have the runs for a week on this meatless diet. Either that, or he'd turn into a liberal.

"How's your chest?" Her back was turned to him as she worked the food processor.

"Ugly." A big yellow and purple bruise covered the left side of his chest where the bullets had hit him, but the crushing chest pains never came back. They took an EKG at the hospital last night, and the doctor told him not to worry. He hadn't had a heart attack. Residual muscle spasms caused by the impact of the bullets after the pain-killers and the booze wore off. He hadn't told Lorraine anything about the chest pains or the EKG. Why worry her?

Lorraine shut off the food processor. "I'm sorry."

"About what?"

Lorraine turned around. Her face was red. "I'm sorry that I didn't cry for you." She sniffed and wiped the corner of her eye with the back of her hand. "When you got shot yesterday, and you were lying on the floor in Macy's? I didn't cry. It just

288

wouldn't come. I just stared at you and accepted it . . . that you were dead. I couldn't cry. I'm sorry."

Gibbons swallowed hard. His stomach sank, weighed down by that feeling of dread he always got whenever Lorraine sprang one of these emotional discussions on him, the ones where she aired her feelings and expected him to do the same. He always felt like he was being put on the spot whenever she did this. He believed in people being honest with each other, but these kind of deep confessionals weren't for everyone. Christ, if everyone started confessing what they really felt about each other, there'd be more domestic violence than there already was. God made people repressed for a reason.

Silent tears brimmed in Lorraine's eyes as she stood there, wringing her mashed-potatoey hands on a dish towel.

Gibbons really felt cornered now. Shit.

He got up and went to her, starting to give her a hug, which was always a good way to get out of these situations. Give her a hug, let her cry it out, and hope it passes quick. But as he went to put his arms around her, she raised her hand to push him away, and he froze, afraid that she'd touch his sore chest.

"What'sa matter?" he said.

"I don't want to be comforted. I want to tell you how I feel."

Gibbons sighed. There was no way out.

"What happened yesterday really opened my eyes to a lot of things. I guess the biggest shock is that we're getting old."

Gibbons scowled. "What's that got to do with anything?" He hated talking about his age.

"I think I couldn't cry for you because we're not young lovers. We're not Romeo and Juliet. I guess when you get older, deep down you know that loss is inevitable, so you can't cry about it. I wanted to, though. I apologize."

289

Gibbons just looked at her. He was nervous. He wasn't sure if it was his turn to say something, or she was just pausing.

"Did you notice that I didn't cry? Or were you too fuzzy from the pain?"

He licked his lips. "Well, to be honest, that didn't cross my mind. The only thing I was worried about was you. I was afraid you were gonna get hurt with all those crazy wiseguys around."

She nodded, looking down at the linoleum. He thought maybe she'd be happy or touched or something. After all, he was being honest; that really was how he felt when all that shit was going down. But now he felt like he'd said something wrong.

She lifted her eyes and let out a long sigh. "I guess you still think of me as the damsel in distress while I've moved on to thinking of you as the old monarch. The two of us, actually. The old king and queen." She went back to inspecting the linoleum.

"Lorraine—" He cleared his throat. "Lorraine, you're getting all medieval on me. I mean, I know medieval history is what you teach and all, but I think you're—you know—making things more dramatic than they really are."

She wrinkled her brow. "Dramatic? How do you mean?"

"Well . . ." He didn't want to hurt her, but he did want to be honest. "Well, this old king and queen jazz. It's all very symbolic and all, but that's term paper stuff. It's not real. It's not us. I love you. I married you, for chrissake. Why the hell shouldn't I worry about you taking a slug from one of those mutts? So you didn't cry for me, so what? Some people just don't cry. It doesn't mean they're not human. I don't need for you to cry. I know you care about me."

She looked up, and a tear dripped down her cheek. "You've never said that."

"Yeah, I know. But I know you know I care about you. Why else would you be making me mashed potatoes, when I know what you think of mashed potatoes? For you, making mashed potatoes is like voting Republican. Right?"

She tried to sit on her smile, but she couldn't. She reached for his hand and shook her head. "You're really something, Gibbons. You really are."

He put his arm around her waist and pulled her close. "You're something, too." He kissed her, and when she tried to cut it short, he tightened his grip and kept her there. It hurt his chest to hug her like that, but so what? They needed this.

"I better stir the soup," she murmured, their lips pressed together. "I think it's burning."

No loss, he thought as he let her go. Who the hell ever heard of cream of carrot soup? Rabbits who don't care about cholesterol, that's who.

As Lorraine went to stir the soup pot, Gibbons peeked into the living room. Tozzi was gone. Back in the bedroom calling Gina again, no doubt. Gibbons had eavesdropped on him on the kitchen extension while Lorraine was in the bathroom.

He reached up and quietly lifted the receiver on the wall phone, covering the mouthpiece as he brought it to his ear and heard Gina's voice.

". . . *Will you please leave me alone about this? To tell you the truth, I don't know what I meant. Don't make a federal case about it.*"

"*But, Gina, I heard you say it. You said you'd call me. Is that what you really meant? I mean—*"

Gibbons carefully hung up the phone, shaking his head. What a sorry piece of work that guy was.

He went over to Lorraine at the stove. "So whatta we gonna do about your cousin? He's like a dog in the desert looking for a tree."

"What do you mean? He's the big hero, isn't he? He survived

being kidnapped and marked for death by Tony Bells. He saved Gina DeFresco's life. He assisted in the arrests of Bells and Freshy, and you told me they're both going to go away forever."

Gibbons nodded. "Freshy'll do time for attempted murder. They found the rest of the counterfeit bills at his house in Bayonne, which pretty much proves that he was the one who shot Petersen. As for Bells, he'll never see the light of day again. They'll get him on murder, kidnapping, and everything else under the sun."

"So what's wrong with Michael?" Lorraine looked very concerned about her dear cousin. "Is it postcaptivity stress syndrome, something like that?"

Gibbons glanced into the living room to make sure that Tozzi was still out of earshot. "Lorraine, I'm surprised at you. Isn't it obvious?"

"What? Him and Gina?"

"Of course. Whatta'ya think? Romeo's looking for a Juliet again. He never learns, this guy. They never work out, these women. He oughta try being gay. Maybe he'd have more luck."

Lorraine put the lid back on the soup pot. "I don't know. I have a feeling this time it might be different."

"Get outta here. It's always the same old story with him. He finds a new woman, and he's in love, he's in love, then—*boom*—she's gone. Something always happens to screw it up for him. But if you notice, it's never *his* fault. It's always them. You watch. It'll be the same deal with Gina. If it ever gets that far."

"You think so? I'm not so sure." Lorraine started to whisper. "He's always like a kid with a new toy when he meets somebody new, always very hopeful. But not this time. He's been moping around all day."

"He always wears a big puss when he doesn't get what he wants when he wants it."

292

"Maybe so, but I don't think I've ever seen him quite like this —so distracted, so out of it. I think Gina's done a real number on him. But Gina isn't like the other ones. I really have a feeling it might be different this time."

"Yeah, but Gina doesn't want any part of him. That's why he's sulking."

"Well, maybe he'll have to put some effort into it for a change. And for Gina, I bet he will."

Gibbons shook his head. "No way. Not Tozzi. The first time Gina rubs him the wrong way, he'll be out the door, looking for someone else. You watch."

"I don't think so. I think Gina's gonna be the one. I just have a feeling." Lorraine had this funny little grin.

"Get outta here. You don't know what you're talking about."

"You want to bet?"

"How much?"

"You name it."

"Ten bucks."

"You're on."

Tozzi appeared in the doorway then. His brows were furrowed as he stared at the window in the oven as if it were the television. He seemed confused. Maybe he wanted it to be the parade. He wandered into the kitchen and lifted the lid on the soup pot, brow still furrowed. He paused by the food processor filled with mashed potatoes and stared at that for a while.

"We gonna be eating soon?" he asked.

"In a little while," Lorraine said.

"Oh . . ." He kept staring at the mashed potatoes.

"Are you hungry?"

"No . . . not really."

Lorraine shot a knowing look at Gibbons. Tozzi was always hungry.

"The turkey should be done in about a half-hour. Can you hold out that long?"

"Ummm . . ." Tozzi didn't seem to be listening.

Gibbons just shook his head. What a piece of work.

"Why don't you see if the football games are on yet?" Lorraine suggested.

"Football?"

"Yes. There must be some bowl game on."

"Yeah . . . I guess . . ."

"Why don't you go see?"

"Okay . . ."

Tozzi gazed at the mashed potatoes a little while longer, then went back to the couch in the living room and started changing channels.

Gibbons and Lorraine looked at each other.

"You still want to bet?" she asked.

Gibbons stared at the back of Tozzi's head set against a green football field on the TV screen. "I don't know. . . ."

When he turned around again, Lorraine was wearing that funny little grin. "You want to make it twenty?" She looked pretty confident.

He rubbed his jaw. He had his doubts now. She could be right about this. "I don't know," he said. "I may have to rethink this."

"How about a hundred?"

Gibbons winced as he touched the sutures through his cheek. Son of a bitch.

When he opened his eyes, Lorraine was looking at him, her arms crossed. "We still on?" she asked. She was smiling like a crocodile.